YELLOWFACE

Writing as R.F. Kuang

The Poppy War

The Dragon Republic

The Burning God

Babel

YELLOWFACE

REBECCA F. KUANG

THE BOROUGH PRESS

The Borough Press
An imprint of HarperCollins*Publishers* Ltd
1 London Bridge Street
London SE1 9GF

www.harpercollins.co.uk

HarperCollins*Publishers*
Macken House, 39/40 Mayor Street Upper,
Dublin 1, D01 C9W8, Ireland

First published in Great Britain by HarperCollins*Publishers* 2023
2 4 6 8 10 9 7 5 3 1

A catalogue record for this book is available from the British Library

ISBN: 978-0-00-853278-9

FICTION

Set in Adobe Garamond

Printed and bound in India by Thomson Press India Ltd

To Eric and Janette

One

THE NIGHT I WATCH ATHENA LIU DIE, WE'RE CELEBRATING HER TV deal with Netflix.

Off the bat, for this story to make sense, you should know two things about Athena:

First, she has everything: a multibook deal straight out of college at a major publishing house, an MFA from the one writing workshop everyone's heard of, a résumé of prestigious artist residencies, and a history of awards nominations longer than my grocery list. At twenty-seven, she's published three novels, each one a successively bigger hit. For Athena, the Netflix deal was not a life-changing event, just another feather in her cap, one of the side perks of the road to literary stardom she's been hurtling down since graduation.

Second, perhaps as a consequence of the first, she has almost no friends. Writers our age—young, ambitious up-and-comers just this side of thirty—tend to run in packs. You'll find evidence of cliques all over social media—writers gushing over excerpts of one another's unpublished manuscripts (LOSING MY HEAD OVER THIS

WIP!), squealing over cover reveals (THIS IS SO GORGEOUS I WILL DIE!!!), and posting selfies of group hangs at literary meet-ups across the globe. But Athena's Instagram photos feature no one else. She regularly tweets career updates and quirky jokes to her seventy thousand followers, but she rarely @s other people. She doesn't name-drop, doesn't blurb or recommend her colleagues' books, and doesn't publicly rub shoulders in that ostentatious, desperate way early career writers do. In the entire time I've known her, I've never heard her reference any close friends but me.

I used to think that she was simply aloof. Athena is so stupidly, ridiculously successful that it makes sense she wouldn't want to mingle with mere mortals. Athena, presumably, chats exclusively with blue check holders and fellow bestselling authors who can entertain her with their rarefied observations on modern society. Athena doesn't have time to make friends with proletarians.

But in recent years, I've developed another theory, which is that everyone else finds her as unbearable as I do. It's hard, after all, to be friends with someone who outshines you at every turn. Probably no one else can stand Athena because they can't stand constantly failing to measure up to her. Probably I'm here because I'm just that pathetic.

So that night it's only Athena and me at a loud, overpriced rooftop bar in Georgetown. She's flinging back cocktails like she has a duty to prove she's having a good time, and I'm drinking to dull the bitch in me that wishes she were dead.

ATHENA AND I ONLY BECAME FRIENDS BY CIRCUMSTANCE. WE LIVED on the same floor at Yale our freshman year, and because we've both known we wanted to be writers since we were sentient, we ended up in all the same undergraduate writing seminars. We both published short stories in the same literary magazines early on in our careers and, a few years after graduation, moved to the same city—Athena for a prestigious fellowship at Georgetown, whose faculty, according to rumor, were so impressed by a guest lecture she gave at American University that its English department inaugurated a creative writing post just for her, and I because my mother's cousin owned a condo in Rosslyn that she would rent to me for the cost of utilities if I remembered to water her plants. We'd never experienced anything like kindred spirit recognition, or some deep, bonding trauma—we were just always in the same place, doing the same things, so it was convenient to be friendly.

But although we started out in the same place—Professor Natalia Gaines's Introduction to Short Fiction—our careers spiraled in wildly different directions after graduation.

I wrote my first novel in a fit of inspiration during a year spent bored out of my skull working for Teach for America. I'd come home after work every day to meticulously draft the story I'd wanted to tell since my childhood: a richly detailed and subtly magical coming-of-age story about grief, loss, and sisterhood titled *Over the Sycamore.* After I'd queried nearly fifty literary agents without luck, the book was picked up by a small press named Evermore during an open call for submissions. The advance seemed like an absurd amount of money to me at the time—ten thousand dollars up front, with royalties to come once I'd earned out—but that was before I learned Athena had gotten six figures for her debut novel at Penguin Random House.

Evermore folded three months before my book went to print.

My rights reverted back to me. Miraculously, my literary agent—who had signed me after Evermore's initial offer—resold the rights to one of the Big Five publishing houses for a twenty-thousand-dollar advance—a "nice deal," read the Publishers Marketplace announcement. It seemed like I had finally Made It, that all my dreams of fame and success were about to come true, until my launch day drew closer, and my first print run was reduced from ten thousand to five thousand copies, my six-city book tour was reduced to three stops in the DMV area, and the promised quotes from famous writers failed to materialize. I never got a second printing. I sold two, maybe three thousand copies total. My editor was fired during one of those publishing squeezes that happen every time the economy dips, and I got passed along to some guy named Garrett who has so far shown so little interest in supporting the novel that I often wonder whether he's forgotten about me entirely.

But that's par for the course, everyone told me. Everyone has a shitty debut experience. Publishers are Just Like That. It's always chaos in New York, all the editors and publicists are overworked and underpaid, and balls get dropped all the time. The grass is never greener on the other side. Every author hates their imprint. There are no Cinderella stories—just hard work, tenacity, and repeat attempts at the golden ticket.

So why, then, do some people rocket to stardom on their first try? Six months before Athena's debut novel came out, she got a big, sexy photo spread in a widely read publishing magazine under the title "Publishing's Newest Prodigy Is Here to Tell the AAPI Stories We Need." She sold foreign rights in thirty different territories. Her debut launched amidst a fanfare of critical acclaim in venues like the

New Yorker and the *New York Times*, and it occupied top spots on every bestseller list for weeks. The awards circuit the following year was a foregone conclusion. Athena's debut—*Voice and Echo*, about a Chinese American girl who can summon the ghosts of all the deceased women in her family—was one of those rare novels that perfectly straddled the line between speculative and commercial fiction, so she accrued nominations for the Booker, Nebula, Hugo, and World Fantasy awards, two of which she won. And that was only three years ago. She's published two more books since, and the critical consensus is that she's only gotten better and better.

It's not that Athena isn't talented. She's a fucking *good* writer—I've read all her work, and I'm not too jealous to acknowledge good writing when I see it. But Athena's star power is so obviously not about the writing. It's about *her*. Athena Liu is, simply put, so fucking cool. Even her name—Athena Ling En Liu—is cool; well done, Mr. and Mrs. Liu, to choose a perfect combination of the classical and exotic. Born in Hong Kong, raised between Sydney and New York, educated in British boarding schools that gave her a posh, unplaceable foreign accent; tall and razor-thin, graceful in the way all former ballet dancers are, porcelain pale and possessed of these massive, long-lashed brown eyes that make her look like a Chinese Anne Hathaway (that's not racist for me to say—Athena once posted a selfie of her and "Annie" from some red carpet event, their four enormous doe eyes squeezed side by side, captioned simply, Twins!).

She's unbelievable. She's literally unbelievable.

So of course Athena gets every good thing, because that's how this industry works. Publishing picks a winner—someone attractive enough, someone cool and young and, oh, we're all thinking it, let's just say it, "diverse" enough—and lavishes all its money and resources on them. It's so fucking arbitrary. Or perhaps not arbitrary, but it hinges on factors that have nothing to do with the strength of one's prose. Athena—a beautiful, Yale-educated, international, ambiguously queer woman of color—has been chosen by the Powers That Be. Meanwhile, I'm just brown-eyed, brown-haired June Hayward, from Philly—and no matter how hard I work, or how well I write, I'll never be Athena Liu.

I'd expected her to skyrocket out of my orbit by now. But the friendly texts keep coming—how's writing going today? hitting that word count target? good luck with your deadline!—as do the invitations: happy hour margaritas at El Centro, brunch at Zaytinya, a poetry slam on U Street. We have one of those skin-deep friendships where you manage to spend a lot of time together without really getting to know the other person. I still don't know if she has any siblings. She's never asked me about my boyfriends. But we keep hanging out, because it's so convenient that we're both in DC, and because it's hard to make new friends the older you get.

I'm honestly not sure why Athena likes me. She always hugs me when she sees me. She likes my social media posts at least twice a week. We get drinks at least every other month, and most of the time it's by her invitation. But I've no clue what I have to offer her—I don't possess anywhere near the clout, the popularity, or the connections to make the time she spends with me worthwhile.

Deep down, I've always suspected Athena likes my company precisely because I can't rival her. I understand her world, but I'm not a threat, and her achievements are so far out of my reach that she doesn't feel bad squealing to my face about her wins. Don't we all want a friend who won't ever challenge our superiority, because they already know it's a lost cause? Don't we all need someone we can treat as a punching bag?

"IT CAN'T BE ALL THAT BAD," SAYS ATHENA. "I'M SURE THEY JUST mean they're pushing the paperback off a few months."

"It's not delayed," I say. "It's canceled. Brett told me they just . . .couldn't see a place for it in their printing schedule."

She pats my shoulder. "Oh, don't worry. You get more royalties off hardcovers anyways! Silver linings, right?"

Bold of you to assume I'm getting royalties at all. I don't say that out loud. If you tell Athena off for being tactless, she gets overly, exaggeratedly apologetic, and that's harder to put up with than just swallowing my irritation.

We're at the Graham's rooftop bar, sitting on a loveseat facing the sunset. Athena is guzzling her second whisky sour, and I'm on my third glass of pinot noir. We've wandered onto the tired subject of my troubles with my publisher, which I deeply regret, because everything Athena thinks is comfort or advice always only comes off as rubbing it in.

"I don't want to piss Garrett off," I say. "Well, honestly, I think he's just looking forward to rejecting the option so they can be done with me."

"Oh, don't sell yourself short," says Athena. "He acquired your debut, didn't he?"

"He didn't, though," I say. I have to remind Athena this every single time. She has a goldfish's memory when it comes to my problems—it takes two or three repetitions for anything to stick. "The editor who did got fired, and the buck passed to him, and every time we talk about it, it feels like he's just going through the motions."

"Well, then fuck him," Athena says cheerfully. "Another round?"

The drinks are stupidly expensive at this place, but it's okay because Athena's buying. Athena always buys; at this point, I've stopped offering. I don't think Athena's ever really grasped the concepts of "expensive" and "inexpensive." She went from Yale to a fully funded master's degree to hundreds of thousands of dollars in her bank account. Once, when I told her that entry-level publishing jobs in New York only make about thirty-five thousand dollars a year, she blinked at me and asked, "Is that a lot?"

"I'd love a malbec," I say. It's nineteen dollars a glass.

"Got it, babe." Athena gets up and saunters toward the bar. The bartender smiles at her and she exclaims in surprise, hands flying to mouth like she's Shirley Temple. It seems that one of the gentlemen at the counter has sent her a glass of champagne. "Yes, we *are* celebrating." Her dainty, delighted laughter floats over the music. "But can I get one for my friend as well? On me?"

No one's out here sending me champagne. But this is typical. Athena gets showered by attention every time we go out—if not by eager readers who want a selfie and an autograph, then by men and women alike who find her ravishing. Me, I'm invisible.

"So." Athena settles back down beside me and hands me my glass. "Do you want to hear about the Netflix meeting? Oh my God, Junie, it was insane. I met the guy who produced *Tiger King. Tiger King!*"

Be happy for her, I tell myself. *Just be happy for her, and let her have this night.*

People always describe jealousy as this sharp, green, venomous thing. Unfounded, vinegary, mean-spirited. But I've found that jealousy, to writers, feels more like fear. Jealousy is the spike in my heart rate when I glimpse news of Athena's success on Twitter—another book contract, awards nominations, special editions, foreign rights deals. Jealousy is constantly comparing myself to her and coming up short; is panicking that I'm not writing well enough or fast enough, that *I* am not, and never will be, enough. Jealousy means that even just learning that Athena's signing a six-figure option deal with Netflix means that I'll be derailed for days, unable to focus on my own work, mired by shame and self-disgust every time I see one of her books in a bookstore display.

Every writer I know feels this way about someone else. Writing is such a solitary activity. You have no assurance that what you're creating has any value, and any indication that you're behind in the rat race sends you spiraling into the pits of despair. *Keep your eyes on your own paper,* they say. But that's hard to do when everyone else's papers are flapping constantly in your face.

Though I feel the vicious kind of jealousy, too, watching Athena talk about how much she adores *her* editor, a literary powerhouse named Marlena Ng who "plucked me from obscurity" and who "just really understands what I'm trying to do on a craft level, you know?" I stare at Athena's brown eyes, framed by those ridiculously large lashes that make her resemble a Disney forest animal, and I wonder, *What is it like to be you?* What is it like to be so impossibly perfect, to have every good thing in the world? And maybe it's the cocktails, or my overactive writer's imagination, but I feel this hot coiling in my stomach, a bizarre urge to stick my fingers in her berry-red-painted mouth and rip her face apart, to neatly peel her skin off her body like an orange and zip it up over myself.

"And it's like, she just *gets* me, like she's having sex with my words. Like, mind sex." Athena giggles, then scrunches her nose up adorably. I suppress the impulse to poke it. "You ever think of the revision process as like, having sex with your editor? Like you're making a great big literary baby?"

She's drunk, I realize. Two and a half drinks in, and she's smashed; she's already forgotten once again that I, in fact, hate my editor.

Athena doesn't know how to hold her alcohol. I learned this a week into freshman year, at some senior's house party in East Rock, at which I held her hair as she vomited into the toilet bowl. She has fancy taste; she loves to show off everything she knows about scotch (she only calls it "whisky," and sometimes "whisky from the Highlands"), but she's barely had anything and her cheeks are already bright red, her sentences rambling. Athena loves to get drunk, and drunk Athena is always self-aggrandizing and dramatic.

I first noticed this behavior at San Diego Comic-Con. We were clustered around a big table in the hotel bar and she was laughing too loudly, cheeks bright red while the guys sitting beside her, one of whom would soon be outed on Twitter as a serial sex pest, stared eagerly at her chest. "Oh my God," she kept saying. "I'm not ready for this. It's all going to blow up in my face. I'm not ready. Do you think they hate me? Do you think everyone secretly hates me, and no one will tell me? Would *you* tell me if you hated me?"

"No, no," the men assured her, petting her hands. "No one could ever hate you."

I used to think this act was a ploy for attention, but she's also like this when it's only the two of us. She gets so vulnerable. She starts sounding like she's going to burst into tears, or like she's bravely revealing secrets she's told no one else before. It's hard to watch.

There's something desperate about it, and I don't know what frightens me more—that she's manipulative enough to pull off such an act, or that everything she's saying might be true.

For all the blaring music and bass vibrations, the Graham feels dead—unsurprising; it's a Wednesday night. Two men come up to try to give Athena their numbers, and she waves them off. We're the only women in the place. The rooftop feels quiet and claustrophobic in a way that's frightening, so we finish our drinks and leave. I think, with some relief, that this will be the end of it—but then Athena invites me over to her apartment, a short Lyft ride away, near Dupont Circle.

"Come on," she insists. "I have some amazing whisky saved, precisely for this moment—you have to come try it."

I'm tired, and I'm not having that much fun—jealousy feels worse when you're drunk—but I'm curious to see her apartment, so I say yes.

It's really fucking nice. I knew Athena was rich—bestseller royalties do count for something—but I hadn't processed *how* rich until we step into the ninth-floor, two-bedroom unit where she lives alone—one room for sleeping, one room for writing—with tall ceilings, gleaming hardwood floors, floor-to-ceiling windows, and a balcony that wraps around the corner. She's decorated it in that ubiquitous, Instagram-famous style that screams minimalist but bougie: sleek wooden furniture, sparely designed bookshelves, and clean, monochrome carpets. Even the plants look expensive. A humidifier hisses beneath her calatheas.

"So then, whisky? Or something lighter?" Athena points to the wine fridge. She has a fucking wine fridge. "Riesling? Or I have this *lovely* sauvignon blanc, unless you want to stick to red—"

"Whisky," I say, because the only way to get through the rest of this night is to get as drunk as possible.

"Neat, on the rocks, or old-fashioned?"

I have no clue how to drink whisky. "Um, whatever you're having."

"Old-fashioned, then." She darts into her kitchen. Moments later, I hear cupboards opening, dishes clanging. Who knew old-fashioneds were such a hassle?

"I have this beautiful eighteen-year WhistlePig," she calls out. "It's so smooth, like toffee and black pepper mixed together—just wait, you'll see."

"Sure," I call back. "Sounds great."

She's taking a while, and I really have to pee, so I wander around the living room searching for the bathroom. I wonder what I'll find in there. Maybe a fancy aromatherapy diffuser. Maybe a basket of jade vagina rocks.

I notice then that the door to her writing office is wide open. It's a gorgeous space; I can't help but take a peek. I recognize it from her Instagram posts—her "creativity palace," she calls it. She has a huge mahogany desk with curved legs beneath a window framed by Victorian-style lacy curtains, atop which sits her prized black typewriter.

Right. Athena uses a typewriter. No Word backups, no Google Docs, no Scrivener: just scribbles in Moleskine notebooks that become outlines on sticky notes that become fully formed drafts on her Remington. It forces her to focus on the sentence level, or so she claims. (She's given this interview response so many times I've nearly memorized it.) Otherwise, she digests entire paragraphs at a time, and she loses the trees for the forest.

Honestly. Who talks like that? Who *thinks* like that?

They make these ugly and overpriced electronic typewriters, for authors who can't string together more than a paragraph without losing focus and hopping over to Twitter. But Athena hates those; she uses a *vintage* typewriter, a clunky thing that requires her to buy special ink ribbons and thick, sturdy pages for her manuscripts. "I just can't write on a screen," she's told me. "I have to see it printed. Something about the reassuring solidity of the word. It feels permanent, like everything I compose has weight. It ties me down; it clarifies my thoughts and forces me to be specific."

I wander farther into the office, because I'm exactly drunk enough to forget that this is bad manners. There's a sheet of paper still in the carriage, upon which are written just two words: *THE END*. Sitting next to the typewriter is a stack of pages nearly a foot tall.

Athena materializes by my side, a glass in either hand. "Oh, that's the World War One project. It's finally done."

Athena is famously cagey about her projects until they're finished. No beta readers. No interviews, no sharing snippets on social media. Even her agents and editors don't get to see so much as an outline until she's finished the whole thing. "It has to gestate inside me until it's viable," she told me once. "If I expose it to the world before it's fully formed, it dies." (I'm shocked no one has called her out for this grotesque metaphor, but I guess anything's okay if Athena says it.) The only things she's revealed over the past two years are that this novel has something to do with twentieth-century military history, and that it's a "big artistic challenge" for her.

"Shit," I say. "Congrats."

"Typed up the last page this morning," she chirps. "No one's read it yet."

"Not even your agent?"

She snorts. "Jared pushes paper and signs checks."

"It's so long." I wander closer to the desk, reach for the first page, then immediately withdraw my hand. Stupid, drunk—I can't just go around touching things.

But instead of snapping at me, Athena nods her permission. "What do you think?"

"You want me to read it?"

"Well, I guess, not all of it, right now." She laughs. "It's *very* long. I'm just—I'm just so glad it's finished. Doesn't this stack look pretty? It's hefty. It . . . carries significance."

She's rambling; she's as drunk as I am, but I know exactly what she means. This book is huge, in more ways than one. It's the sort of book that leaves a mark.

My fingers hover over the stack. "Can I . . . ?"

"Sure, sure . . ." She nods enthusiastically. "I have to get used to it being out there. I have to give birth."

What a bizarre, persistent metaphor. I know reading the pages will only fuel my jealousy, but I can't help myself. I pick a stack of ten or fifteen pages off the top and skim through them.

Holy God, they're good.

I'm not great at reading when I'm tipsy, and my eyes keep sliding to the end of every paragraph, but even from a sloppy once-over, I can tell this book is going to dazzle. The writing is tight, assured. There are none of the juvenile slipups of her debut work. Her voice has matured and sharpened. Every description, every turn of phrase—it all sings.

It's better than anything I could write, perhaps in this lifetime.

"You like it?" she asks.

She's nervous. Her eyes are wide, almost scared; she's fiddling with her necklace as she watches me. How often does she put on this act? How forcefully do people shower her with praise when she does?

It's petty, but I don't want to give that validation to her. Her game works with adoring reviewers and fans; it won't with me.

"I don't know," I say flatly. "I can't really read drunk."

She looks crestfallen, but only for a moment. I watch her hastily plaster on a smile. "Right, duh, that was stupid, of course you don't want to . . ." She blinks at her glass, then at me, and then at her living room. "Well, then do you want to just . . . hang?"

So here's me, just hanging with Athena Liu.

When she's hammered, it turns out, she's shockingly banal. She doesn't quiz me about Heidegger, or Arendt, or the half-dozen philosophers she loves to name-drop in interviews. She doesn't go off about what a good time she had guest modeling for Prada this one time in Paris (which was completely by accident; the director just saw her sitting outside a café and asked her to step in). We cackle about celebrities. We both profess that the latest twink with puppy-dog eyes in fact does nothing for us, but that Cate Blanchett can step on us, always. She compliments my style. She asks where I got my shoes, my brooch, my earrings. She marvels at my skill at thrifting—"I still get half my stuff from Talbots, I'm such an old lady." I make her laugh with stories about my students, a procession of pimply, dull-eyed kids who could waltz into a lower tier Ivy on their parents' legacy connections if they could only score two hundred points higher on the SAT, and how their ghostwritten college essays are all an exercise in inventing some personal hardship when it's clear they've never experienced any. We trade stories about bad dates, about people we knew from undergrad, about how we've somehow hooked up with the same two guys from Princeton.

We end up sprawled on her couch, laughing so hard our ribs ache. I didn't realize it was possible to have so much fun with Athena. I've never been so *myself* with her. We've known each other for over nine years now, but I've always been so guarded in her presence—in part because I'm nervous she'll realize I'm not half as brilliant or interesting as she thinks, and in part because of what happened freshman year.

But tonight, for the first time in a long time, I don't feel like I have to filter every word I say. I'm not struggling to impress Athena Fucking Liu. I'm just hanging with Athena.

"We should do this more," she keeps saying. "Junie, honestly, how have we never done this before?"

"I don't know," I say, and then, in an attempt to be deep, "Maybe we were afraid of how much we'd like each other."

It's a stupid thing to say, and not remotely true, but this apparently delights her.

"Maybe," she said. "Maybe. Oh, Junie. Life is so short. Why do we build up these walls?"

Her eyes are shining. Her mouth is wet. We're sitting side by side on her futon, knees so close they're almost touching. For a moment I think she's going to lean over and kiss me—and what a story *that* would be, I think; what a plot twist—but then she jumps back and yelps, and I realize my whisky glass has tilted so much I've spilled on the floor; thank God it's all hardwood, because if I'd ruined one of Athena's expensive rugs I would have just flung myself off the balcony. She laughs and runs to the kitchen for a napkin, and I take another sip to calm myself, wondering at my racing heart.

Then suddenly it's midnight and we're making pancakes—from scratch, no box mix, and embellished with several dollops of pandan extract in the now-neon-green batter because Athena Liu doesn't do *normal* pancakes. "Like vanilla, but better," she explains. "It's fragrant and herbal, like you're taking a big breath of the forest. I can't *believe* white people haven't learned about pandan yet." She flips them off the pan and onto my plate. The pancakes are burnt and uneven, but they smell incredible, and I realize then that I'm starving. I wolf one down with my hands, then look up to see Athena staring at me. I wipe my fingers, terrified I've disgusted her, but then she laughs and challenges me to an eating contest. And then there's a timer going and we're shoveling down the gloppy, half-cooked pancakes as quickly as we can, swigging milk in between to help the bulging lumps down our throats.

"Seven," I gasp, coming up for air. "Seven, what did—"

But Athena's not looking at me. She's blinking very hard, brows furrowed. One hand goes to her throat. The other frantically taps my arm. Her lips part, and out comes this muted, sickening rasp.

She's choking.

Heimlich, I know the Heimlich—at least, I think I do? I haven't thought about it since grade school. But I get behind her and wrap my arms around her waist and jerk my hands against her stomach, which should dislodge the pancake—holy *shit*, she's skinny—but she's still shaking her head, tapping my arm. It's not coming out. I jerk in again. And again. This isn't working. It crosses my mind to pull out my phone to Google "Heimlich," maybe watch a YouTube tutorial. But there's no time, that'll take forever.

Athena's banging against the counters. Her face has turned purple.

I remember reading a news article a few years ago about a sorority girl who choked to death at a pancake-eating contest. I remember sitting on my toilet, scrolling through the details in prurient fascination, because it seemed like such a sudden, ridiculous, and devastating way to die. *The pancakes were like a lump of cement in her throat*, said the EMT. A lump of cement.

Athena yanks at my arm; points at my phone. *Help*, she mouths. *Help, help*—

My fingers keep shaking; it takes me three tries to unlock my phone to call 911. They ask me what my emergency is.

"I'm with a friend," I gasp. "She's choking. I've tried the Heimlich; it's not coming out—"

Beside me, Athena is folded over a chair, jamming her sternum against the back, trying to perform the Heimlich on herself. Her movements get more and more frantic—*She looks like she's humping the chair*, I think stupidly—but it doesn't seem to work; nothing comes flying out of her mouth.

"Ma'am, what is your location?"

Oh, fucking hell, I don't know Athena's address. "I don't know, it's my friend's place." I try to think. "Um, across the taco place, and the bookstore, I don't know exactly . . ."

"Can you be more specific?"

"Dupont! Dupont Circle. Um—it's a block from the metro station, there's this nice revolving door—"

"Is it an apartment building?"

"Yes—"

"The Independent? The Madison?"

"Yes! The Madison. That one."

"Which unit?"

I don't know. I turn to Athena, but she's curled on the ground, jerking back and forth in a way that's awful to watch. I hesitate, torn between helping her and checking the door number—but then I remember, the ninth floor, so far up you can see all of Dupont Circle from the balcony. "Nine-oh-seven," I gasp. "Please, come quick, oh my God—"

"An ambulance is on its way to you now, ma'am. Is the patient conscious?"

I glance over my shoulder. Athena has stopped kicking. The only thing moving now is her shoulders, heaving in wild jerks like she's been possessed.

Then those stop, too.

"Ma'am?"

I lower the phone. My vision swims. I reach out and shake her shoulder: nothing. Athena's eyes are wide, bulging open; I can't bear to look at them. I touch my fingers to her neck for her pulse. Nothing. The dispatcher says something else, but I can't understand her; I can't understand my own thoughts, and everything that happens next, between the banging at the door and the rush of EMTs into the apartment, is a dark, bewildering blur.

I DON'T GET HOME UNTIL EARLY THE NEXT MORNING.

Documenting death, apparently, takes a very long time. The EMTs have to check every fucking detail before they can officially write on their clipboards: *Athena Liu, twenty-seven, female, is dead because she choked, to death, on a fucking pancake.*

I give a statement. I stare very hard into the eyes of the EMT in front of me—they're a very pale blue, and big black globs of mascara are stuck to her outer lashes—to distract from the stretcher in the kitchen behind me, the uniformed people pulling a plastic sheet over Athena's body. *Oh my God. Oh my God, that's a body bag. This is real. Athena is dead.*

"Name?"

"June—sorry, Juniper Hayward."

"Age?"

"Twenty-seven."

"How do you know the deceased?"

"She's—she was—my friend. We've been friends since college."

"And what were you doing here tonight?"

"We were celebrating." Tears prickle behind my nose. "We were celebrating, because she'd just signed a Netflix deal, and she was so fucking happy."

I'm weirdly terrified that they're about to arrest me for murder. But that's stupid—Athena choked, and the globule (they kept calling it a globule—what kind of word is "globule"?) is right there in her throat. There are no signs of struggle. She let me in, people saw us being friendly at the bar—*Call the guy at the Graham*, I want to say, *he'll back me up.*

But why am I even trying to come up with a defense? These details shouldn't matter. I didn't do it. I didn't kill her. That's ridiculous; it's ridiculous I'm even worried about it. No jury would convict.

At last, they let me go. It's four in the morning. An officer—at some point the police arrived, which I guess happens when there's a dead body—offers me a ride home to Rosslyn. We spend most of it in silence, and as we pull up to my building, he offers some condolences that I hear but don't process. I stagger into my apartment, rip off my shoes and bra, gargle some mouthwash, and collapse onto my bed. I cry for a while, great howling sobs to vent out this awful clawing energy in my body, and then one melatonin and two Lunestas later, I manage to fall asleep.

Meanwhile, in my bag, tossed at the floor of my bed, Athena's manuscript sits like a hot sack of coals.

Two

MOURNING IS STRANGE. ATHENA WAS ONLY A FRIEND, NOT A close friend. I feel like a bitch saying it, but she just wasn't that important to me, and she doesn't leave a hole in my life that I now need to build detours around. I don't feel the same black, suffocating loss I did when my father died. I don't struggle to breathe. I don't lie awake in the mornings debating whether it's worth crawling out of bed. I don't resent every stranger I encounter, wondering how they can keep moving around the world as if it hasn't stopped turning.

Athena's death didn't break my world, it just made it . . . weirder. I go about my days as normal. For the most part, if I don't think too hard about it, if I don't dwell on the memories, I'm fine.

Still, I was *there*. I watched Athena die. My feelings those first few weeks are dominated less by grief and more by an awed shock. That really happened. I really watched her feet drumming against her hardwood floors, her fingers clawing at her neck. I really sat next to her dead body for ten whole minutes before the EMTs arrived. I really saw her eyes bulging open, stricken, unseeing. Those memories don't make me cry—I couldn't describe this as pain—but I do stare at the wall and mutter, "What the *fuck*?" several times a day.

Athena's death must have made the news, because my phone blows up with friends trying to say the correct, concerned thing (Hey, I'm just reaching out, how have you been?) and acquaintances trying to seek out all the juicy details (OMG I saw on Twitter, were you actually THERE?). I don't have the energy to respond. I watch the red numbers tick higher and higher in the corners of my messaging apps with thrilled, amazed disgust.

On my sister Rory's advice, I visit a local support group and make an appointment with a therapist specializing in grief. Both only make me feel worse, because they assume a version of a friendship that didn't exist, and it's too hard to explain why I'm not more broken up about Athena, so I don't follow up with either. I don't want to talk about how much I miss her, or how my days feel so empty without her. The problem is that my days feel completely normal, except for the singular, bewildering fact that Athena is fucking *dead*, that she's gone, just like that, and I don't know how I'm even supposed to feel about it, so I start drinking and panic-eating whenever the blues creep up in the evenings, and I get pretty bloated for a few weeks from all the ice cream and lasagna, but that's as bad as things get.

I am, in fact, rather astounded by my mental resilience.

I break down only once, a week after it happened. I'm not sure what triggers it, but I do spend that night watching Heimlich tutorials on YouTube for hours, comparing them to what I did, trying to remember if I positioned my hands the same way, if I yanked with enough force. I could have saved her. I keep saying this out loud, like Lady Macbeth yelling about her damned spot. I could have kept my head on, taught myself how to do it properly, put my fists correctly over her navel, cleared the obstruction, and let Athena breathe again.

I am the reason why she died.

"No," says Rory when I call her at four in the morning, weeping so hard I can barely speak. "No, no, no, don't you think that for a second, do you understand? You are not guilty for anything. *You did not kill that girl. You are innocent.* Do you understand?"

I feel like a toddler as I mumble back, "Yes. Okay. Yeah."

But that's what I need right now: a child's blind faith that the world is so simple, and that if I didn't mean to do a bad thing, then none of this is my fault.

"Are you going to be okay?" Rory presses. "Do you want me to call Dr. Gaily?"

"No—God, no, I'm fine. Don't call Dr. Gaily."

"Okay, it's just, she told us that if you were ever backsliding—"

"I'm not backsliding." I take a deep breath. "This isn't like that. I'm all right, Rory. I didn't know Athena that well anyways. It's fine."

A few days after the news breaks, I write a long Twitter thread about what happened. It feels like I'm writing from a template, drawing on the countless bereavement threads I have pruriently scrolled through in the past. I use phrases like "tragic accident" and "hasn't sunk in" and "still feels unreal to me." I don't delve into details—that's vile. I write about how shaken I am, what Athena meant to me, and how much I'll miss her.

Strangers keep telling me how sorry they are, how I should be gentle with myself, how it's totally valid to be reeling like I am from such a traumatic incident. They call me a good person. They send me hugs and well-wishes. They ask if they can set up a GoFundMe for my therapy, and I'm tempted by the money, but I feel too uncomfortable to say yes. Someone even offers to drive over and bring me home-cooked meals every day for the next month. I ignore that, though, because you can't trust anyone on the internet and who knows if they're really coming to poison me?

My tweet racks up thirty thousand likes in one day. It's the most attention I've ever gotten on Twitter, much of it from literary luminaries and internet personalities with verified checkmarks. It all makes me strangely excited, watching my follower count tick up by the second. But then that makes me feel gross, the same way I feel after masturbating when I only started out of boredom, so then I block Twitter on all my devices (I'm taking a hiatus for my mental health, but thank you everyone for your concern) and vow not to log back in until at least a week has passed.

I ATTEND ATHENA'S FUNERAL, WHERE ATHENA'S MOTHER HAS INVITED me to speak. She called me a few days after the accident, and I nearly dropped the phone when she told me who she was; I had this sudden fear that she would interrogate me, or accuse me of killing her daughter—but instead she kept apologizing, as if Athena had been very rude to die in my presence.

The funeral is at a Korean church out in Rockville, which is strange to me because I thought Athena was Chinese, but whatever. I'm struck by how few people present are my age. It's mostly old Asian people, probably friends of her mother. Not a single writer I recognize, nor anyone from college. Though maybe this funeral is just a community affair—probably Athena's actual acquaintances went to the virtual service that the Asian American Writers' Collective set up.

It's closed casket, thank God.

A lot of the eulogies are in Chinese, so I sit there awkwardly, looking around for cues on when to laugh or shake my head and cry. When it's my turn, Athena's mother introduces me as one of her daughter's closest friends.

"Junie was there the night my Athena died," said Mrs. Liu. "She did her best to save her."

That's all it takes for my tears to start flowing. *But that's a good thing,* says an awful, cynical voice in my mind. Crying makes my grief look genuine. It deflects from the fact that I don't know what the fuck I'm doing here.

"Athena was dazzling," I say, and I do mean it. "She was larger than life. Untouchable. Looking at her was like looking at the sun. She was so brilliant that it hurt to stare for too long."

I suffer through half an hour of the wake before I make up an excuse to leave—I can only take so much pungent Chinese food and old people who can't or won't speak in English. Mrs. Liu presses against me, sniffling, as I say my goodbyes. She makes me promise to keep in touch, to let her know how I'm doing. Her tear-smudged mascara leaves clumpy stains on my velvet blouse that won't come out, even after half a dozen washes, so eventually I throw the whole outfit away altogether.

I CANCEL MY TUTORING SESSIONS FOR THE REST OF THE MONTH. (I work part-time at the Veritas College Institute, coaching the SAT test and ghostwriting common app essays, which is the default landing job for every Ivy League graduate without better prospects.) My boss is annoyed, and the parents who booked me are understandably pissed, but I cannot sit in a windowless room and go over multiple-choice reading comprehension answers with gum-chewing, braces-wearing brats right now. I simply cannot. "Last week I watched a friend thrash around on the ground until she died," I snap when a student's mother calls me to complain. "So I think I can take some bereavement leave, all right?"

I don't go out those next few weeks. I stay in my apartment, wearing pajamas all day. I order Chipotle at least a dozen times. I watch old episodes of *The Office* until I can quote them word for word, just for something to calm my mind.

I also read.

Athena was right to be excited. *The Last Front*, simply put, is a masterpiece.

I have to tunnel down a Wikipedia rabbit hole for a bit to situate myself. The novel is about the unsung contributions and experiences of the Chinese Labour Corps, the 140,000 Chinese workers who were recruited by the British Army and sent to the Allied Front during World War I. Many were killed by bombs, accidents, and diseases. Most were mistreated upon arrival in France, cheated out of their wages, assigned to dirty and cramped living quarters, denied interpreters, and attacked by other laborers. Many never made it back home.

It's a running joke that every Serious Author at some point does a grand and ambitious war novel, and I suppose this one is Athena's. She has the confidence, the understated and lyrical prose necessary to tell such a heavy story without coming across as pompous, juvenile, or sanctimonious. Most grand war epics by young writers tend to read like mere imitations of grand war epics; their authors come off as toddlers riding toy horses. But Athena's war epic sounds like an echo from the battlefield. It rings *true*.

It's clear what she meant when she called this an evolution in her craft. So far her novels had presented linear narratives, all told in the past tense from the third person perspective of a singular protagonist. But here Athena does something similar to what Christopher Nolan does in the movie *Dunkirk*: instead of following one particular story, she layers disparate narratives and perspectives together to form a moving mosaic, a crowd crying out in unison. It's cinematic in effect; you can almost see it in your head, documentary style: a multiplicity of voices unburying the past.

A story with no proper protagonist shouldn't be this compelling. But Athena's sentences are so engaging, I keep getting lost in the story, reading ahead instead of transcribing it to my laptop. It's a love story disguised as a war story, and the details are so shockingly vivid, so particular, it's hard to believe it's not a memoir, that she didn't simply transcribe the words of ghosts speaking in her ear. I understand now why this took so very long to write—the painstaking research bleeds through in every paragraph, from the standard-issue fur-lined hats to the enamel mugs the laborers used to drink their watered-down tea.

She has this sorcerous ability to keep your eyes riveted to the page. I have to know what happens to A Geng, the spindly student translator, and Xiao Li, the unwanted seventh son. I'm in tears at the end, when I find out that Liu Dong never made it back home to his waiting bride.

But it needs work. It's far from a first draft—it's not even a proper "draft," really; it's more like an amalgamation of startlingly beautiful sentences, bluntly stated themes, and the occasional "[and then they travel - complete later]." But she's laid out enough breadcrumbs that

I can follow the trail. I see where it's all going, and it's gorgeous. It's simply, breathtakingly gorgeous.

So gorgeous I can't help but give finishing it a try.

It's just a lark at first. A writing exercise. I wasn't rewriting the manuscript so much as seeing if I could fill in the blanks; if I had enough technical knowhow to shade, fine-tune, and extrapolate until the picture was complete. I was only going to play around with one of the middle chapters—one that had so many unfinished scenes that you could only tell what it was trying to say if you were intimately acquainted with the writing, and the writer.

But then I just kept going. I couldn't stop. They say that editing a bad draft is far easier than composing on a blank page, and that's true—I feel so *confident* in my writing just then. I keep finding turns of phrases that suit the text far better than Athena's throwaway descriptions. I spot where the pacing sags, and I mercilessly cut out the meandering filler. I draw out the plot's through line like a clear, powerful note. I tidy up; I trim and decorate; I make the text *sing*.

I know you won't believe me, but there was never a moment when I thought to myself, *I'm going to take this and make it mine*. It's not like I sat down and hatched up some evil plan to profit off my dead friend's work. No, seriously—it felt *natural*, like this was my calling, like it was divinely ordained. Once I got started, it felt like it was the most obvious thing in the world that I should complete, then polish Athena's story.

And then—who knows? Maybe I could get it published for her, too.

I work so damn hard on it. I write every day from dawn to past midnight. I've never worked so hard on any writing project before, not even my debut. The words burn like coals inside my chest, fueling me, and I must pour them all out at once before they consume me.

I complete the first draft in three weeks. I take a week off, during which all I do is take long walks and read books, just to gain a fresh set of eyes, and then I have the whole thing printed at Office Depot so I can go over it all with a red pen. I flip slowly through the pages, murmuring every sentence out loud to get a feel for the sound, the shape of the words. I stay up all night to incorporate the changes back into Word.

In the morning, I compose an email to my literary agent, Brett Adams, who I haven't spoken to for months, since I've been deleting all his polite-but-urgent inquiries about how my second book is going:

> Hey, Brett.
>
> I know you're waiting to hear about my second book, but I've actually got

I pause for a moment, and then delete that last sentence.

How am I going to explain all this to Brett? If he knows Athena wrote the first draft, he'll need to get in touch with Athena's agent, Jared. There will be messy negotiations with her literary estate. I don't have written evidence that Athena wanted me to finish the book—though I'm sure that's what she would have preferred, since what writer wants their work to languish in obscurity? Without proof of permission, however, my version might never be authorized at all.

But then. No one knows Athena wrote the first draft, do they?

Does the way that it's credited matter as much as the fact that, without me, the book might never see the light of day?

I can't let Athena's greatest work go to print in its shoddy, first-draft state. I can't. What kind of friend would I be?

Hey, Brett.

Here's the manuscript. It's a little different from the direction we'd discussed, but I've found a new voice, and I like it. What do you think?

Best,

June

Done; sent; *woosh* goes my mail app. I shut the lid and push my laptop across the desk, breathless at my own audacity.

WAITING IS THE HARDEST PART. I SEND THAT EMAIL ON MONDAY; Brett doesn't get back to me until Thursday, when he lets me know he's reserved the weekend for having a look. I can't tell if he means it, or if he's stalling so that I won't bother him. By the time the next Monday rolls around, I'm a mass of anxiety. Every minute feels like an eternity. I've paced outside my apartment block a million times, and I've resorted to leaving my phone in my microwave so that I'm not tempted to check it all the time.

I first met Brett through a pitch event on Twitter. Several days a year, authors will write a tweet-length query about their book and add the event hashtag, so that agents can scroll through the hashtag liking tweets they're intrigued by. I wrote:

> Over the Sycamore: Sisters Janie and Rose are having the worst summer of their lives. Their father is dying. Their mother's never around. All they have is each other—and a mysterious door in the backyard. A portal to another land. #Adult #ComingofAge #Litfic

Brett requested my manuscript, I sent it off, mentioned that I already had a publishing contract in hand, and he offered to chat on the phone with me a week later. He struck me as a little dude-bro-ey—his speech was peppered with words like "rad" and "super pumped," and he seemed awfully young. He'd graduated two years ago from Hamilton with a master's in publishing, and he hadn't been at his agency for more than a few months. But the agency was reputable, and his client referrals seemed to really like him, so I agreed to sign with him. That, plus I didn't have any better offers.

He's done okay for me over the years. I've always felt like a bit of a lower priority for him, especially since I don't make him that much money, but he at least answers all my emails within the week and hasn't lied to me about my royalties or the state of my rights, which you hear horror stories about all the time. Sure, I feel awkward and embarrassed reading curt, impersonal emails like Hi June, so the publisher won't be taking your book to paperback because they aren't sure it'll keep selling, or Hey June, so no one's biting on the audio rights front, so I'm going to take it off submission for now; just wanted to keep you updated. And sure, I'd thought occasionally about leaving Brett and querying again for an agent who might make me feel like more of a person. But it would have been terrifying to be out on my own again, without a single advocate in the industry.

I think Brett was expecting I'd quietly give up on writing on my own. I'd give anything to have seen his face when I dropped that bomb in his inbox.

He finally emails me back around midnight on Tuesday. It's short.

Hey June,

Wow, this is really special. I don't blame you for dropping everything to work on this project. It's a little different from your range, but this could be a great opportunity for you to grow. I don't think Garrett is right for this book—we should definitely take it out on wider submission. I'll handle that on my end.

I only have a few editorial suggestions. See attached.

Regards,
Brett

Brett's edits are light, noninvasive. Aside from line edits, they're mostly cuts for pacing (Athena could get *so* wrapped up in the sound of her own prose), moving some flashback scenes around so the narrative is more linear, and reemphasizing certain themes at the end. I sit down with some canned espressos and do them all over seventy-two hours. The words come easily to me—revisions are usually like pulling teeth, but I'm having fun with this. I'm having more fun with writing than I have in years. Maybe because it's someone else's words I'm chopping, so I don't feel like I'm killing my darlings. Maybe because the raw material is so *good*, and I feel like I'm sharpening gems, trimming away the rough patches to let them shine.

Then I send it back off to Brett, who submits it first to Garrett, since he's technically allowed the right of first refusal. Garrett passes, just as we'd hoped. I don't think he even bothered to open the file. Brett then immediately sends the novel to a half-dozen editors, all senior decision-makers at powerhouse publishers. ("Our reach list," he calls it, as if these are college applications. He's never submitted any of my work to a "reach list" before.) And then we wait.

THREE WEEKS LATER, AN EDITOR AT HARPERCOLLINS TAKES MY BOOK to acquisitions—the meeting where all the important people sit around a desk and decide whether to buy a book. They phone Brett with an offer that afternoon, and the number makes my jaw drop. I didn't know people *paid* that much money for books. But then Simon & Schuster wants in; then Penguin Random House, too, then Amazon (nobody in their right mind goes with Amazon, Brett assures me; they're here just to drive price up), and then all the smaller, prestigious independent houses that somehow still exist. We go to auction. The number keeps going up. They're talking about payment schedules, earn-out bonuses, world rights versus North American rights, audio rights, all these things that weren't even part of the conversation for my debut sale. Then at the end of it all, *The Last Front* sells to Eden Press, a midsize indie publisher that has a reputation for cranking out award-winning prestige fiction, for more money than I'd dreamed I would make in a lifetime.

When Brett calls to tell me the news, I lie down on my floor and don't get up until the ceiling stops spinning.

I get a huge, splashy deal announcement in *Publishers Weekly*. Brett starts talking about interest for foreign rights, film rights, mixed media rights, and I don't even know what any of that means except that there's more money coming through the pipeline.

I call my mother and sister to brag, and though they don't really know what this news means, they're glad that I have some stable income for the next few years.

I call the Veritas College Institute and let them know I'm quitting for good.

Writing friends I catch up with about twice a year text me CONGRATULATIONS, messages I just know are dripping in jealousy. Eden's official Twitter account blasts the news, and I get several hundred new followers. I go out for drinks with colleagues from Veritas, friends I don't even like that much and who clearly aren't interested in hearing more about the book, but after three shots it doesn't matter because we're drinking to me.

The whole time I'm thinking, *I've made it. I've fucking made it.* I'm living Athena's life. I'm experiencing publishing the way it's supposed to work. I've broken through that glass ceiling. I have everything I ever wanted—and it tastes just as delicious as I always imagined.

Three

I KNOW WHAT YOU'RE THINKING. *THIEF. PLAGIARIZER.* AND PERhaps, because all bad things must be racially motivated, *Racist.*

Hear me out.

It's not so awful as it sounds.

Plagiarism is an easy way out, the way you cheat when you can't string words together on your own. But what I did was not *easy*. I did rewrite most of the book. Athena's early drafts are chaotic, primordial, with half-finished sentences littered all over the place. Sometimes I couldn't even tell where she was going with a paragraph, so I excised it completely. It's not like I took a painting and passed it off as my own. I inherited a sketch, with colors added only in uneven patches, and finished it according to the style of the original. Imagine if Michelangelo left huge chunks of the Sistine Chapel unfinished. Imagine if Raphael had to step in and do the rest.

This whole project is beautiful, in a way. A never-before-seen kind of literary collaboration.

And so what if it was stolen? So what if I lifted it wholesale?

Athena died before anyone knew the manuscript existed. It would never have been published, or if it had, in its current state, it would always have been known as Athena's half-finished manuscript, as overhyped and disappointing as F. Scott Fitzgerald's *The Last Tycoon.* I gave it a chance to go out into the world without the judgment that multiple authorship always entails. And for all the work I put into it, all those hours of effort—why shouldn't it be my name on the title?

Athena is, after all, thanked in the acknowledgments. My treasured friend. My greatest inspiration.

And maybe Athena would have even wanted this. She was always into trippy literary hoaxes like this. She loved talking about how James Tiptree Jr. had fooled people into thinking she was a man, or how so many readers still think Evelyn Waugh was a woman. "People come to a text with so many prejudices formed by what they think they know about the author," she's said before. "I sometimes wonder how my work would be received if I pretended to be a man, or a white woman. The text could be exactly the same, but one might be a critical bomb and the other a resounding success. Why is that?"

So perhaps we can view this as Athena's great literary prank, as my complicating the reader-author relationship in a way that will provide juicy fodder for scholars for decades to come.

Okay—perhaps that last one is a bit of a stretch. And if this sounds like me assuaging my own conscience—fine. I'm sure you'd rather believe I spent those few weeks tortured, that I struggled constantly with my guilt.

But the truth is, I was too excited.

For the first time in months, I was happy about writing again. I felt like I'd been given a second chance. I was starting to believe in the dream again—that if you hone your craft and tell a good story, the industry will take care of the rest. That all you have to do is put a pen to paper, that if you work hard enough and write well enough, the Powers That Be will transform you overnight into a literary star.

I'd even begun toying around with some of my old ideas. They felt fresh now, vivid, and I could think of a dozen new directions in which to take them. The possibilities felt endless. It was like driving a new car or working on a new laptop. I'd somehow absorbed all the directness and verve of Athena's writing. I felt, as Kanye put it, harder, better, faster, and stronger. I felt like the kind of person who now listened to Kanye.

I once went to a talk by a successful fantasy writer where she claimed her fail-safe for getting over writer's block was to read a hundred or so pages of very good prose. "It makes my fingers itch to see a good sentence," she'd said. "It makes me want to imitate the same."

That's precisely how I felt about editing Athena's work. She made me a better writer. It was eerie, how quickly I absorbed her skill; as if upon death, all that talent needed to go somewhere, and ended up right inside me.

I felt like now I was writing for both of us. I felt like I was carrying on the torch.

Is that justification enough for you? Or are you still convinced that I'm some racist thief?

Fine. Here's how I really felt, when things came down to it.

At Yale, I once dated a graduate student in the philosophy department who did population ethics. He wrote papers on thought experiments so implausible that I often thought he would have been better off writing science fiction—whether we have obligations to future, unborn peoples, for example, or whether you can desecrate bodies if it will cause no harm to the living. Some of his arguments were a little extreme—he didn't think, for instance, that there is any moral obligation to follow wills of the deceased if there is an overriding interest in redistributing wealth elsewhere, or that there are strong moral objections to using cemetery grounds for, say, housing for the poor. The general theme of his research was under what circumstances someone counts as a moral agent that deserves consideration. I didn't understand much of his work, but his central argument was quite compelling: we owe nothing to the dead.

Especially when the dead are thieves and liars, too.

And fuck it, I'll just say it: taking Athena's manuscript felt like reparations, payback for the things that Athena took from me.

Four

PUBLISHING MOVES SLOWLY, UNTIL IT DOESN'T. THE TRULY EXCITing moments—going to auction, negotiating deals, fielding calls from potential editors, choosing a publisher—are a dizzying whirlwind, but the rest involves a lot of staring at your phone and waiting for updates. Most books are sold up to two years before they're released. The big announcements we're always seeing online (Book deal! Movie deal! TV deal! Awards nominations!) have been open secrets for weeks, if not months. All the excitement and surprise are feigned for social clout.

The Last Front won't come out until fifteen months after I sign my contract. Until then, there's production.

I receive my edit letter two months after the deal. My editor at Eden is Daniella Woodhouse, a deep-voiced, no-nonsense, fast-talking woman who both intimidated and intrigued me during our first phone call. I remembered she'd gotten into some kerfuffle at a conference last year when she called a fellow female panelist "pathetic" for arguing that sexism in the industry remained an obstacle, after which all sorts of online personalities labeled her an enemy of women and demanded she make a public apology, if not resign. (She did neither.) That doesn't seem to have impacted her career. In the last year, she's published three bestsellers: a novel about the interior lives of murderous and sexy housewives, a thriller about a classical pianist who makes a deal with the literal devil in exchange for a legendary career, and a memoir by a lesbian beekeeper.

I was hesitant about signing with Eden Press at first, especially since it was an indie publisher instead of one of the Big Five—HarperCollins, Penguin Random House, Hachette, Simon & Schuster, and Macmillan. But Brett convinced me that at a midsize house, I'd be a big fish in a small pond; that I'd get all the care and attention I never felt at my first publisher. Sure enough, compared to Garrett, Daniella practically coddles me. She responds to all my emails within the day, often within the hour, and always in depth. She makes me feel like I matter. When she tells me this book will be a hit, I know that she means it.

I like her editorial style, too. Most of her requested changes are simple clarifications. *Are American audiences going to know what this phrase means? Should this flashback be placed in this early chapter when we haven't met the character in the proper timeline yet? This dialogue exchange is artful, but how does it move the story along?*

Honestly, I'm relieved. Finally someone's calling Athena out on her bullshit, on her deliberately confusing sentence structures and cultural allusions. Athena likes to make her audience "work for it." On the topic of cultural exposition, she's written that she doesn't "see the need to move the text closer to the reader, when the reader has Google, and is perfectly capable of moving closer to the text." She drops in entire phrases in Chinese without adding any translations—

her typewriter doesn't have Chinese characters, so she left spaces and wrote them out by hand. It took me hours of fiddling with an OCR to search them online, and even then I had to strike out about half of them. She refers to family members in Chinese terms instead of English, so you're left wondering if a given character is an uncle or a second cousin. (I've read dozens of guides to the Chinese kinship nomenclature system by now. It makes no goddamn sense.)

She's done this in all her other novels. Her fans praise such tactics as brilliant and authentic—a diaspora writer's necessary intervention against the whiteness of English. But it's not good craft. It makes the prose frustrating and inaccessible. I am convinced it is all in service of making Athena, and her readers, feel smarter than they are.

"Quirky, aloof, and erudite" is Athena's brand. "Commercial and compulsively readable yet still exquisitely literary," I've decided, will be mine.

The hardest part is keeping track of all the characters. We change almost a dozen names to reduce confusion. Two different characters have the last name Zhang, and *four* have the last name Li. Athena differentiates them by giving them different first names, which she only occasionally uses, and other names that I assume are nicknames (A Geng, A Zhu; unless A is a last name and I'm missing something), or Da Liu and Xiao Liu, which throws me for a loop because I thought Liu was a last name, so what are Da and Xiao doing there? Why are so many of the female characters named Xiao as well? And if they're family names, does that mean everyone is related? Is this a novel about *incest*? But the easy fix is to give them all distinct monikers, and I spend hours scrolling through pages on Chinese history and baby name sites to find names that will be culturally appropriate.

We cut out thousands of words of unnecessary backstory. Athena likes to write in a rhizomatic fashion: jumping back ten or twenty years to explore a character's childhood; lingering in rural Chinese landscapes for long, unrelated chapters; introducing characters who have no clear relevance to the plot, and then forgetting about them for the rest of the novel. I can tell she's trying to add texture to her characters' lives, to show the readers where they come from and the webs in which they exist, but she's gone way overboard. It's distracting from the central narrative. Reading should be an enjoyable experience, not a chore.

We soften the language. We take out all references to "Chinks" and "Coolies." *Perhaps you mean this as subversive*, writes Daniella in the comments, *but in this day and age, there's no need for such discriminatory language. We don't want to trigger readers.*

We also soften some of the white characters. No, it's not as bad as you think. Athena's original text is almost embarrassingly biased; the French and British soldiers are cartoonishly racist. I get she's trying to make a point about discrimination within the Allied front, but these scenes are so hackneyed that they defy belief. It throws the reader out of the story. Instead we switch one of the white bullies to a Chinese character, and one of the more vocal Chinese laborers to a sympathetic white farmer. This adds the complexity, the humanistic nuance that perhaps Athena was too close to the project to see.

In the original draft, several laborers are driven to suicide by their mistreatment at the hands of the British, and one man hangs himself in the captain's dugout. The captain, upon finding the body, tells an interpreter to order the rest of the laborers to hang themselves in their own dugouts if they must, for "We don't like such a mess in ours." This whole scene, apparently, was lifted straight from the historical record—Athena's copy had handwritten notes in the margin emphasizing: *COMMENT ON IN ACKNOWLEDGMENTS—CAN'T MAKE THIS SHIT UP. MY GOD.*

It's a powerful scene, and I felt a curdle of horror when I read it for the first time. But Daniella thinks it's too over the top. *I get that they're army men, and they're uncouth, but this feels like tragedy porn*, she comments. *Cut for pacing?*

The largest change we make is to the last third of the book.

The pacing really flags here, reads Daniella's comment. *Do we need all this context about the Treaty of Versailles? Seems out of place—focus is not Chinese geopolitics, surely?*

At the end of the book, Athena's original draft is unbearably sanctimonious. Here she leaves the more engaging personal narratives behind to hit the reader over the head with the myriad ways in which the laborers have been forgotten and ignored. The laborers killed in action could not be buried in plots near European soldiers. They were not eligible for military awards because they were purportedly not in combat. And—the part that Athena was angriest about—the Chinese government was still fucked over in the Treaty of Versailles at the conclusion of WWI, with the territory of Shandong ceded from Germany to Japan.

But who's going to follow all of that? It's hard to sympathize with the stakes in the absence of a main character. The last forty pages read more like a history paper than a gripping wartime narrative. They feel out of place, like a senior term paper attached haphazardly to the end. Athena did always have such a didactic streak.

Daniella wants me to cut it altogether. Let's end the novel with A Geng on the boat heading home, she suggests. It's a strong final image, and it carries the momentum of the previous burial scene. The rest can go in an afterword, perhaps, or a personal essay we can put out in an outlet closer to publication. Or perhaps as additional material in the paperback, for book clubs?

I think that's brilliant. I make the cut. And then, just to add some flair, I include a short epilogue after the A Geng scene consisting of one line from a letter one of the laborers later wrote Kaiser Wilhelm II in 1918 pleading for world peace: *I am convinced that it is the will of Heaven that all mankind should live as one family.*

This is brilliant, Daniella writes in response to my turnaround. *You are so wonderfully easy to work with. Most authors are pickier about killing their darlings.*

This makes me beam. I want my editor to like me. I want her to think I'm easy to work with, that I'm not a stubborn diva, that I'm capable of making any changes she asks for. It'll make her more likely to sign me on for future projects.

It's not all about pandering to authority. I do think we've made the book better, more accessible, more streamlined. The original draft made you feel dumb, alienated at times, and frustrated with the self-righteousness of it all. It stank of all the most annoying things about Athena. The new version is a universally relatable story, a story that anyone can see themselves in.

The whole process takes three editorial rounds over four months. By the end, I've become so familiar with the project that I can't tell where Athena ends and I begin, or which words belong to whom. I've done the research. I've read a dozen books now on Asian racial politics and the history of Chinese labor at the front. I've lingered over every word, every sentence, and every paragraph so many times that I nearly know them by heart—hell, I've probably been over this novel more times than Athena herself.

What this whole experience teaches me is that I *can* write. Some of Daniella's favorite passages are the ones original to me. There's one part, for instance, where a poor French family wrongly accuses a group of Chinese laborers of stealing a hundred francs from their house. The laborers, determined to make a good impression of their race and nation, collect two hundred francs among them and gift it to the family even though it's clear they are innocent. Athena's draft only made a brief mention of the wrongful accusation, but my version turns it into a heartwarming illustration of Chinese virtue and honesty.

All of my confidence and verve, dashed after my horrific debut experience, come rushing back. I'm brilliant with words. I've studied writing for nearly a decade now; I know what makes a direct, punchy sentence, and I know how to structure a story so that the reader stays riveted all the way through. I've labored for years to learn my craft. Perhaps the core idea of this novel wasn't mine, but I'm the one who rescued it, who freed the diamond from the rough.

But the thing is, no one will ever understand how much I put into this novel. If news ever breaks that Athena wrote the first draft, the whole world will look at all the work I did, all those beautiful sentences I produced, and all they'll ever see is Athena Liu.

But no one ever has to know, do they?

THE BEST WAY TO HIDE A LIE IS IN PLAIN SIGHT.

I lay the groundwork long before the novel is out, before early versions of it are off to reviewers and book bloggers. I've never made a secret of my relationship to Athena, and I'm even less subtle about it now. I am, after all, currently best known as the person who was at her side when she died.

So I play up our connection. I mention her name in every interview. My grief over her death becomes a cornerstone of my origin story. All right, maybe I exaggerate the details a bit. Quarterly drinks become monthly, sometimes weekly drinks. I only have two selfies of us saved on my phone, which I never meant to share because I hate how frumpy I look beside her, but I upload them on my Instagram under a black-and-white filter and pen a touching tribute poem to accompany it. I've read all her work, and she mine. Often we traded ideas. I saw her as my greatest inspiration, and her feedback on my drafts was foundational to my growth as a writer. This is what I tell the public.

See, the closer we seem, the less mysterious that resemblances to her work will appear. Athena's fingerprints are all over this project. I don't wipe them off. I just provide an alternative explanation for why they're there.

"I was in a really difficult place with my writing after my debut flopped," I tell *Book Riot*. "I didn't know if I even wanted to keep going. Athena's the one who convinced me to give the manuscript another try. And she helped me with all my research—she navigated the Chinese primary sources, and she helped me hunt down texts at the Library of Congress."

It's not *lying*. I swear, it was never as psychopathic as it sounds. It's all just stretching reality a bit, putting the right spin on the picture so that the lurking social media outrage mob doesn't get the wrong idea. Besides, the train has left the station—coming clean at this point would tank the book, and I couldn't do that to Athena's legacy.

No one is suspicious. Athena's aloofness helps me out here. She did have other friends, according to all the Twitter eulogies I read after her funeral, but they're all spread out across different states and continents. There's no one else she was regularly hanging out with in DC. There's no one who can contradict my account of our relationship. The whole world seems ready to believe that I was Athena Liu's closest friend. And who knows? Maybe I was.

And yes—this is incredibly cynical, but the fact of our friendship casts an awful light on any future detractors. If anyone criticizes me for imitating her work, they're coming after a friend who's still in mourning, which makes them a monster.

Athena, the dead muse. And I, the grieving friend, haunted by her spirit, unable to write without invoking her voice.

See, who ever said I wasn't a good storyteller?

I set up a scholarship in Athena's name at the Asian American Writers' Collective's annual workshop, where Athena had spent one summer as a student and three as a guest instructor. The director, Peggy Chan, had sounded confused and suspicious when I called about Athena, but changed her tone quickly enough when she realized that I was offering money. Since then she's been retweeting all of my book news, spamming my Twitter feed with messages like CONGRATULATIONS! and CAN'T WAIT TO READ THIS!!! #GoJune!

Her enthusiasm makes me a bit uncomfortable, especially since the rest of her feed is exclusively stuff about racism in publishing and the industry's shoddy treatment of marginalized writers. But, if she's going to use me, then I'm going to use her right back.

MEANWHILE, I DO MY DUE DILIGENCE.

I research. I read every single one of the sources that Athena cited in her draft, until I'm as much an expert on the Chinese Labour

Corps as anyone can be. I even try to teach myself Mandarin, but no matter how hard I try, all the characters look as unrecognizable as chicken scratch, and the different tones feel like an elaborate practical joke, so I give up. (It's all right, though: I find an old interview where Athena admitted that she didn't even speak Mandarin fluently herself, and if Athena Liu couldn't read primary sources, well, then why should I?)

I set up Google Alerts for my name, Athena's name, and both of our names in conjunction. Most of my search results are publishing press releases that say nothing new—splashy information about my book deal, memorials to Athena's work, and occasionally mentions about how my work is influenced by hers. Someone writes a long and thoughtful piece on the history of literary friendships, and it tickles me to see me and Athena compared to Tolkien and Lewis, Brontë and Gaskell.

For a few weeks, it all feels like I'm in the clear. No one asks questions about how I came to my source material. No one seems to even have known what Athena was working on.

One day, I see a headline from the *Yale Daily News* that makes my stomach drop.

"Yale Acquires Athena Liu's Drafting Notes," it reads. From the opening paragraph: "Late novelist and Yale alumna Athena Liu's notebooks will soon become part of the Marlin Literary Archive at the Sterling Memorial Library. The notebooks have been donated by Liu's mother, Patricia Liu, who has expressed her gratitude that her daughter's notebooks will be memorialized by her alma mater . . ."

Shit. Shit, shit, shit.

Athena did all her outlining in those stupid Moleskine notebooks.

She's spoken publicly about this process. "I do all my brainstorming and research by hand," she's said. "It helps me think better, to identify themes and linkages. I think it's because the act of physical writing forces my mind to slow down, to examine the potential of every word I'm scribbling out. Then, when I've filled up six or seven notebooks this way, I pull out the typewriter and start drafting properly."

I don't know why I never thought of taking the notebooks as well. They were right there on the desk—at least three of them, two lying open next to the manuscript. I was so panicked that night. I suppose I thought they'd go into storage with the rest of her belongings.

But a public archive? I mean, fuck. The first person who goes in to write a paper about her—and there will be many, I'm sure—will see the notes for *The Last Front* right away. I'm sure they're extensive, detailed. That'll be a dead giveaway. Then this whole artifice unravels.

I don't have time to calm myself, to think things through. I need to nip this in the bud. Heart racing, I reach for my phone and call Athena's mother.

MRS. LIU IS GORGEOUS. IT'S TRUE WHAT THEY SAY—ASIAN WOMEN don't age. She must be in her midfifties by now, but she doesn't look a day over thirty. You can see, in that elegant, petite frame and sharp cheekbones, the wispy beauty Athena would have grown into. Mrs. Liu's face had been so puffy from crying at the funeral, I hadn't noticed how striking she was; now, up close, she looks so much like her daughter that it's disorienting.

"Junie. So good to see you." She embraces me on her doorstep. She smells like dried flowers. "Come in."

I sit down at her kitchen table, and she pours and places a steaming cup of a very fragrant tea before me before sitting down. Her slender fingers curl around her own cup. "I understand you wanted to talk about Athena's things."

She's so direct, I wonder for a moment if she's onto me. She's nothing like the warm, welcoming woman I'd met at the funeral. But then I notice the tired sag of her mouth, the shadows beneath her eyes, and I realize she's only trying to get through the day.

I had a whole arsenal of small talk planned: stories about Athena, stories about Yale, observations on grief and how hard it is to make it through every minute of every day when one of your pillars has vanished overnight. I know loss. I know how to talk to people about loss.

Instead I cut straight to the chase. "I read that you're going to donate Athena's notebooks to the Marlin Archive?"

"I am." She cocks her head. "You don't think that's a good idea?"

"No, no, Mrs. Liu, I don't mean that, I'm just . . . I'm wondering if you mind telling me how you made that decision?" My cheeks are burning. I can't hold her gaze. I drop my eyes. "I mean, only if you want to talk about it. I know all of this is—it's impossible to really talk about, I know, and it's not like you know me all that well . . ."

"I received an email from the librarian in charge of the project a few weeks ago," says Mrs. Liu. "Marjorie Chee. Very nice girl. We spoke on the phone, and she seemed so familiar with Athena's work." She sighs, takes a sip of tea. For some reason, I keep thinking about how good her English is. There's only a hint of an accent, and her vocabulary is rich, her sentence structures complex and varied. Athena had always made a big deal about how her parents had immigrated to the States without speaking a word of English, but Mrs. Liu's English sounds fine to me. "Well, I don't know much about these things. But it seems like a public archive is a good way to let people remember Athena. She was so brilliant—well, you know that; her mind worked in such fascinating ways. I'm sure some literary scholars might be interested in doing a study. Athena would like that. She was always so thrilled when academics wrote about her work; she said it was better validation than the . . . the adoration of the masses. Her words. Anyhow, it's not like I'm doing anything important with them." She nods to the corner. I follow her gaze, and my breath catches. The notebooks are right there, piled unceremoniously together in a big cardboard box, shelved beneath a large bag of rice and what looks like a smooth, unstriped watermelon.

Wild fantasies flood my mind. I could grab them and run out, be halfway down the block before Mrs. Liu realizes what's happening. I could douse this whole place in oil while she's out and burn them, and no one would be any wiser.

"Have you read what's in them?" I ask cautiously.

Mrs. Liu sighs again. "No, I've thought about it, but I . . . It's very painful. You know, even when Athena was alive, it was difficult for me to read her novels. She drew so much from her childhood, from stories her father and I told her, from things . . . things in our past. Our family's past. I did read her first novel, and that's when I realized it's very hard to read about these memories from someone else's point of view." Her throat pulses. She touches her collar. "It makes me wonder if we should have spared her all that pain."

"I understand," I say. "My relatives are the same way with my work."

"Oh yes?"

No, that's a lie; I don't know what compelled me to say it. My folks couldn't care less about what I write. My grandfather griped about having to pay the cost of my useless English degree all four years that I was at Yale, and my mother still phones once a month to ask whether I've decided yet to try something that will let me earn real money, like law school or consulting. Rory did read my debut novel, though she didn't understand it at all—she kept asking why the sisters were so insufferable, which baffled me, because the sisters were supposed to be *us*.

But what Mrs. Liu wants right now is company and sympathy. She wants to hear the right words. And words are, after all, what I'm good at.

"They feel too close to the subject matter," I say. "I draw a lot on my own life in my novels, too." This part is true; my debut novel was nearly autobiographical. "And I didn't exactly have a smooth childhood, so it's hard for them . . . I mean, they don't like to be reminded of their mistakes. They don't like seeing things through my eyes."

Mrs. Liu nods vigorously. "I can understand that."

I see my way in. And it's so obvious, it almost feels too easy.

"And, well, that's sort of why I wanted to come talk to you today." I take a breath. "I'll be honest with you, Mrs. Liu. I don't think putting her notebooks up for public access is a good idea."

Her brows furrow. "Why not?"

"I don't know how much you know about your daughter's writing process . . ."

"Not much," she says. "Almost nothing. She hated talking about her work until it was finished. She got so snippy if I even brought it up."

"Well, that's just it," I say. "Athena was so private with her stories while she was putting them together. They draw from such painful histories—we spoke about it once; she described it as mining her past for scars and ripping them open so that they bleed fresh again." We never spoke about writing quite so intimately; I read the part about ripping scars open in an interview. But it is true; that really is how Athena thought about her works in progress. "She couldn't show that pain to anyone else until she'd perfected the way she wanted to tell it, until she had complete control over the narrative. Until she'd polished it into a version and argument that she was comfortable with. But those notebooks are her original thoughts, raw and unfiltered. And I just can't help but . . . I don't know, I feel like donating them to an archive would be a violation. Like putting her corpse on display."

Maybe I'm a bit heavy-handed with the imagery there. But it works.

"My goodness." Mrs. Liu touches a hand to her mouth. "Oh my goodness, I can't believe—"

"Of course it's up to you," I say hastily. "It's entirely your right to do as you like with them. I just thought, as a friend, I feel obligated to tell you. I don't think that's what Athena would have wanted."

"I see." Mrs. Liu's eyes are red, watery with tears. "Thank you, June. I never even considered . . ." She's silent for a moment, staring at her teacup. She blinks hard, then glances up at me. "Do you want them, then?"

I flinch back. *"Me?"*

"It hurts to have them around." Her shoulders sag; the whole of her seems to wilt. "And since you knew her so well . . ." She shakes her head. "Oh, what am I saying? It's such an imposition. No, forget about it."

"No, no, it's just that . . ." Should I say yes? I would have complete control over Athena's notes for *The Last Front*, and who knows what else. Ideas for future novels? Full drafts, even?

No, best not to get greedy. I have what I want. Any more, and I risk leaving a trail. Mrs. Liu might be discreet, but what might happen if the *Yale Daily News* reports, however innocuously, that I now own all those notebooks?

And it's not like I'm trying to build an entire career on repurposing Athena's work. *The Last Front* was a special, happy accident—a melding of two modes of genius. Whatever work I produce from here on out will be my own. I don't need the temptation.

"I couldn't," I say gently. "I wouldn't feel right. Perhaps you could leave them in the family?"

What I would like is for her to burn them, to scatter the ashes along with Athena's so that no one, no curious relative decades from now, can go poking through them to dredge up what should be left alone. But I have to make her think she came up with the idea herself.

"There's no one else." Mrs. Liu shakes her head again. "No, after her father went back to China, it was me and Athena, just the two of us." She sniffles. "That's why I said yes to the Marlin people, you see—they would at least take it off my hands."

"I just wouldn't trust a public archive," I say. "You don't know what they'll uncover."

Mrs. Liu's eyes widen. Suddenly she seems greatly disturbed, and I wonder what she's thinking about, but I know it's best not to pry. I've already gotten what I came for. I'll let her imagination do the rest.

"Oh my goodness," she says again. "I can't believe . . ."

My stomach twists. She looks so distressed. Jesus Christ. What am I *doing*? Suddenly all I want is to be out of there, notebooks be damned. This is so fucked up. I can't believe I had the nerve to come here. "Mrs. Liu, I don't mean to pressure you—"

"No." She sets down her teacup with a thud. "No. You're right. I will not put my daughter's soul on display."

I exhale, watching her cautiously. Have I won? Could it have been that easy? "If that's what you—"

"That is what I have decided." She glares at me, as if I'm about to try to talk her out of it. "No one will see those notebooks. No one."

I stay for another half an hour before I go, making small talk and telling Mrs. Liu about how I've been doing since the funeral. I tell her about *The Last Front*, about how much Athena inspired my work and that I hope she'd be proud of what I've written. But she's not interested; she's distracted, asking me thrice if I want some more tea although I've already said no, and it's obvious she wants to be left alone but is too polite to ask me to leave.

When I finally get up to go, she's staring at the boxes, clearly terrified of what lies within.

I KEEP TABS ON THE MARLIN ARCHIVE WEB PAGE FOR THE NEXT FEW weeks, scanning for any updates about the Athena Liu collection.

But there's nothing. January thirtieth comes and goes, which is the date the notebooks would have been made available to the public. One day I search the *Yale Daily News* website to find that the original announcement has simply been taken down without acknowledgment, its URL broken, as if the story had never existed.

Five

THAT WEDNESDAY I HAVE MY FIRST VIDEOCONFERENCE MEETING with my new publicity and marketing teams.

I'm so nervous I could puke. My last experience working with a publicist was awful. She was a pinched-face blonde woman named Kimberly who only ever sent me interview requests from bloggers that had, maybe, five followers. When I asked for anything more, like maybe coverage at a website that people had actually heard of, she'd say, "We'll look into that, but it depends on interest." Kimberly, like everyone else, had known early on that my debut was dead in the water. She just didn't have the heart to say it to my face. Half the time, she misspelled my name as "Jane." When I left my old publisher, she sent me a curt little email that read only, It's been such a pleasure to work with you.

But this time around, I'm struck by everyone's enthusiasm. Emily, who does publicity, and Jessica, who does digital marketing, kick things off by telling me how much they adore the manuscript. "It just *exudes* the gravitas of a much older writer," Jessica gushes. "And

I think we'll be able to position it really well between historical fiction, which women really enjoy, and military fiction, which suits a male audience."

I'm shocked. Jessica seems to have actually read my book. That's a first—Kimberly always seemed confused as to whether I'd written a novel or a memoir.

Next, they walk me through their marketing strategy. I'm overwhelmed by how comprehensive it is. They're talking Facebook ads, Goodreads ads, maybe even metro station ads, although it's not clear if anyone pays attention to those anymore. They're also investing big in bookstore placement, which means that from the day that it's out, my book will be the first thing people see when they walk into any Barnes & Noble across the country.

"This will, for sure, be *the* book of the season," Jessica assures me. "At least, we're doing everything we can to make it so."

I'm speechless. Is this what it was like to be Athena? To be told, from the beginning, that your book will be a success?

Jessica wraps up the marketing plan with some dates and deadlines for when they'll need promotional materials from me. There's a short pause. Emily clicks and double-clicks her pen. "So then the other thing we wanted to ask you is, uh, positioning."

I realize I'm supposed to answer. "Right—sorry, what do you mean?"

She and Jessica exchange a glance.

"Well, the thing is, this novel is set in large part in China," says Jessica. "And given the recent conversations about, you know—"

"Cultural authenticity," Emily jumps in. "I don't know if you follow some of the conversations online. Book bloggers and book Twitter accounts can be pretty . . . picky about things these days . . ."

"We just want to get ahead of any potential blowups," says Jessica. "Or pile-ons, as it were."

"I did hours and hours of research," I say. "It's not like I, you know, wrote from stereotypes; this isn't that kind of book—"

"Of course," Emily says smoothly. "But you're . . . that is, you are not . . ."

I see what she's getting at. "I am not Chinese," I say curtly. "If that's what you're asking. It's not 'own voices,' or whatever you want to call it. Is that a problem?"

"No, no, not at all, we're just covering our bases. And you're not . . . anything else?" Emily winces the moment those words leave her mouth, like she knows she shouldn't have said that.

"I am white," I clarify. "Are you saying we'll get in trouble because I wrote this story and I'm white?"

I immediately regret phrasing it like that. I'm being too blunt, too defensive; wearing my insecurities on my sleeve. Both Emily and Jessica begin blinking very quickly, glancing at each other as if hoping the other will speak first.

"Of course not," Emily says finally. "Of course, anyone should be able to tell any kind of story. We're just thinking about how to position you so that readers trust the work."

"Well, they can trust the work," I say. "They can trust the words on the page. The blood and sweat that went into telling the story."

"No, of course," says Emily. "And we don't mean to invalidate that."

"Of course not," says Jessica.

"Again, we think anyone should be able to tell any kind of story."

"We're not censors. That's not our culture here at Eden."

"Right."

Emily then shifts the conversation to where I'm based, where I might be up to travel, etc. The meeting fizzles out pretty quickly after that, before I've gotten a chance to get my bearings back. Emily and Jessica tell me again how excited they are about the book, how wonderful it was to meet me, and how they can't wait to keep working with me. Then they're gone, and I'm staring at an empty screen.

I feel awful. I shoot off an email to Brett, airing out all my anxieties. He responds an hour later, assuring me not to worry. They just want to be clear, he says. On how exactly they can position me.

As it turns out, they want to position me as "worldly." Jessica and Emily send us a longer email detailing their plans the next Monday: We think June's background is very interesting, so we want to make sure readers are aware of that. They highlight all the different places I lived when I was little—South America, Central Europe, a half-dozen cities in the US that were stops on my dad's never-ending tour as a construction engineer. (Emily really likes the word "nomad.") They highlight the year I spent in the Peace Corps in my newly written author biography, although I never went near Asia (I was in Mexico, making use of my high school Spanish, and I quit early because I got a debilitating stomach virus and had to be medically evacuated). And they suggest I publish under the name Juniper Song instead of June Hayward ("Your debut didn't reach quite the same market we're hoping for, and it's better to have a clean start. And Juniper is so, so unique. What kind of name is that? It sounds Native, almost."). Nobody talks about the difference in how "Song" might be perceived versus "Hayward." No one says explicitly that "Song" might be mistaken for a Chinese name, when really it's the middle name my mother came up with during her hippie phase in the eighties and I was very nearly named Juniper Serenity Hayward.

Emily helps me pitch an article about authorial identities and pen names to *Electric Lit*, where I explain that I've chosen to rebrand myself as Juniper Song to honor my background and my mother's influence in my life. "My debut, *Over the Sycamore*, written as June Hayward, was rooted in my grief over my father's death," I write. "*The Last Front*, written as Juniper Song, symbolizes a step forward in my creative journey. This is what I love most about writing—it offers us endless opportunities to reinvent ourselves, and the stories we tell about ourselves. It lets us acknowledge every aspect of our heritage and history."

I never lied. That's important. I never pretended to be Chinese, or made up life experiences that I didn't have. It's not fraud, what we're doing. We're just suggesting the right credentials, so that readers take me and my story seriously, so that nobody refuses to pick up my work because of some outdated preconceptions about who can write what. And if anyone makes assumptions, or connects the dots the wrong way, doesn't that say far more about them than me?

THINGS RUN MORE SMOOTHLY ON THE EDITORIAL SIDE. DANIELLA loves what I've done in the revisions. All she requests in her third pass are some light line edits, and a suggestion that I add a dramatis personae, which is a fancy term for a list of all the characters accompanied by short descriptions so that readers don't forget who they are. Then it's off to a copyeditor, who from my experience are these superhuman, eagle-eyed monsters that catch continuity errors unseen to the naked eye.

We only run into one wrinkle, a week before my copyedit pass is due.

Daniella emails me out of the blue: Hey June. Hope you've been well. Can you believe we're already six months out from publication? Wanted to bring up something to get your opinion—Candice suggested that we get a Chinese or Chinese diaspora sensitivity reader, and I know it's late in the process, but do you want us to look into things for you?

Sensitivity readers are readers who provide cultural consulting and critiques on manuscripts for a fee. Say, for example, a white author writes a book that involves a Black character. The publisher might then hire a Black sensitivity reader to check whether the textual representations are consciously, or unconsciously, racist. They've gotten more and more popular in the past few years, as more and more white authors have been criticized for employing racist tropes and stereotypes. It's a nice way to avoid getting dragged on Twitter, though sometimes it backfires—I've heard horror stories of at least two writers who were forced to withdraw their books from publication because of a single subjective opinion.

I don't see why, I write back. I'm pretty comfortable with the research I did.

A response instantly pings my inbox. It's Candice, following up. I feel strongly we ought to hire a reader familiar with the history and language. June is not Chinese diaspora, and we run the risk of doing real harm if we don't check any of the Chinese phrases, naming conventions, or textual recounting of racism with a reader better suited to catch mistakes.

I groan.

Candice Lee, Daniella's editorial assistant, is the only person at Eden who doesn't like me. She never makes it so evident that I have grounds to complain about it—she's unfailingly polite in emails, she likes and retweets everything I post about the book on social media, and she always greets me with a smile during videoconference meetings. But I can tell it's all forced—there's something in her pinched expression, the curtness of her words.

Maybe she knew Athena. Maybe she's one of those wannabe writers daylighting as an underpaid, overworked publishing junior staff member with a China-inspired manuscript of her own, and she's jealous I've made it big when she hasn't. I get that—in publishing, that's a universal dynamic. But that's not my problem.

Again, I'm quite comfortable with the research I did in preparation for this book. I don't find it necessary to delay things for a sensitivity read at this point in production, especially since we have a tight turnaround for review copies to early readers. Send.

That should be the end of it. But an hour later, my inbox pings again. It's Candice, doubling down. She's addressed the email to me, Daniella, and the entire publicity team.

> Dear all,
>
> I want to emphasize again how important I feel it is that we get a sensitivity reader for this project. In this current climate, readers are bound to be suspicious of someone writing outside of their lane—and for good reason. I understand this would slow down production, but an SR would protect June from accusations of both cultural appropriation and, worse, cultural leeching. It would show that June meant to represent the Chinese diaspora community in good faith.

Jesus Christ. Cultural appropriation? Cultural *leeching*? What is her *problem*?

I forward her email to Brett. Can you tell her to step off? I ask. Agents are wonderful intermediaries during heated exchanges like this; they let you keep your hands clean while they drive in the knife. I think I've made my stance pretty clear, so why is she still bothering me with this?

Brett proposes that perhaps, instead of bringing in an outsider, we can have Candice do the sensitivity read instead. Candice responds curtly that she is Korean American, not Chinese American, and that Brett's assumption otherwise is a racist microaggression. (It is at this point that I determine Candice exists entirely to complain about microaggressions.) Daniella jumps in to smooth things over. Of course they'll default to my authorial judgment. Hiring a sensitivity reader is entirely my choice, and I've made it clear that I don't want one. We'll stick to the original production timeline. Everything is fine.

The following week, Candice sends me an email apologizing for her tone, on which Daniella is cc'd. It's not a real apology; in fact, it's passive-aggressive as fuck: I'm sorry if you felt offended by my editorial suggestions. As you know, June, I only want to help publish *The Last Front* as well as we can.

I roll my eyes, but I take the high road. I've won my battle, and it never pays to bully a poor editorial assistant. My reply is succinct:

Thank you, Candice. I appreciate that.

Daniella follows up in a private thread to inform me that Candice has been taken off the project. I won't have to interface with her anymore. All further communications about *The Last Front* can go directly through Daniella, Emily, or Jessica.

I am so sorry you had to deal with this, Daniella writes. Candice clearly had some strong feelings about this project, and it's affected her judgment. I want you to know that I've had a serious conversation with Candice about respecting boundaries with authors, and I will make sure this never happens again.

She sounds so apologetic that for a moment I feel embarrassed, nervous I've blown this out of proportion. But that's nothing compared to the relief that finally, for once, my publisher is firmly on my side.

HAVE YOU EVER SEEN SOMEONE YOU KNOW GO FROM ORDINARY TO, suddenly, semifamous—a polished, artificial front familiar to hundreds of thousands of people? A musician from high school who made it big, perhaps, or a film star you recognize as the blonde girl on your freshman floor with the eating disorder? Have you ever wondered at the mechanics of popularization? How does someone go from being a real person, someone you actually knew, to a set of marketing and publicity points, consumed and lauded by fans who think they know them, but don't really, but understand this also, and celebrate them regardless?

I watched all this happen with Athena the year after we graduated college, in the run-up to the launch of her first novel. Athena was a Known Entity at Yale, a campus celebrity who received regular declarations of love in that year's iteration of the Secret Valentines Facebook group, but she wasn't yet so famous that she had a Wikipedia page, or that the average reader's eyes would light up with recognition when you said her name.

That changed when the *New York Times* ran a hype piece on her titled "Yale Graduate Lands Six-Figure Deal with Random House," centering a photograph of Athena in a low-cut blouse so sheer you could see her nipples, posing in front of Sterling Memorial Library. They ran a quote from a famous poet then adjuncting at Yale dubbing her a "worthy successor to the likes of Amy Tan and Maxine Hong Kingston." Everything ramped up from there. Her Twitter follow count shot up to the mid–five figures; her Instagram numbers hit six figures. She did puff-piece interviews with the *Wall Street Journal* and *HuffPost*; once, while driving to a doctor's appointment, I was startled to hear her crystalline, unplaceable, occasionally suspiciously fake, somewhat-British accent drifting through my Uber.

Cue the mythmaking in real time, the constructed persona deemed maximally marketable by her publishing team, paired with a healthy dose of neoliberal exploitation. Complex messages reduced to sound bites; biographies cherry-picked for the quirky and exotic. This in fact happens to every successful author, but is weirder to witness when you've been friends with the source material. Athena Liu writes only on a Remington typewriter (true, but only after her senior year, after she got the idea from a famous visiting lecturer). Athena Liu was a finalist for a national writing competition when she was only sixteen (also true, but come on; every high schooler who can string sentences together places in those competitions at one point or another; it's not hard to beat out other kids whose definition of art consists of plagiarized Billie Eilish lyrics). Athena Liu is a prodigy, a genius, the Next Big Thing, the voice of her generation. Here are six books that Athena Liu can't live without (including, invariably, Proust). Here are five affordable notebook brands Athena Liu recommends (she writes only on Moleskines, but check these other brands out if you're poor)!

This is so wild, I'd texted her, along with the link to a recent *Cosmo* shoot. I didn't realize Cosmo readers were, like, literate.

HAHAH I know! she'd responded. I don't even recognize that girl on the front page, they've airbrushed me to death. Those are not my eyebrows.

It's the hyperreal. Back then it was still cool to quote Baudrillard as if you'd read him in full.

Exactly, she'd said. Athena.0, and Athena.1. I'm a work of art. All construct. I'm Athena Del Rey.

So when it was my turn to release a novel, I had wild expectations that publishing would do the same thing for me and *Over the Sycamore*, that some well-oiled machine would build my public persona without my lifting a finger, that the marketing department would take me by the hand and coach me on precisely the right things to wear and say when I showed up for all the major media interviews they had set up for me.

Instead my publisher threw me to the wolves. Everything I learned about self-promotion I learned from conversations on a debut writer's Slack, where everyone was as lost as I was, throwing out outdated blog posts they'd dredged up from the corners of the internet. One absolutely had to have an author website, but was WordPress better or Squarespace? Did newsletters drive sales, or were they a waste of money? Should you hire a professional for your author photographs, or was a selfie taken with Portrait mode on your iPhone sufficient? Should you create a separate Twitter account for your author persona? Could you shitpost on it? If you got into public beef with other writers, would that tank your sales or drive up your visibility? Was it still cool to have public beef on Twitter? Or was beef now reserved only for Discord?

Needless to say, the high-profile interviews never materialized. The closest I got was an invitation by some guy named Mark, whose podcast had five hundred followers, and which I immediately regretted saying yes to when he began ranting about the overpoliticization of contemporary genre fiction and I began to worry that he was maybe a Nazi.

This time around, I get far more support from Eden. Emily and Jessica are on hand to answer all my questions. Yes, I should be active on all my social media platforms. Yes, I should include preorder links on every post—Twitter's algorithm reduces visibility for tweets with links, but you can get around that by including links farther down the thread or in your bio. No, starred reviews don't actually mean anything, but yes, I should still brag about them because artificial hype is still hype. Yes, the book has been sent to reviewers at all the major outlets, and we're expecting at least a few to run something positive. No, we're probably not going to get a profile in the *New Yorker*, though perhaps a few books down the road we can talk.

I have actual money now, so I hire a photographer to take a new set of author photos. My old set was done by my sister's friend from college, an amateur photographer named Melinda who happened to be in the area and charged me a fraction of the rates I'd found elsewhere online. I contorted my face in a number of different ways, trying to evoke the sultry, mysterious, and serious vibes of the photos of Serious Famous Woman Writers. Channel Jennifer Egan. Channel Donna Tartt.

Athena always looked like a model in hers: hair floating loose around her face, skin porcelain pale and glowing, full lips loose and slightly curled up at the edges as if she knew a joke that you weren't in on, one eyebrow arched as if to say, *Try me.* It's easy to sell books if you're gorgeous. I made peace a long time ago with the fact that I'm only passably hot, and only from the right angles and lighting, so I tried for the next best thing, which is "tortured in a very deep and brilliant way." It's hard to transpose those thoughts to the camera, though, and the results horrified me when Melinda sent them in. I looked like I was trying to hold in a sneeze, or like I had to take a shit but was too afraid to tell anyone. I wanted to take them all again, this time with maybe a mirror in the background so I could see what the fuck I was doing, but I felt bad for wasting Melinda's time, so I picked the one where I looked the most like a human being and the least like myself and paid her fifty bucks for her trouble.

This time I drop half a grand on a professional photographer in DC named Cate. We shoot in her studio, where she employs all sorts of lighting equipment I've never seen before, and which I can only hope will wash out my acne scars. Cate is brisk, friendly, professional. Her instructions are clear and direct. "Chin up. Relax your face a bit. Now I'm going to tell a joke, and just react however you want, just don't pay attention to the lens. Lovely. Oh, that's lovely."

She sends me a selection of watermarked photos a few days later. I'm amazed by how good I look, especially in the photos we took outside. During golden hour I come off as nicely tanned, which makes me look sort of racially ambiguous. My eyes are cast demurely to the side, my mind full of profound and cryptic thoughts. I look like someone who could write a book about Chinese laborers in World War I and do it justice. I look like a Juniper Song.

At Emily's suggestion, I start cultivating a social media presence. Until now, I've only tweeted random shitposts and jokes about Jane Austen. I had barely any followers, so it didn't matter what I was tossing out. But now that I'm drawing attention for my book deal,

I want to give off the right impression. I want bloggers, reviewers, and readers to know I'm the kind of person who, you know, cares about the right issues.

I study the Twitter feeds of Athena and her mutuals to see which community figures I should follow, which conversations I should be a part of. I retweet hot takes about bubble tea, MSG, BTS, and some drama series called *The Untamed*. I learn it's important to be anti-PRC (that's the People's Republic of China) but pro-China (I'm not terribly sure how that's different). I learn what "little pinks" and "tankies" are and make sure I don't inadvertently retweet support for either. I decry what's happening in Xinjiang. I Stand with Hong Kong. I start gaining dozens more followers a day once I've started vocalizing on these matters, and when I notice that many of my followers are people of color or have things like #BLM and #FreePalestine in their bios, I know I'm on the right track.

And just like that, my public persona springs into being. Farewell June Hayward, little-known author of *Over the Sycamore*. Hello Juniper Song, author of this season's biggest hit—brilliant, enigmatic, the late Athena Liu's best friend.

IN THE MONTHS BEFORE *THE LAST FRONT* COMES OUT, EDEN'S PUBLICity team does everything it can to make sure all of America is aware of its existence.

They send ARCs—that's "advanced reader copies"—out to other big-name authors at Eden, and though not everyone has time to read it, a handful of bestselling writers do say kind things like "Engrossing!" and "A compelling voice," which Daniella will have printed on the jacket cover.

The cover art was finalized about a year before the release date. Daniella asked me to put together a Pinterest board of ideas for the design. (Authors usually get some input on themes and general design ideas, but otherwise, we accept that we know nothing about cover art and leave the process alone.) I tooled around Google for some photographs of the Chinese Labour Corps and found some nice black-and-white photographs of the laborers themselves—there's one in particular that I thought was charming: eight or so laborers crowded beaming around the camera. I sent it off to Daniella. *What about this?* I asked. *It's in the public domain now, so we wouldn't have to get the rights.*

But Daniella and the art department didn't think that was quite the right vibe. *We don't want it to look like a nonfiction history book,* she responded. *Would you pick that up if you were strolling through the bookstore?*

In the end, we went with a more modern theme. The words THE LAST FRONT are printed in massive block letters, against an abstract duo-chrome rendering of what looks like some French village on fire. *We want colors that emphasize bold, epic, and romantic,* wrote Daniella. *And you'll notice the Chinese characters on the edges of the inner jacket—that'll let readers know they can expect something different with this one.*

The cover felt hefty, serious, attractive. It was somehow simultaneously every World War I novel that had been published in the last ten years, and also something new, exciting, and original. *Perfect,* I wrote to Daniella. *That's perfect.*

Now that we're much closer to release, I start seeing ads for it everywhere—Goodreads, Amazon, Facebook, and Instagram. They even get an ad for the subway. Either they didn't tell me about it, or

I forgot, because when I get off the train to Franconia-Springfield and see my book cover plastered on the opposite wall, I'm so stunned that I stand frozen on the platform. *That's my book. That's my name.*

"*The Last Front*," a woman behind me reads out loud to her companion. "By Juniper Song. Huh."

"Looks good," says the man. "We should check it out."

"Sure," says the woman. "Maybe."

A thrum of joy comes over me in that instant, and though it's so trite you'd think I was imitating an actress in a CW pilot, I ball both hands into fists and jump high into the air.

The good news keeps piling up. Brett emails me with updates on foreign rights sales. We've sold rights in Germany, Spain, Poland, and Russia. Not France, yet, but we're working on it, says Brett. But nobody sells well in France. If the French like you, then you're doing something very wrong.

The Last Front starts making it onto all sorts of lists with titles like "Ten Best Books of the Summer," "Debuts We Can't Wait For," and incredibly, PopSugar's "15 Must-Read Summer Beach Reads." Not everyone wants to read about World War I at the beach, I joke on Twitter. But if you're a freak like me, you might enjoy this list!

My book even gets chosen for a national book club run by a pretty white Republican woman who is mostly famous for being the daughter of a prominent Republican politician, and this gives me some moral discomfort, but then I figure that if the book club reader base is largely Republican white women, then wouldn't it be good for a novel to broaden their worldviews?

In the UK, *The Last Front* is chosen for the Readaholics Book Box. I didn't know book boxes were such a major industry, but apparently subscription services like Readaholics send books out in cute crates with accompanying merchandise to tens of thousands of customers a month. The Readaholics Book Box edition of *The Last Front* will have special deckled edges, and ship out along with a cruelty-free vegan leather tote bag, a collectible key chain featuring various jade Chinese zodiac animals (for a special fee you can take a personality quiz online to determine your zodiac affinity), and a selection of sustainably sourced, single-origin green teas from Taiwan.

Barnes & Noble decides to do an exclusive special signed edition, which means that four months before release date, I get eight giant packages delivered to my apartment containing tip-in sheets, which are blank title pages that will be inserted into the printed books once I've signed them. Signing thousands of tip-in sheets takes *forever*, and I spend the next two weeks doing "wine and sign" nights, where I sit in front of my TV with a pile of pages to my right and a bottle of merlot, watching *Bling Empire* as I write "Juniper Song" in big, looping script.

Are these the signs of a bestseller in the making? I wonder. They must be. Why doesn't anyone tell you, right off the bat, how important your book is to the publisher? Before *Over the Sycamore* came out, I worked my ass off doing blog interviews and podcasts, hoping that the more sweat I put into publicity, the more my publisher would reward my efforts. But now, I see, author efforts have nothing to do with a book's success. Bestsellers are chosen. Nothing you do matters. You just get to enjoy the perks along the way.

EARLY REVIEWS START POURING IN TWO MONTHS BEFORE THE RELEASE date.

I make it a nightly habit to scroll through new Goodreads reviews, just for that little boost of serotonin. They tell authors never to look at Goodreads, but nobody follows that advice—none of us can resist the urge to know how our work is being received. In any case, *The Last Front* is killing it; its review average is a healthy 4.89, and most of the top reviews are so gushingly positive that the occasional ambivalent three-star review hardly fazes me.

One night, though, I glimpse something that makes my heart stop.

One star. *The Last Front* has received its first one-star review, from a user named CandiceLee.

No way. I click over to her profile, wondering if it's just a coincidence. Nope—CandiceLee, NYC, works in publishing. Favorite authors: Cormac McCarthy, Marilynne Robinson, and Jhumpa Lahiri. She's not particularly active on Goodreads—her last review is for a poetry collection from 2014—meaning this was no accident. Her thumb didn't just slip. Clearly, Candice went out of her way to log in and give my book one star.

Fingers trembling, I screenshot the rating and send it to my editor.

Hey Daniella,

I know you said not to look at GR, but a friend sent me this and I'm a bit concerned. It seems like a pretty large lapse in professionalism. I guess technically Candice has the right to review my work however she likes in her off time, but after what happened with the SR this feels intentional . . .

Best,

June

Daniella gets back to me first thing in the morning.

Thank you for letting me know. That is quite unprofessional. We will handle this internally.

I know Daniella's email voice well enough by now to tell when she's irritated. Curt, choppy sentences. She didn't even sign off. Daniella is *pissed.*

Good. Hot vindication coils in my gut. Candice deserves it—putting the sensitivity read kerfuffle aside, what kind of psychopath would fuck around with an author's feelings like this? Shouldn't she know how stressful and terrifying it is to launch a book? I bask for a moment, imagining what kind of chaos I've sown over at Eden's office this morning. And though I would never say this out loud about a fellow woman—the industry is tough enough as it is—I hope I got that bitch fired.

Six

Months become weeks become days, and then the book is out.

Last time, I learned the hard way that for most writers, the day your book goes on sale is a day of abject disappointment. The week beforehand feels like it should be the countdown to something grand, that there will be fanfare and immediate critical acclaim, that your book will skyrocket to the top of all the sales rankings and stay there. But in truth, it's all a massive letdown. It's fun to walk into bookstores and see your name on the shelves, that's true (unless you're not a major front-list release, and your book is buried in between other titles without so much as a face out, or even worse, not even carried by most stores). But other than that, there's no immediate feedback. The people who bought the book haven't had time to finish reading it yet. Most sales happen in preorders, so there's no real movement on Amazon or Goodreads or any of the other sites you've been checking like a maniac the whole month prior. You have all this hope and energy bubbled up inside you, but none of it . . . goes anywhere.

There's no single, crushing moment of realization when your book tanks, either. There's only a thousand disappointments, stacked on top of one another as the days tick by, as you compare your own sales numbers to those of other authors, as you keep seeing the same signed, unbought copy sitting on the shelf of your local bookstore every time you pop in to check. There's only a slow trickle of "sales are a bit lower than we'd expected but we hope they'll pick up" emails from your editor, followed by total, inscrutable silence. There's only a growing sense of dread and disappointment, until the bitterness becomes too much, until you start to feel stupid for believing that you could be an author at all.

So I learned, from the release of *Over the Sycamore*, not to get my hopes up.

But this time feels special. This time I learn again how vastly different the world is as experienced by writers like Athena. The morning of my launch day, Eden has a massive crate of champagne delivered to my apartment. *Congratulations*, reads the attached handwritten note from Daniella. *You earned it.*

I extract a bottle from the wrapping, take a selfie as I hold it up, and upload it to Instagram with the caption: TODAY'S THE DAY! Feeling grateful, overwhelmed, and nervous. Blessed to have the best team in the business. It gets two thousand likes in an hour.

Watching those hearts pile up gives me the flood of serotonin that I've always hoped for on launch day. Throughout the morning, strangers keep tagging me in congratulations posts, reviews, and photographs of my book on the New Releases pile at Barnes & Noble, or face out with a recommendation tag at their local indie bookstores.

One bookseller tags me in a literal *pyramid* of her books, captioned: DETERMINED TO SELL 100 COPIES OF THE LAST FRONT ON DAY ONE! WITNESS MEEEE

Common wisdom says that social media is a bad metric for gauging how well a book is doing. Twitter doesn't reflect the larger book-buying ecosphere, for example, and books that seem to be getting lots of hype are usually explained by an overactive Twitter presence by the author's team. Likes and followers don't necessarily translate into sales.

But shouldn't all this hype signal something? I'm reviewed in *NPR*, the *New York Times*, and the *Washington Post*. With *Over the Sycamore*, I'd felt lucky to even get a *Kirkus* review, and that had been little more than a plot summary. Meanwhile, everyone's talking about *The Last Front* like they know it's going to be a hit. And I wonder if that's the final, obscure part of how publishing works: if the books that become big do so because at some point everyone decided, for no good reason at all, that this would be the title of the moment.

Arbitrary as it is, I'm glad that it's working for me.

That night, I have a launch event scheduled at Politics and Prose near the Waterfront. I've been here a dozen times as part of the audience. It's the kind of bookstore that ex-presidents and celebrities speak at on book tours; a few years ago, I came here to see Hillary Clinton give a reading. Athena did the launch for her debut here. When Emily told me she'd booked me at P and P, I'd shrieked at my screen.

I have to steel myself before I walk through the doors. My publisher for *Over the Sycamore* set up a "multi-city" bookstore tour for me, but each store I visited never had an audience of more than ten people. And it is painful, truly painful, to struggle through a reading and Q&A when people keep leaving in the middle of your sentences. It's even worse to sit and sign a pile of unpurchased stock after the events, while the store manager hovers and makes awkward small talk about how it's probably because it's the holidays, and people are busy shopping, and they didn't have quite enough time to advertise that the attendance numbers were so low. After the second stop I wanted to call it quits, but it's more humiliating to cancel a book tour altogether than to struggle through it, minute by minute, your heart sinking the entire time as you realize your irrelevance, your foolishness to ever hope.

Tonight, though, the store is packed—there's so little standing room, people are sitting cross-legged in the aisle. I almost walk back out. I hover at the entrance, checking my phone, making sure the time and date are right, because this can't be real. Did I mix my reading date up with Sally Rooney's? But the store manager sees me and ushers me into the back office, where he offers me a water bottle and some mints, and then it sinks in—this isn't a mistake, this is real, and all these people are here to see *me*.

Applause echoes around me as I walk out to the front. The store manager introduces me, and then I take my place at the podium, knees trembling. I've never spoken to this many people in my life. Thankfully, I'm set to do a reading before the Q&A, so I have a moment to get my bearings. I've selected an excerpt from the very middle of the book—a self-contained vignette that will serve as an easy entry point for the audience. More important, it's one of the scenes that was largely written by me. These are my sentences, my brilliance.

"'The British officer assigned to direct the men of Ah Lung's squadron seemed perpetually afraid that these foreigners would turn on him any moment.' " My voice trembles but steadies. I cough, take a sip from my water bottle, and keep going. I'm okay. I can do this. " ' "Keep 'em contained," his colleague had advised upon his station. "They do good work, but you've got to make sure they don't become a general nuisance." So he ordered that the men were not allowed to leave their barbed-wire enclosure for any reason without express permission, and Ah Lung spent his first few weeks in France tiptoeing around warning bells and trip wires, wondering why, if he was here to aid the war effort, he was being treated as a prisoner.' "

It goes over so well. You can tell when you have command of a room. There's a certain hushed silence, a tension, like you have a grappling hook in everyone's chest and the lines are pulled taut. My voice has smoothed out; it's clear, attractive, and wobbly enough to make me seem vulnerable and human, yet composed. And I know I look good in the gray leggings, brown boots, and tight burgundy turtleneck I chose for this night. I'm a Serious Young Author. I'm a Literary Star.

I finish reading to enthusiastic applause. The Q&A goes equally well. The questions are either softballs which give me a chance to show off ("How did you balance research for such a niche historical topic with your day job?" "How did you make the historical setting feel so rich and realized?") or baldly flattering ("How do you stay grounded while being so successful at such a young age?" "Did you feel any pressure after receiving such a major book deal?").

My answers are funny, articulate, thoughtful, modest:

"I don't know that I'm balancing anything. I still don't know what day of the week it is. Earlier tonight I forgot my own name." Laughter.

"Of course everything I wrote in college was utter tripe, because college students don't know how to write about anything other than the romance of being a college student." More laughter.

"As for my approach to historical fiction, I think what I'm drawing from is Saidiya Hartman's technique of critical fabulation, which is a way of writing against the grain, of injecting empathy and realism to the archival record of a history that feels abstract to us." Thoughtful, impressed nods.

They love me. They can't look away from me. They're here for me, they're hanging on to my every word, the whole of their focus is consumed with *me*.

And for the first time it really sinks in that I did it, it happened, it worked. I have become one of the chosen ones, one deemed by the Powers That Be to matter. I'm riding high off my rapport with the crowd, laughing when they laugh, riffing off of the wording of their questions. I've forgotten about my stilted, prewritten answers; I'm going completely off the cuff now, and every word out of my mouth is clever, adorable, engaging. I'm killing it.

And then I see her.

Right there, in the front row, flesh and blood, casting her own shadow, so solid and present that I can't be hallucinating. She's dressed in an emerald-green shawl, one of her signature looks, looped over her slender frame in such a way that makes her shoulders look thin, vulnerable, and elegant all at once. She's slouched gracefully against her plastic pull-out chair, pushing her shiny black locks back over her shoulders.

Athena.

Blood thunders in my ears. I blink several times, hoping desperately she's an apparition, but every time I open my eyes she's still there, smiling expectantly at me with bright, berry-red lips. *Stila Stay All Day*, I think wildly, because I know this, because I read that stupid *Vogue* feature with Athena's makeup tips a dozen times before my launch. *Beso shade.*

Calm down. Perhaps there's some other explanation. Perhaps it's her sister, someone who looks exactly like her—a cousin, a twin? But Athena doesn't have a sister, or any extended family in her generation; her mother had made that very clear. *It was just me and my daughter.*

The spell breaks. Dizzy, dry-mouthed, I stumble through the rest of the Q&A. I've lost whatever hold I had over the audience. Someone asks me whether any of my coursework at Yale influenced *The Last Front*, and suddenly I can't remember the names of any classes I've ever taken.

I keep glancing down at Athena, hoping she'll have disappeared and that she was a trick of my imagination, but every time I do she is still *right there*, watching in that cool, inscrutable way of hers, judging every word that comes out of my mouth.

Then the hour's up. I sit through the applause, trying desperately not to faint. The store manager guides me over to a table at the front of the signing line, and I force a grin on my face as I greet reader after reader. There's an art to smiling, making eye contact, making small talk, and signing a book without misspelling your own name or the name of the person you're personalizing it to. I've had some practice at prerelease stock-signing events now, and on a good day I can juggle it all with only one or two awkward silences. Today, I keep fumbling. I ask the same person "So, how's your evening been?" twice, and I flub one customer's name so badly that the store offers them a free replacement copy.

I'm terrified Athena will appear before me, book in hand. I keep craning my head to search for her green shawl in the line, but she seems to have vanished.

Has no one else noticed? Am I the only one who's seen her?

The store staff can tell something is wrong. Without consulting me, they rush the rest of the signing line along, reminding everyone to keep their questions short as it's getting late. When we're done, they don't ask me out to dinner or drinks; they merely shake my hand and thank me for coming. The store manager offers to call me an Uber back to my apartment, and I gratefully accept.

At home, I kick off my shoes and curl into bed.

My heart races; my breaths are shallow. My brain buzzes so loudly that I can hardly hear my own thoughts, and I feel a tug at the base of my skull, like I'm withdrawing into and then away from my body. I can feel a panic attack oncoming—no, not oncoming, *peaking*; I've been low-key suffering an attack for the past hour, and I'm only now in an environment private enough to experience the full range of symptoms. My chest constricts. My vision fades to a pinprick.

I try going through the checklist Dr. Gaily taught me. What do I see? This beige comforter, stained on one side with my foundation and streaks of my mascara. What do I smell? The Korean food that I ordered for lunch today that's still sitting out on the table because I was too jittery before the event to eat; the clean detergent scent of my freshly laundered sheets under my nose. What do I hear? Traffic outside, my own heartbeat in my eardrums. What do I taste? Stale champagne, since I've just noticed the half-empty bottle from this morning.

It all brings me back down a bit, but my mind is still racing, my stomach still curdling with nausea. I ought to stumble to the bathroom, should at least take a shower and wipe off all this makeup, but I'm too dizzy to get up.

Instead I reach for my phone.

I search Twitter for Athena's name, and then my own, and then our names in conjunction. First names only, last names only, first and last names; hashtag, no hashtag. I search for mentions of Politics and Prose. I search for the Twitter handles of every bookstore staff member whose name I remember.

But there's nothing. I'm the only one who saw Athena. All everyone's talking about on Twitter is how brilliant the event was, how passionate and articulate I sounded, and how very excited they are to read *The Last Front*. My search for "June+Athena" yields only one new tweet in the past hour, written by someone I assume is a random audience member:

> Juniper Song's reading from The Last Front tonight was absolutely gorgeous, and it's clear why she feels this book is a homage to her friend; indeed, as she spoke about her creative process, it felt as if Athena Liu's ghost was right there in the room with us.

Seven

I HIT NUMBER THREE ON THE *NEW YORK TIMES* BESTSELLER LIST THE following Wednesday. Daniella emails me with the news: Congratulations, June! No one's surprised here, but I know you were anxious, so here's the official proof. You did it :)

Brett follows up a few minutes after that. WOOOHOOO!

Emily in publicity puts out a blast on Twitter, which sparks a flurry of joyful tweets, Instagram posts, and DMs. Eden's official account tags me in a tweet with that GIF of the two ladies jumping around over a bottle of champagne. JUNIPER SONG, NEW YORK TIMES BESTSELLING AUTHOR!

Oh my God.

Oh my *God*.

This is everything I've ever wanted. We'd known from the pre-order numbers that my hitting the list was likelier than not, but seeing the evidence printed in black and white sends me into paroxysms of delight. Here is my stamp of approval. I'm a bestselling writer. I've made it.

For a full half hour I sit at my desk, staring blankly at my phone as more congratulations messages trickle in. I want to call someone and scream all my joy into their ear—but I don't know who. My mother won't care, or she might only pretend to care, and ask inane questions about how the list works, which will feel worse. Rory will be happy for me, but she won't understand why it's such an achievement. The fourth name down my call history is an ex, attempting a booty call when he was swinging by DC for work, and I certainly can't tell *him*. I'm not close enough with any of my writer friends that the news wouldn't come off like a classless brag, and there's no satisfaction in telling my friends who aren't writers—I want someone who is in the know, who can really understand that this is a Big Fucking Deal.

It takes me a minute to realize that the first person I would have called, the only person who would have understood this news for what it was, and wouldn't have reacted with petty jealousy or feigned support, is Athena.

Congratulations, I tell her ghost, because I can afford this generosity, because by now the disturbing sight of her at my reading has faded to the back of my memory, crowded out by my present, vicious delights. It's easy, now, to chalk that vision up to nervous hallucinations; easier still to forget that it happened at all.

I tweet my news to the public instead. I write up a long thread about why hitting the list means so much to me, especially after the failure of my first book; about the long, painful slog in publishing that has finally, finally paid off. Not everyone becomes a bestseller overnight, I observe sagely. For some of us, it takes years of hard work and hoping and dreaming. I always hoped my moment would come. And here, now, I guess it has.

The infusion of likes and CONGRATULATIONS responses are precisely what I need to fill the void. I sit in front of my screen, watching the numbers tick up, enjoying that little serotonin boost every time I get another flurry of notifications.

At last I have to pee, which forces me to tear myself away from the screen. While I'm up, I order a box of a dozen cupcakes from Baked & Wired, one of every flavor they have on sale that day. When it arrives, I sit down on my floor with a fork and eat until it tastes good.

THE LAST FRONT HANGS ON TO THE LIST AT NUMBER SIX FOR ANOTHER week, and at number ten for the week after that, where it sits for an entire month. That means I didn't hit the list by accident. I'm selling well, and selling steadily. Eden's investment in my advance has paid off. I am, by every possible metric, a major success.

Everything changes. I've now moved into an entirely different class of writer. I receive a half-dozen invitations to speak at various literary events in the next month alone, and after attending a few, I find I enjoy them. I used to hate these events. Big author gatherings—awards ceremonies, conferences, conventions—are like the first day of high school, but even worse, because the cool kids actually are that cool, and there's nothing more humiliating than being shut out of a conversation circle because your book didn't sell enough copies, didn't get enough marketing, or wasn't critically acclaimed enough for everyone else to treat you like a human being. At one of my first literary conferences, I bashfully introduced myself to a writer whose work I'd loved since middle school. He squinted at my name tag, uttered the words "Oh, I don't think I've ever heard of you," and promptly turned his back on me.

Suddenly now, I'm important enough to acknowledge. Now, guys hit on me and buy me drinks at the bar. (We call bar gatherings at literary events "barcons"—watering holes for people who have been waiting all year to rub shoulders and get into dick-measuring contests over their advances and print runs.) An editor from a small press corners me in the bathroom to tell me what a big fan of my work she is. Film agents give me their cards and encourage me to be in touch. Writers who have snubbed me ever since my first novel flopped start acting like we're best friends. *Oh my God, how have you been? Funny how time flies, huh? Hey, would you consider blurbing my next book? Would you introduce me to your editor?*

At this summer's BookCon, which you can think of as publishing prom, I receive invitations to multiple after-parties around the Javits Center, where I'm passed around and introduced to a series of successively more important industry people until I find myself in a circle with Daniella and three of her bestselling authors—Marnie Kimball, who's written several bestsellers about a sexy blonde waitress fighting supernatural crime and romancing vampires in seedy bars; Jen Walker, who's just been on the *Today* show to talk about her memoir about becoming a rich and powerful CEO before she turned thirty; and Heidi Steel, a severe and handsome romance novelist whose titles I've seen on Target racks since I was a child.

"Is it just me or are the debut writers getting younger?" asks Marnie. "They look like children."

"They're all getting signed right out of college these days." Heidi shakes her head. "No offense, June. I had a girl on my romance panel who was still a sophomore. She's not even old enough to drink."

"Is that wise, though?" asks Jen. "Giving them book deals before they've had time to develop frontal lobes?

"One of them came up to me in a signing line and asked for a blurb," says Jen. "Can you believe it? Title I've never heard of, from some small press I've never heard of, and she comes up to me with a bound ARC, beaming, like of course I'm going to say yes."

Marnie shudders with horror. "What did you say?"

"I said I don't have the bag space for print books, but she could have her agent send an epub file to mine. Of course I'll never open it." Jen makes a *whoosh* noise with her lips. "Straight into the trash."

They all chuckle.

"Diplomatic," says Heidi.

"Go easy on them," says Marnie. "They're not getting marketing support, poor things."

"Yes, it's a real pity," sighs Daniella. "I hate watching these small presses acquire good novels just to throw them to the wolves."

"It's diabolical," says Jen. "Their agents should know better. This industry is vicious."

"Oh, I *know*."

We all nod and sip our wine, relieved that we are not part of the unfortunate masses. The conversation moves on to the latest independent publisher that's recently laid off half its staff, including all but one senior editor, and whether the writers in their stable should try their luck in the imminent shuffle or try to get their rights reverted and jump ship to another house. Publishing gossip, it turns out, is a lot of fun when you're speculating about other people's misfortune.

"So what got you interested in the Chinese Labour Corps?" Marnie asks me. "I'd never heard of them before your book."

"Most people hadn't." I preen, flattered that Marnie knows what my book is about at all. I won't inquire further about her thoughts—

it's good etiquette among writers not to ask if someone has read your work or is just pretending. "I took a course on East Asian history at Yale. A professor referenced it in a discussion section, and I thought it was surprising that there weren't any novels in English about it, so I thought I'd make that necessary addition to the canon." The first part is true; the rest is not—I spent most of that class reading about Japanese art history, meaning tentacle porn, but it's been a convenient cover story for questions like this.

"That's precisely my approach," Heidi exclaims. "I look for the gaps in history, the stuff no one else is talking about. That's why I wrote an epic fantasy romance about a businessman and a Mongolian huntress. *Eagle Girl.* It's out next year. I'll have Daniella send you a copy. It's so important to think about what perspectives aren't embraced by Anglophone readers, you know? We must make space for the subaltern voices, the suppressed narratives."

"Right," I say. I'm a little surprised Heidi knows the word "subaltern." "And without us, these stories wouldn't get told."

"Precisely. *Precisely.*"

Near the end of the party, I run into my former editor while standing in line at the coat check. He comes in for a hug like we're best friends, like he didn't butcher my very first book baby, set it up to fail, and then leave me out in the cold.

"Congratulations, June," he says, smiling broadly. "It's been wonderful to watch you succeed."

I've wondered often for the past year what I would say to Garrett if I ever came across him again. I always held my tongue while I was his author; I was terrified of burning bridges, of him spreading the word that I was impossible to work with. I've wished I could say to his face how small he made me feel, how his curt, dismissive emails made me convinced the publisher had already given up on my work, how he nearly made me quit writing with his indifference.

But the best revenge is to thrive. Garrett's imprint has been struggling. He hasn't landed anything on a bestseller list aside from titles from the literary estates of famous, deceased authors that he's clinging to like a lifeboat. When the next economic contraction comes, I wouldn't be surprised if he's out of a job. And I know what the whisper networks are saying behind his back—*Garrett McKintosh had Juniper Song on his list, and he let* The Last Front *go. How stupid do you have to be?*

"Thank you," I say. And then, because I can't help it, "I've been really happy with the support I'm getting at Eden. Daniella is wonderful."

"Yeah, she's brilliant. We were interns together at Harper." He doesn't elaborate, just smiles at me expectantly.

I realize, horrified, that he's trying to make small talk. I don't need to impress him. I'm impressive enough as is. *He* wants to be seen with *me*.

"Yeah," I say, smiling tightly. "She's so awesome." And then, because I'm irritated now and because I want to twist the knife, "She really gets my vision, you know, in a way that's wonderfully collaborative. I've never worked with someone so incisive before. I owe all my success to her."

He gets the hint. His expression sags. We trade some other niceties, give all the usual updates—I'm working on something new; he's just signed an author he's excited about—and then he makes his excuses. "Sorry to dip out, Junie, but I'd better go say hi to my UK counterpart before she leaves. She's only in town for the weekend." I shrug and wave. He walks off, and hopefully out of my life for good.

THE FOLLOWING JANUARY, I GET MY FIRST ROYALTIES STATEMENT FOR *The Last Front*. I've earned out. This means that I've sold enough copies to cover my already sizable advance, and that from here on out I get to keep a percentage of all future sales. And sales, if this statement is anything to go by, are astounding.

I've been wary of spending any of my advance money so far. I've read enough cautionary tales to know that advance money dries up fast, that there is no guarantee of earning out, or of securing another book deal approaching the amount of the first. But I treat myself this month. I buy a new laptop; finally, a MacBook Pro that doesn't shriek and shut down whenever I try to open a Word file bigger than two hundred pages. I move to a nicer apartment—nothing quite as fancy as the Dupont place Athena had leased, but nice enough that anyone who visits will assume I have inherited wealth. I go to IKEA, order whatever I want without looking at the prices, and pay the extra fees to have it all delivered and assembled by two very handsome college seniors I solicited on TaskRabbit. I let them flirt with me. I tip well.

I get a liquor cabinet. I am now the sort of person who has a liquor cabinet.

I write a check for the entirety of my remaining student debt, lick the envelope, and send it off to the Department of Education. No more Nelnet emails for the rest of my life, thank God. I get health insurance. I go to the dentist, and when it turns out I'll have to fork over several thousand dollars to get all these undetected cavities drilled out, I pay the bill without blinking. I see a primary care physician, even though there's nothing wrong with me, just for a physical, just because I can.

I start buying nice whisky, even though I can't taste whisky without thinking of Athena and those stupid old-fashioneds. I start shopping at Whole Foods. I become addicted to their jalapeño corn bread. I start getting my clothes at brand-name outlets instead of the thrift store. I throw out my cheap Etsy jewelry and stop wearing anything that doesn't feature ethically, sustainably sourced gemstones.

When tax season rolls around, I ask my sister, Rory, who's an accountant, to handle things. I send her my 1099s for this year; within minutes she responds, Jesus Christ, are you serious???

Hell yeah, I email her back. Told you writing would work out.

I DO PAY THINGS FORWARD. I'M NOT LYING WHEN I SAY I WANT TO make a positive contribution to the Asian community. I make a check out to the Asian American Writers' Collective for two thousand dollars, just as I'd promised, and I'll keep making those yearly contributions so long as my royalties are this good. I graciously accept a request to serve as a mentor for Scribblers' Fairy Godmothers, a program that pairs an underrepresented writer with a published writer who can coach them through the vicissitudes of the industry.

I'm glad to be spreading my generosity. Athena never made efforts to send the ladder down to her fellow writers of color. If anything, she found them annoying. "My inbox keeps filling up with wannabe writers who think I'll spend hours writing them advice letters just because we have the same vaguely ethnic background," she'd complain contemptuously. "'Hi Miss Liu, I'm a sophomore in high school, and as a fellow Asian American woman I admire you so much.' Shut up. You're not special; you're a dime a dozen."

Athena seemed more than just minorly irritated that Asian American writers clustered admiringly around her. She seemed to actively despise them. She hated it whenever I brought up debut novels that were compared to hers in the press. She'd bitch about how they were unoriginal, too try-hard, too obviously catered to an ethnic niche in the marketplace. "Write something else!" she'd complain. "No one wants another feel-good immigrant story. Boohoo, did they think your lunch smelled bad? Did they make fun of your eyes? God, I've read it all before. There's no originality."

Maybe it was Highlander Syndrome—I've read about that before, the way members of marginalized groups feel threatened if someone else like them starts finding success. I've experienced that, too—every time I see a publishing announcement about a young girl hitting it big with her debut, I want to claw my eyes out. Maybe she was terrified someone was going to replace or surpass her.

But I'm going to be better than Athena. I am a woman who helps other women.

I'm matched with a girl named Emmy Cho, who sends me an effusive email about how much she admires my books. Emmy is based out in San Francisco, so we do our first mentoring session over Zoom. She's pretty in a fresh-faced, innocent way—like a cute bunny rabbit, like a defanged Athena, and I instinctively feel an urge to sweep her under my coat and protect her.

She tells me about her current work in progress, a coming-of-age novel about a queer Korean American girl growing up in the Midwest in the nineties, based largely on her own experiences. "It's a bit like that film *The Half of It*, if you've seen it?" She has this adorable habit of tucking her hair behind her ears every time she finishes a sentence. "I'm kind of worried, you know, that the industry isn't that interested in this kind of story. Like, growing up, I didn't see any books like that on shelves, and it's more of a quiet, introspective literary novel instead of, like, a high-octane thriller, so I don't know . . ."

"I don't think you have anything to worry about," I assure her. "If anything, it's easier now than ever to be Asian in the industry."

Her brows furrow. "Do you really mean that?"

"Absolutely," I say. "Diversity is what's selling right now. Editors are *hungry* for marginalized voices. You'll get plenty of opportunities for being different, Emmy. I mean, a queer Asian girl? That's every checkbox on the list. They'll be slobbering all over this manuscript."

Emmy laughs nervously. "Well, okay."

"Just write the best thing you can and put it out there," I say. "You'll be a hit, I promise."

We chat a little bit more about how her querying process has gone so far (lots of partial requests, but no solid offers yet) and about her feelings toward the manuscript (she's confident in her narrative voice, but doesn't know if she's attempted too many overlapping timelines).

As the hour draws to a close, Emmy clears her throat and says, "Um, if you don't mind me asking, are you white?"

My surprise must show on my face, because she immediately apologizes. "Sorry, I don't know if that's cool to say, I just, um, like, *Song*, that's kind of ambiguous, so I just wanted to know."

"I am white," I say, more frostily than I'd intended. What is she insinuating? That I can't be a good mentor to her unless I'm Asian? "Song is my middle name. My mother gave it to me."

"Okay," Emmy says, and tucks her hair back behind her ears again. "Um, cool. I was just asking."

Eight

OF COURSE, I HAVE MY DETRACTORS. THE MORE POPULAR A BOOK becomes, the more popular it becomes to hate on said book, which is why revulsion for Rupi Kaur's poetry has become a millennial personality trait. The majority of my reviews on Goodreads are five stars, but the one-stars are *vitriolic.* Uninspired colonizer trash, one reads. Another iteration of the white woman exploitation sob story formula: copy, paste, change the names, and voila, bestseller, reads another. And a third, which seems way too personal to be objective: What a stuck-up, obnoxious bitch. Brags too much about being a Yalie. I got this during a Kindle sale, and you can bet I made sure to get every one of the two hundred and ninety-nine cents I spent back.

The first time I get tagged in a bad review on Twitter (All the hype led me wrong, won't be reading anything more from this author), I text Marnie Kimball and Jen Walker, my new friends from the BookCon after-party. They'd given me their numbers and insisted that I reach out if I was ever having a hard time navigating the industry. Since then our group chat, cheekily named "Eden's Angels," has been my go-to source of support and industry gossip.

How do you get over rude shit people say about you online? I ask. This is so demoralizing. It's like they have a personal vendetta. Like I, personally, once kicked their dog or something.

Rule one: Do Not Read Reviews. Marnie does that weird thing older women do where she uses extra spaces and capitalizations, though I can never tell if they're intentional or typos. If they had anything good to say, they would have written their own books. They are Petty Little People.

Let them scream in their own echo chambers, writes Jen. Performing outrage is a bonding activity for them. Gives them serotonin hits, literally, there's research on this. Don't let it get to you. They're sheep.

That's good advice, if only I had the mental fortitude to not care so much about what people think of me. I keep reading through Goodreads tirades, vicious tweet threads, and condescending Reddit posts. I keep clicking on negative articles when they show up in my Google Alerts, even when the title promises nothing but self-righteous vehemence.

I can't help it. I need to know what the world is saying about me. I need to sketch out the contours of my digitally perceived self, because at least if I know the extent of the damage then I'll know how much I should be worried.

The most widely circulated hate piece is an essay review in the *Los Angeles Review of Books* by a critic named Adele Sparks-Sato, whose work I actually enjoy, because she's good at pointing out that the novels everyone else touts as "the voice of a generation" are actually self-indulgent, narcissistic nonsense. She's published some of the harshest criticisms of Athena's work in the past (on Athena's debut: "Here, Liu falls into the novice trap of mistaking a lyrical, self-othering sentence for a profound observation. Unfortunately, you can still be Orientalist even if you're Asian. My read? Athena Liu needs to get over her own yellow fever."). This time, she's come after me:

"In *The Last Front*, Juniper Song misses an excellent opportunity to excavate a forgotten history and instead uses the suffering of thousands of Chinese laborers as a site for melodrama and white redemption," she writes. "She could have, for instance, interrogated the use of Christian missionaries to convince young, illiterate Chinese men to work and die overseas, and who in France were largely recruited to keep the Chinese docile, tame, and cooperative. Instead she unabashedly praises the missionaries' role in converting laborers. *The Last Front* hardly breaks new ground; instead, it joins novels like *The Help* and *The Good Earth* in a long line of what I dub historical exploitation novels: inauthentic stories that use troubled pasts as an entertaining set piece for white entertainment."

Whatever. Who is Adele to tell me off about authenticity? Isn't the name "Sato" Japanese? Isn't there a whole discourse about how being Chinese and Japanese are totally different experiences?

Can this Adele bitch take a fucking chill pill? I text Eden's Angels.

Marnie: With initials like ASS . . . no?

Jen: Critics build an audience by dragging others down. It's the only way they can legitimize themselves. It's a toxic culture. Don't get pulled in. We're better than that.

Some undergraduate at UCLA named Kimberly Deng puts up a twelve-minute YouTube video titled "ALL THE CULTURAL

MISTAKES IN THE LAST FRONT!!!" which racks up a hundred thousand views within a week. I watch for a bit out of curiosity, but I'm unimpressed more than I am insulted. It's full of trivial stuff like "Chinese soldiers wouldn't have eaten foods like mince pie for a holiday meal" (How would she know what they were eating, and when?) or ad hom details about naming conventions ("Ah Kay? Did she get this shit from a Hong Kong crime drama?") that Athena herself wrote in. The comments are all shit like YAAAS KWEEN and OMG GO OFF KIMMY and LOLLLL THAT WHITE GIRL IS QUAKING. Kimberly later has the nerve to DM me on Instagram asking if I'd like to be a guest on her channel, and I take some vindictive pleasure in instructing her to contact me through my publicist, Emily, and then instructing Emily to ghost her.

Another online firebrand, a guy named Xiao Chen, puts out a Substack essay arguing that *The Last Front* should never have been published. I'm actually quite familiar with Xiao Chen's brand—Athena had complained about him viciously and often. Xiao Chen had gone viral the previous year for a piece in *Vox* titled "Enough with Diaspora Fiction," which argued essentially that no one in the current wave of Chinese American novelists was producing anything of value, because none of them had lived through things like the Tiananmen Square massacre or the Cultural Revolution, and that spoiled Bay Area kids who couldn't even speak Mandarin and who thought that Asian identification boiled down to being annoyingly obsessed with bubble tea and BTS were diluting the radical force of the diaspora canon. I've seen him getting in vicious spats with other writers on Twitter; LEARN CHINESE, he would snap, or SHUT UP, BRAINWASHED WESTERN PUPPETS. His modus operandi seems to be ascribing everything wrong with a text to some armchair-diagnosed psychological problem with the writer; in my case, Xiao Chen thinks I wrote *The Last Front* because I am "one of the many white women, like those who write queer fan fiction of *The Untamed*, who not only have an unexamined fetish for feminine-looking Asian men, but who think Chinese history is something to cherry-pick from in search of intriguing and shiny nuggets, like nice Ming vases to set in the corner."

Honestly, his vitriol makes me laugh. Some critical pieces are cold and condescending enough to wound, but this one is *so* emotional, *so* angry, that it only reveals Xiao Chen's own insecurities and bottomless, inexplicable rage. I imagine him hunched over a laptop in his basement, snarling and spitting to an audience of none. I wonder what Xiao Chen would do if he ever saw me in person—punch me in the face, or utter some inane niceties and slink away. People like him are always braver online than they are in the flesh.

Jen: People like that just can't stand to see women succeed.
Marnie: Misogynism at its worst. Also, what's The Untamed?

There's one scene, which occurs two hundred pages into the novel, that all the critics are obsessed with. Indeed, every negative review mentions it by at least the third paragraph. Annie Waters—a character I'd expanded from Athena's draft, the seventeen-year-old daughter of YMCA missionaries—visits the laborers' camp alone to hand out Bibles and Christmas biscuits. The men, who haven't seen their wives or any women of their kind in months, understandably ogle over her. She's blonde, slim, and pretty; of course they can't get enough of her. One asks if he can kiss her on the cheek, and since it's Christmastime, she bashfully permits it.

I thought the scene was touching. Here we have people divided by language and race, who are nonetheless able to share a tender moment in the middle of a war. The scene also fixed an earlier gripe Daniella had with the novel, which was that it centered almost entirely on men. *The era of the macho war story is over,* she'd written. *We need to start elevating female perspectives.*

Athena's original draft didn't include the kiss. In her version, Annie was a sheltered, fidgety girl who thought the laborers were dirty, frightening thugs. Athena's Annie told the men a frigid "Merry Christmas" and left the biscuits at the edge of the barbed-wire enclosure, then skirted timidly away like the men were dogs that would break free of their leashes and maul her to death if given the chance.

It's clear Athena was trying to point out all the racism the laborers suffered from people fighting on their own side. But there was already so much of that throughout the book. It was starting to feel heavy-handed, repetitive. Why not include a scene that showed the potential for interracial love, instead? Can't we all get behind decrying antimiscegenation?

This is, apparently, the most racist artistic choice I could have made.

From Adele Sparks-Sato: "Song, rather than exploring the kind of real challenges posed against interracial romances between French women and Chinese laborers, decides instead to portray Chinese workers as animalistic creatures who cannot control their lust for the white woman."

From Xiao Chen: Do all white women think we're obsessed with fucking them??? Imagine the arrogance. Trust me, Juniper, you're not that hot.

"For my next video," drawls Kimberly Deng, "I will be doing an Annie Waters makeup tutorial, featuring a turmeric face mask and white tears."

The whole conversation sparks the creation of the "Annie Waters meme," which involves pictures of bland and mediocre-looking white women paired with the caption, taken from the book, "She was a lithe young thing, with hair the color of the rising sun and eyes like the ocean, and the men could not keep their eyes off her as she floated past." Quite a lot of these memes employ the least flattering photographs of me my haters can find online.

I want to point out how outrageously cruel and sexist this is, but the Eden's Angels assure me that silence is my best defense. When you let trolls know they've hurt you, they win, says Jen. You can't let them think they're getting to you.

Since I can't issue any takedowns in person, I often rehearse pretend arguments in the shower.

"Actually," I tell my shampoo bottle, "just because Chinese people were being discriminated against doesn't mean that they couldn't be racist as well. And actually, it's well documented that the Chinese laborers did not get along with Arabs and Moroccans—according to one of my sources, the Chinese would call them 'black devils.' Interethnic conflicts *are* a thing, you know."

In response to accusations that I glorified Western missionaries, I would say, "It's just as essentialist to claim broadly that not a single Chinese soldier found comfort in Christianity. The missionaries were often discriminatory and patronizing, yes, but we know from reports and memoirs that there were true converts, and it seems racist in turn to argue that conversion was impossible just because they were Chinese."

And in response to Kimberly Deng's idiotic clickbait, I would say, "Actually, it does fucking make sense that there are scenes set in Canada, because the laborers were first shipped to Canada, and then to France. You could have learned that from Wikipedia."

I bask in imagining my critics' crestfallen faces as they realize that simply being Asian doesn't make them historical experts, that consanguinity doesn't translate into unique epistemological insight, that their exclusive cultural snobbishness and authenticity testing are only a form of gatekeeping, and that when it all comes down to it, they haven't a fucking clue what they're talking about.

I've gotten so good at having these arguments in my head that I am, in fact, extremely well prepared when one of my detractors confronts me in person. That night, I'm at a historical fiction speaker series hosted by an indie bookstore in Cambridge. The audience has been polite so far, if a little challenging with their questions. It's mostly Harvard and MIT students, and I remember well from my time at Yale that undergraduates at elite universities always think they know more than they do, and that they consider it their greatest achievement to take down a public intellectual. So far I've fielded off questions about my name change ("As I've said before, I chose to write under my middle name to signify a fresh start"), my research process (I have a standard bibliography that I rattle off now), and my engagement with the Chinese American community (here, I trot out the Athena Liu Scholarship I fund at the Asian American Writers' Collective's summer workshop).

Then a girl in the front row takes the mic. I know before she opens her mouth that this will go badly. She's dressed like a right-wing meme of a social justice warrior—dyed purple hair buzzed into an undercut; floppy beanie, knit arm warmers, and a dozen pins and badges on her vest proclaiming her loyalty to BLM, BDS, and AOC. (Look, we're all liberals here. But come *on*.) She's got this breathless, wild-eyed look on her face, like she's been waiting her entire life for this chance to take me down.

"Hi," she says, and her voice wavers for a moment. She's not used to picking fights in front of a live audience. "I'm Chinese American, and when I read *The Last Front*, I thought . . . I mean, I found a lot of deeply painful histories. And I wanted to ask you, why do you think it's okay for a white author—I mean, an author who isn't Chinese—to write, and profit from, this kind of story? Why do you think you're the right person to tell it?"

She lowers the mic. Her cheeks are flushed. She's gotten a big rush from this. No doubt she thinks that this is some grand public callout, that this is the first time I've ever heard this objection. No doubt everyone's riveted, glancing between her and me as if expecting us to go to blows.

But I've prepared this answer. I've been preparing this answer ever since I started writing the book.

"I think it's very dangerous to start censoring what authors should and shouldn't write." I open strong, and this gets some approving murmurs from the crowd. But I still see some skeptical faces, especially from the other Asians present, so I continue. "I'd hate to live in a world where we tell people what they should and shouldn't write based on the color of their skin. I mean, turn what you're saying around and see how it sounds. Can a Black writer not write a novel with a white protagonist? What about everyone who has written about World War Two, and never lived through it? You can critique a work on the grounds of literary quality, and its representations of history—sure. But I see no reason why I shouldn't tackle this subject if I'm willing to do the work. And as you can tell by the text, I did do the work. You can look up my bibliographies. You can do the fact-checking yourself. Meanwhile, I think writing is fundamentally an exercise in empathy. Reading lets us live in someone else's shoes. Literature builds bridges; it makes our world larger, not smaller. And as for the question of profit—I mean, should every writer who writes about dark things feel guilty about it? Should creatives not be paid for their work?"

Profiting from someone else's suffering. God, what a cruel way to put it. Athena used to struggle with this, publicly, performatively.

"I am ethically troubled by the fact that I can only tell this story because my parents and grandparents lived through it," she once told *Publishers Weekly*. "And sometimes it does feel like I'm exploiting their pain for my profit. I try to write in a way that is honoring them. But I remain aware that I can only do this because I am the privileged, lucky generation. I have the indulgence to look back, to be a storyteller."

Please. I've always found that line to be a cop-out. There's no need to dress it up. We are all vultures, and some of us—and I mean Athena, here—are simply better at finding the juiciest morsels of a story, at ripping through bone and gristle to the tender bleeding heart and putting all the gore on display.

Of course I feel somewhat icky when I inform a captivated audience that British officers were told they could quell disturbances by shooting those laborers responsible. It feels both thrilling and wrong to recount this, the same way racking up likes for my thread about Athena's death felt wrong. But that's the fate of a storyteller. We become nodal points for the grotesque. We are the ones who say, "Look!" while everyone peeks through their eyes, unable to confront darkness in full force. We articulate what no one else can even parse. We give a name to the unthinkable.

"I think this discomfort with my writing about tragedy speaks to our larger discomfort with acknowledging it happened at all," I conclude. "And that is, unfortunately, the lot of anyone who writes a war novel. But I won't let that stop me from telling untold histories. Someone has to do it."

Smattered applause. Not everyone agrees with me, but that's fine—at least I haven't gotten any boos. With questions like this, that in itself is a victory. The SJW girl looks like she wants to say more, but the bookstore staff have already passed the mic on to the next audience member, who wants to know about where and how I get my inspiration. I smile, touch my fist to my chin, and launch into another perfectly rehearsed answer.

WHO HAS THE RIGHT TO WRITE ABOUT SUFFERING?

I once went to a Korean War exhibit at the Smithsonian's National Museum of American History with Athena, back when I was still fooling myself that we could be good friends. I'd just moved to DC after my stint with Teach for America, and I knew Athena had moved there a few months prior for her fellowship at Georgetown, so I'd reached out breezily to see what she was up to. She responded that she was working in the morning, but doing a museum visit in the afternoon, and would love if I came along.

Wandering about an exhibit on the Korean War wasn't my first choice for how to spend a Friday afternoon, but Athena wanted to hang out with me, and back then I still felt a little thrill every time I received any shred of Athena's attention, so I met her at the front doors at three.

"I'm so glad you're in town!" She hugged me in that light, detached way of hers, the way that made it seem like she was a supermodel who'd hugged a line of a hundred fans and now no longer knew how to put real emphasis into this action, hugging. "Shall we go in?"

"Oh—yeah, sure." That was it; no small talk, no *how have you been?* Just a brief hug before we walked straight into the museum's temporary showcase of the experiences of American POWs in North Korea.

I thought this was a joke at first. *Oh, silly, you didn't think I'd want to stroll a stuffy old museum instead of catching up with you, did you?* Or that perhaps, hopefully, we'd spend a few minutes here while she saw whatever she wanted to see and then remove ourselves to a cool, air-conditioned bar where we could sip fruity drinks and talk about, you know, life and publishing. But it was quickly apparent Athena wanted to linger here all afternoon. She would stand for ten minutes or longer in front of each life-size, black-and-white cutout, whispering under her breath as she read about the subject's life story. Then she would touch her fingers to her lips, sigh, and shake her head. Once I even saw her wipe a tear from her eye.

"Imagine," she kept murmuring. "All those lives lost. All that suffering for a cause that they didn't even know if they believed in, just because their government was convinced domino theory was true. My God."

And the whole thing would start again as we moved on to the next. Here we could read the last known letter from nineteen-year-old draftee Ricky Barnes, who'd asked his friend to bring his dog tags back to his mother when he caught diphtheria along the Yalu River.

Athena could not stop talking. At first I thought that maybe she was incredibly sensitive, that she couldn't hear about someone else's suffering without experiencing it acutely as her own. Fucking saint. But as we moved through the exhibit, I noticed she was scribbling things into a Moleskine. This was all research for some writing project.

"Just awful," she whispered. "His widow was only seventeen—only a girl still. And she was pregnant already with his daughter, who would never know her father's face." And on and on. We inched down the exhibit while Athena examined every placard and cutout, announcing every so often what it was that made this particular story so very tragic.

At last I couldn't take the sound of her voice anymore, so I wandered off to get a closer look at the uniform displays. I couldn't find Athena when I exited the exhibit, and for a moment I thought she'd ditched me before I saw her sitting on a bench next to an old man in a wheelchair, jotting things into her notebook while he talked at her boobs.

"And do you remember how that felt?" she asked him. "Can you describe it for me? Everything you can remember?"

Jesus Christ, I thought. *She's a vampire.*

Athena had a magpie's eye for suffering. This skill united all her best-received works. She could see through the grime and sludge of facts and details to the part of the story that bled. She collected true narratives like seashells, polished them off, and presented them, sharp and gleaming, to horrified and entranced readers.

That museum visit was disturbing, but it didn't surprise me.

I'd seen Athena steal before.

She probably didn't even think of it as theft. The way she described it, this process wasn't exploitative, but something mythical and profound. "I try to make sense of the chaos," she told the *New Yorker* once. "I think the way we learn about history in classrooms is so antiseptic. It makes those struggles feel so far away, like they could never happen to us, like we would never make the same decisions that the people in those textbooks did. I want to bring those bloody histories to the fore. I want to make the reader confront how close to the present those histories still are."

Elegantly put. Noble, even. When you phrase it like that, it's not exploitation, it's a service.

But tell me, really, what more right did Athena have to tell those stories than anyone else did? She never lived in China for more than a few months at a time. She was never in a war zone. She grew up attending private schools in England paid for by her parents' tech jobs, summered on Nantucket and Martha's Vineyard, and spent her adult life between New Haven, NYC, and DC. She doesn't even speak Chinese fluently—she's admitted in interviews that she "spoke only English at home in an attempt to better assimilate."

Athena would go on Twitter and talk about the importance of Asian American representation, about how the model minority myth was false because Asians were overrepresented at both the low and high ends of the income spectrum, how Asian women continued to be fetishized and made victims of hate crimes, and how Asians were silently suffering because they did not exist as a voting category to white American politicians. And then she'd go home to that Dupont Circle apartment and settle down to write on a thousand-dollar antique typewriter while sipping a bottle of expensive Riesling her publisher had sent her for earning out her advance.

Athena never personally experienced suffering. She just got rich from it. She wrote an award-winning short story based on what she saw at that exhibit, titled "Whispers along the Yalu." And she wasn't even Korean.

Nine

THE CAMBRIDGE EVENT SPARKS A MINOR TWITTER DISCOURSE, featuring all the usual suspects—lots of threads covering what happened with various degrees of outrage, lots of people weighing in with their own opinions, most of them using it as a chance to grandstand and show off profound thoughts that are only tangentially related to what was actually said. A couple of people agree with the question asker—I learn that she's a sophomore at MIT named Lily Wu, and that she's written a whole angry thread about the encounter in which she calls me, among other things, an oblivious White woman with no real ties to the community and a disingenuous, self-interested faux ally.

But more people are on my side than hers. Her replies are full of comments like Your position sounds like reverse racism to me . . . and Oh, you like censorship? Might I suggest moving back home to communist China! It's a whole mess. I don't comment. By now, I've learned that the best way to deal with negative backlash is to bunker down, silent and unscathed, until the whole thing blows over. In any case, Twitter discourse never *does* anything—it's just an opportunity for firebrands to wave their flags, declare their sides, and try to brandish some IQ points before everyone gets bored and moves on.

A WEEK LATER, I RECEIVE THE FOLLOWING EMAIL:

> Good afternoon,
>
> My name is Susan Lee, and I am the events coordinator for the Rockville chapter of the Chinese American Social Club. I recently read your novel *The Last Front*, and was really impressed by your grasp on this forgotten aspect of Chinese history. Many of our club members would be very curious to hear your story. We would love to host you at one of our club meetings. We usually do a Q&A with an invited guest, followed by a buffet dinner (free of charge to you, of course). Please let me know if that would be of interest.
>
> Thank you,
> Susan

I almost delete the email. At this point, I delete most event invitations that don't offer honorariums unless they're truly prestigious. Susan Lee's tone reads as formal and stilted in a way that makes me suspicious, though I can't quite put my finger on why. (I always briefly worry, before accepting any invitations, whether the organizers are really setting a trap to hold me hostage or kill me.) Besides,

Rockville is all the way in Maryland; it's a pain to get out to from central DC if you don't feel like spending a hundred bucks on an Uber round trip or sitting on the red line for an hour, and it's not a paid gig.

I should have said no and saved myself the humiliation.

But Lily Wu's words echo in my mind—"disingenuous, self-interested faux ally," "oblivious White woman with no real ties to the community." Aside from the Asian American Writers' Collective, which I donate to and which can't exactly shun me, this is the first Asian organization that's wanted to host me since the Cambridge debacle. This could be good for me. This could prove, to the Twitter conspiracy theorists, that my support for Asian Americans isn't an act. That I wrote *The Last Front* because I've studied the history, and because I care about the community. Maybe I'll even make some new friends. I imagine the optics of an Instagram post of me eating catered Chinese food, surrounded by admiring Chinese fans.

I look up the Chinese American Social Club of Rockville. Their website is a dinky little single page featuring Comic Sans text against a bright red background. I scroll down past the giant header to find several badly lit photos of club functions—a buffet dinner with a local business leader, a New Year's banquet where everyone is wearing red, a karaoke night illuminated by garish flash. From what I can tell, the club members range from middle-aged to elderly. They look harmless. Adorable, even.

Oh, what the hell? I wait a respectable few hours so that I don't come off as desperate, and then I email Susan back.

Hi, Susan. I would be happy to come speak to the club. April is quite open for me. Which dates work best for you?

SUSAN LEE GREETS ME AT THE PARKING LOT OF THE SHADY GROVE metro station. I'm not so comfortable with my new wealth that I can just fling money at Ubers, so I've taken the red line all the way to the end, and she's offered to drive me the rest of the way to the club. She's a short, petite woman wearing a very crisp suit jacket. Kim Jong Un's girlboss propagandist sister immediately comes to mind, only because I'd once seen a news photograph of her wearing a similar suit and sunglasses, but of course I can't mention this comparison out loud.

Susan greets me with a firm handshake. "Hi, Juniper. Was the train ride okay?"

"Yeah, fine." I follow her to her blue sedan. She has to toss a few books and blankets into the back to make space for me, and the car is suffused with some cloying, herbal odor. "Sorry about the mess. Here you go—you sit up front."

Her lack of formality strikes me as rather unprofessional. I rankle a bit that Susan's acting like she's picking her daughter up from school instead of chauffeuring an acclaimed guest. But no, no, that's my own bias coming through. *They're not a glitzy bookstore,* I remind myself. *They're just some little social club without a big budget, and they're doing me a favor by wanting to be associated with me.*

"You speak Chinese?" Susan asks as we pull onto the highway.

"Huh? Oh, no—no, sorry, I don't."

"Your mom didn't teach you? Or your dad?"

"Oh—I'm sorry." My gut twists with dread. "You must be mistaken—neither of my parents are Chinese."

"What!" Susan's mouth makes such a perfectly round O of shock, I would laugh if this whole thing weren't so awkward. "But your last name is Song, so we thought maybe . . . You are Korean, then? I know some Korean Songs."

"No, sorry. Song is my middle name, actually. My last name is Hayward. Neither of my parents are, um, Asian." I want to die. I want to open the car door and roll out onto the highway and be obliterated by oncoming traffic.

"Oh." Susan falls silent for a moment. I glance sideways at her, only to catch her sneaking a sideways glance at me. "Oh. I see."

I feel shitty about the mix-up, obviously, but also a little defensive. I've never pretended to be Chinese. I have noticed that people often operate in a gray area with me where they might think I'm Chinese, but don't want to presume or ask me to clarify. I'm not fooling anyone on purpose. I don't have a big sign that says WHITE! stamped to my forehead, but shouldn't the onus be on other people not to presume? Isn't it racist, in a sense, to assume my race based on my last name?

Susan and I don't speak for the rest of the drive. I wonder what she's thinking. Her face looks tight, but maybe it always looks that tight; maybe that's how all middle-aged Asian ladies look. As we pull up to the church—the Chinese American Social Club of Rockville meets Thursday nights at a Presbyterian church, I guess—she asks me if I like Chinese food.

"Sure," I say. "I love it."

"Good." She kills the engine. "Because that's what we ordered."

Inside, metal fold-out chairs are arranged in rows before a pastor's lectern. I've drawn a larger crowd than I expected; there are forty, maybe fifty people here. I thought this was just a club, not a whole congregation. A lot of them are carrying signed copies of my book. A few people wave enthusiastically when I walk through the door, and I feel stabs of guilt in my gut.

"Up this way." Susan gestures for me to follow her to the lectern. She adjusts the mic to her height, and I stand awkwardly behind her, surprised that we're starting so abruptly. I wish someone had offered me a glass of water.

"Hello, everyone," Susan says. The mic screeches; she waits for the feedback to die out before she continues. "Tonight we have a very special guest. Our esteemed speaker has written a beautiful novel about the Chinese Labour Corps, which many of you have read, and she's here to give us a reading and talk to us about being a writer. Please, everyone join me in welcoming Miss Juniper Song."

She claps politely. The audience follows suit. Susan steps back from the lectern and gestures for me to begin. She's still smiling that tight, strained smile.

"Well, hello." I clear my throat. *Come on, this is nothing.* I've done a dozen bookstore talks by now; I can get through a simple club meeting. "I guess, well, I'll start with a reading."

To my surprise, it goes just fine. The audience is tame and quiet, smiling and nodding at all the right moments. A few of them seem confused when I begin to read—they squint and tilt their heads to the side, and I can't figure out if they're hard of hearing or if they can't understand English well, so I slow way down and talk very loudly just in case. It takes me way longer to get through my excerpt as a result, which leaves only twenty minutes for the Q&A, but honestly that's a relief. Anything to burn time.

Though the questions, too, are total softballs. Actually, most of them are quite sweet; they're the sort of questions you might receive from your mom's friends. They ask about how I became so successful at such a young age. How did I balance my studies with my writing career? What other interesting things about Chinese laborers did I encounter in my research? One bespectacled old man asks a very blunt question about the size of my advance and my royalties rate ("I did some math and I have some thoughts on publishing's business model, which I would like to share," he says), which I dodge by telling him I prefer to keep those details private. Another man asks, in broken English, how I think Chinese Americans should better advocate for representation in the American political sphere. I have no idea what to say to this, so I mutter something about social media visibility, coalition with other marginalized groups, and the disappointing centrism of Andrew Yang, and hope that my rapid English confuses him enough that he thinks I've uttered a coherent answer.

One woman, who introduces herself as Grace Zhou, tells me that her daughter Christina is in ninth grade and asks whether I have any advice for her about the college application process. "She loves to write," she says. "But she has trouble fitting in at school, especially because there aren't many other Chinese Americans, you know, and I was wondering if you could offer some advice for her to help her feel comfortable expressing herself."

I sneak a glance at Susan, whose mouth is now pressed so thin it could have been drawn on with a pencil.

"Just tell her to be herself," I offer weakly. "I also had a hard time in high school, but, um, I got through it by throwing myself into the things I loved. My refuge was books. When I didn't like the world around me, I would read, and I think that's what turned me into the writer I am today. I learned the magic of words early on. Maybe the same will be true for Christina."

All that, at least, is true. I can't tell if Grace is happy with this answer or not, but she passes on the microphone.

At last the hour is up. I thank my audience graciously and make for the door, hoping to slip away before anyone drags me into conversation, but Susan materializes by my side just as I step away from the lectern.

"I was hoping—" I begin, but Susan guides me, almost violently, toward the plastic foldout tables at the back of the room.

"Come," she says, "get some dinner while it's hot."

Some volunteers have put out trays of the catered Chinese food, which looks so greasy under the fluorescent lights that it turns my stomach. I thought Chinese people were supposed to be snooty about cheap Chinese takeout. Or maybe it was just Athena who'd obnoxiously declared never to consume a bite of food that came delivered from places named things like "Kitchen Number One" and "Great Wall Express." ("You know that's not authentic," she told me. "They just serve that shit to white people who don't know any better.") I use the plastic tongs to select a single vegetarian egg roll, since it's the one thing that isn't literally glistening with oil, but the tiny grandma at my shoulder insists I also try the kung pao chicken and the sesame noodles, so I let her pile helpings of those onto my plate while I try not to gag.

Susan guides me to a table in the corner and seats me next to an old man she introduces as Mr. James Lee. "Mr. Lee has been very excited about your talk ever since it was announced," says Susan. "He even brought his book for you to sign. Everyone wanted to sit with you—I know Grace wants to bother you about her daughter's college applications—but I told them no."

Mr. Lee beams at me. His face is so brown and wrinkled it has the consistency of a walnut, but his eyes are bright and friendly. He pulls a hardcover edition of *The Last Front* out from his bag and offers it to me with both hands. "Sign, yes?"

Oh my God, I think. *He's adorable.*

"Should I personalize it to you?" I ask gently.

He nods. I can't tell if he can understand what I'm saying, so I glance at Susan, who also nods her permission.

To Mr. Lee, I write. *Was such a pleasure to meet you. Best, Juniper Song.*

"Mr. Lee's uncle was one of the Chinese Labour Corps," Susan informs me.

I blink. "Oh! Really!"

"He settled in Canada afterward," says Mr. Lee. So he does understand what we're saying. His English is slow and halting, but all his sentences are perfectly grammatical. "I used to tell all the children at school that my uncle fought in World War One. So cool, I thought! My uncle, the war hero! But nobody believed me. They said that the Chinese were not in World War One." He reaches out to take my hands in his, and I'm so startled by this that I let him. "You know better. Thank you." His eyes are wet, shining. "Thank you for telling this story."

My nose prickles. I have the sudden urge to bawl. Susan has gotten up to chat at another table, and that's the only thing that gives me the courage to say what I do next.

"I don't know," I murmur. "Honestly, Mr. Lee, I don't know if I was the right person to tell this story."

He clasps my hands tighter. His face is so kind, it makes me feel rotten.

"You are exactly right," he says. "We need you. My English, it is not so good. Your generation has very good English. You can tell them our story. Make sure they remember us." He nods, determined. "Yes. Make sure they remember us."

He gives my hands one last squeeze and tells me something in Chinese, but of course I don't understand a word.

For the first time since I submitted the manuscript, I feel a deep wash of shame. This isn't my history, my heritage. This isn't my community. I am an outsider, basking in their love under false pretenses. It should be Athena sitting here, smiling with these people, signing books and listening to the stories of her elders.

"Eat, eat!" Mr. Lee nods encouragingly at my plate. "You young people work too hard. You don't eat enough."

I want to vomit. I can't stay a moment longer among these people. I need to break free from their smiles, their kindness.

"Excuse me, Mr. Lee." I stand up and hurry across the room. "I have to go," I tell Susan. "I need to—uh, I forgot I have to pick up my mom at the airport."

I know it's an awful excuse the moment I blurt it out—Susan knows I don't have a car, that's the reason she had to come pick me up at the train station in the first place. But she seems sympathetic. "Of course. You can't keep your mother waiting. Just let me get my purse, and I'll drive you to the station."

"No, please, I couldn't impose. I'll get an Uber—"

"Absolutely not! Rosslyn is so far!"

"I really don't want to put you out of the way," I gasp. "You haven't finished your dinner. I had a lovely time, and it was so great meeting everyone, but I—um, I should really just let you enjoy your night."

I burst for the door before Susan can answer. She doesn't chase after me, but if she had, I would have sprinted until I was out of sight. It's so undignified, but all I can perceive then is the relief of cool air on my face outside.

Ten

AFTER THAT, I ASK EMILY TO DECLINE MOST EVENT INVITATIONS on my behalf. I'm done with schools, bookstores, and book clubs. I'm selling at the level where personal appearances aren't going to move the needle on sales, so I don't need to keep exposing myself as bait for further controversy. The only events I keep attending are awards ceremonies at literary conventions, because as much as I now want to hide from the public, I'd hate to give up the rush of validation from *those*.

Awards in this industry are very silly and arbitrary, less a marker of prestige or literary quality and more an indication that you've won a popularity contest with a very small, skewed group of voters. Awards don't matter—at least, I am told this constantly by the people who regularly win them. Athena made an annual point to explain all this on Twitter, always right after she was nominated for something big: Oh, of course I'm so honored, but remember, if you weren't a finalist, that doesn't mean your work doesn't matter! All of our stories are special in their own, important ways.

I do fully believe that awards are bullshit, but that doesn't make me want to win them any less.

And *The Last Front* is, simply put, awards bait. It's brilliantly written—check. It attracts both commercial and "upmarket" readers—check. But most important, it is *about* something; some timely or sensitive issue that the awards committees can point to and say, *Look, we care about what is going on in the world, and since literature is a necessary reflection of our lived reality, this story is what we've chosen to elevate.*

I'm a bit nervous that *The Last Front* is *too* commercially successful to win anything. I'm told that awards committees want to seem more tasteful than the proletariat, so there's always a mega bestseller that doesn't make the ballot in the category it should obviously win, and always a few finalists in every category that no one's ever heard of. But I shouldn't have worried. The nominations trickle in one by one: Goodreads Choice Awards, check; the Indies Choice Book Awards, check. The Booker Prize and the Women's Prize are long shots, so I'm not too disappointed when I don't make the short list for those. Besides, I'm nominated for so many regional awards that I'm swimming in attention regardless.

Adele Sparks-Sato is eating her heart out, texts Marnie when I share the Goodreads Choice Awards news.

From Jen: YES! Good on you. The best revenge is to thrive. Proud of you for handling all this with grace. #StayClassyStayWinning!

I reread my nomination emails several times a day, gloating at those words: Dear Ms. Song, we are delighted to inform you . . . And I dance around my apartment, rehearsing an imaginary acceptance speech, attempting the same mixture of grace and youthful excitement Athena always exuded in hers: "Oh my *God*, I really don't believe it . . . No, really, I didn't think I was going to win . . ."

The nominations bring about a flurry of good press. I'm featured on a lot of BuzzFeed lists. I get to do a profile with the *Yale Daily News*. Winning the Goodreads Choice Award gives me a sizable sales bump, and I end up back on the *New York Times* bestseller list for two weeks. I suppose the awards buzz gets the attention of people in Hollywood, too, because Brett calls me that week to let me know my film agent wants to set up a meeting between me and some people from Greenhouse Productions.

"What's Greenhouse?" I ask. "Are they legit?"

"They're a production company. Pretty standard; we've done a few deals with them in the past."

"I've never heard of them." I type the name into Google. Oh, no, they're actually pretty impressive—their main staff are three producers who have a number of films I recognize under their belts, and notably, one producer-director, Jasmine Zhang, who was an Oscar finalist last year for a film about Chinese migrant workers in San Francisco. I wonder if she's the source of the interest. "Oh, shoot, so they're like actually a big player?"

"You wouldn't have heard the names of most independent production companies," Brett explains. "They largely operate behind the scenes. They package your book, find a screenwriter, attach some talent, etcetera, and then they pitch it to a studio. The studios put up the big money. But the production companies will pay you up front to option it, and this is the strongest option interest we've seen so far. Can't hurt to chat, right? How's next Thursday?"

The Greenhouse Productions people happen to be in DC for a film festival that weekend, so we arrange to meet at a coffee shop in Georgetown. I arrive early—I hate the fluster of shaking hands, then figuring out what to order, and then fumbling with my card at the register—but they're already occupying a booth in the back when I show up. There's two of them—Justin, one of the Greenhouse founders, and his assistant, Harvey. They're both blond, tan, fit, and possessed of dazzlingly white smiles. They look like they could be brothers, maybe cousins, though perhaps that's because their hair is coiffed back in identical crests and they are wearing the same cut of V-neck Henley rolled up to the elbows. Jasmine Zhang does not appear to be present.

"Hey, Juniper!" Justin stands up to hug me. "Wonderful to meet you. Thanks for making time for us."

"Of course," I say, just as Harvey leans out for a hug as well. It's awkward, reaching over the booth toward his outstretched arms, and I strain to meet him in the middle. He smells very clean. "Georgetown is super close."

"Do you come out here a lot?" asks Justin.

Actually, no, because everything in Georgetown is so fucking expensive, and the students who overrun the neighborhood are loud, obnoxious, and way too rich. I've only been here a handful of times with Athena, who was obsessed with this margarita place on Wisconsin Ave. But I picked the venue, mostly because I hoped it would impress, so I can't act like I don't know the area. "Um, yeah, all the time. El Centro is nice. Lots of good seafood places on the waterfront. And the macaron place on M, if you have some free time later."

Justin beams like macarons are his favorite food in the world. "Well, we'll have to try it out!"

"Definitely," says Harvey. "Right after this."

I know their puppy-dog act is meant to set me at ease, but instead I'm now stiff with nerves. Hollywood people mean literally none of what they say, Athena had once complained. They're so friendly and enthusiastic, and they tell you you're the most special snowflake they ever did see, and then they turn around and ghost you for weeks. I see now what she meant. I have no idea how to gauge how genuine Justin and Harvey are, or how they're evaluating my responses, and their blindingly cheerful front makes them so hard to read that it's sending my anxiety into overdrive.

A waitress comes by and asks for my order. I'm too rattled to peruse the menu, so I ask for the same thing Justin is sipping, which turns out to be an iced Vietnamese coffee called "the Miss Saigon."

"Great choice," says Justin. "It's very nice. Very strong—and sweet, too, I think it's made with condensed milk?"

"Oh, um, yeah." I hand my menu back to the waitress. "It's what I always get."

"So! *The Last Front*." Justin slams both hands so hard against the table that I flinch. "What a *book*! I'm surprised no one's snapped up the rights already!"

I don't know what to say to this. Does that mean he feels lucky we're having this meeting, or is he fishing for a reason why the rights haven't been more attractive? Should I pretend like there's been other interest?

"I guess Hollywood isn't too keen on taking a risk on films about Asian people," I say. It's an arch comment, but I mean it, and I've heard the same complaint plenty of times from Athena. "I would love to see this story adapted for the big screen, but I guess it would take a true ally to do it. Someone would really have to understand the story."

"Well, we *loved* the novel," says Justin. "It's so original. And so diverse, in a time when we desperately need diverse narratives."

"I love the mosaic storytelling style," says Harvey. "It reminds me of *Dunkirk*."

"It's precisely like *Dunkirk*. One of my favorite films, actually—I thought it was so brilliant how Nolan kept us guessing at how all the narrative threads would fit together at the end." Justin glances sideways at Harvey. "Actually, Chris would be a pretty fun pick for a director, wouldn't he?"

"Oh, Jesus." Justin nods emphatically. "Yeah, that'd be the dream."

"What about Jasmine Zhang?" I ask. I'm a little surprised neither of them has brought her up. Isn't she the most obvious choice to direct?

"Oh, I don't know if she has the bandwidth for this." Justin fiddles with his straw. "She's a little overwhelmed with work right now."

"Side effects of winning an Oscar," says Harvey. "She's booked up for the next decade."

"Ha. Yeah. But don't worry, we have some really special talent in mind. There's a kid just out of USC, Danny Baker, just wowed everyone with a short film about war crimes in Cambodia—oh, and some girl at Tisch who put out a student documentary on accessing PRC historical archives last year, if it's important that you have an Asian female in charge."

The waitress sets my Miss Saigon in front of me. I take a sip and wince; it's much sweeter than I expected.

"Well, that's very cool," I say, slightly flummoxed. They're talking like they've already decided to option the novel. Am I doing well, then? What else do I need to say to persuade them? "So what can I help you with?"

"Oh, we're just here to hear whatever's on your mind!" Justin laces his fingers together and leans forward. "We care a lot about the author's vision here at Greenhouse. We're not here to mangle your work, or whitewash it or Hollywood-ify it, or whatever. We're all about the story's integrity, so we want your input at every stage."

"Think of it as creating a vision board." Harvey sits ready with a pen poised over a legal pad. "What elements would you absolutely want to see in a movie version of *The Last Front*, Juniper?"

"Well, um, I guess I hadn't thought much about that." I've just remembered why I never order coffee at work meetings. Caffeine goes straight to my bladder, and I have a sudden, vicious urge to pee. "Screenwriting's not really my thing, so I don't know . . ."

"We could start with, like, your dream cast?" Justin prompts. "Any big stars you always had in mind while writing?"

"I—uh, I don't know, really." My face burns. I feel like I'm failing a test I didn't bother to study for, though in retrospect it feels obvious I should have put some thought into what I wanted from a film adaptation before I met with producers. "I didn't have any actors when I was writing in mind, to be honest; I'm not super visual like that . . ."

"Well, how about this Colonel Charles Robertson character?" asks Harvey. "The British attaché? We could invest in getting someone really major, like Benedict Cumberbatch, or Tom Hiddleston . . ."

I blink. "But he's not even a main character." Colonel Charles Robertson gets barely a passing mention in the first chapter.

"Well, right," says Justin. "But maybe we could expand his role a bit, give him some more dramatic presence—"

"I mean, I guess." I frown. "I'm not sure how that would work—it'd ruin the pacing of the first act—but we could look into it . . ."

"See, the trick with big war epics is that you need someone really charismatic to ground it all," says Justin. "You don't get broad crossover appeal if military history is the only marketing point. But put in a British heartthrob, and then you've got your women, your middle-aged moms, your teenage girls . . . Again, it's the Dunkirk principle. What the fuck is Dunkirk? Who knows? We went to see Tom Hardy."

"And Harry Styles," says Harvey.

"Right! Exactly. What we're saying is, your film needs a Harry Styles."

"What about that little kid from *Spider-Man*?" says Harvey. "What's his name?"

Justin perks up. "Tom Holland?"

"Oh yeah. I would love to see him in a war movie. Logical next step, for a career like that." Harvey glances my way, like he's just remembered I exist. "What do you think, June? You like Tom Holland?"

"I—yeah, I like Tom Holland." My bladder bulges. I squirm in my seat, trying to find a better equilibrium. "That would work, I guess, sure. I mean, I'm not sure who he would play, but—"

"Then for A Geng, we were thinking some Chinese talent—a pop star, maybe," says Justin. "Then that gets us the Chinese box office, which is huge—"

"The problem with Asian pop stars is that they have shit English, though," says Harvey. "*Herro.* Production nightmare."

"Harvey!" Justin laughs. "You can't say that."

"Ah! You caught me! Don't tell Jasmine."

"But that wouldn't be a problem," I cut in. "The laborers are supposed to have bad English."

I must sound snarkier than I intended, because Justin quickly amends, "I mean, we would never alter the story in a way you aren't comfortable with. That's not what we're trying to do here. We want to totally respect the project—"

I shake my head. "No, no, yeah, I don't feel disrespected—"

"And we're just spitballing ideas to package things more attractively, and to, uh, broaden the audience . . ."

I sit back and lift my hands in surrender. "Look. You guys are the Hollywood experts. I'm just the novelist. All of that sounds fine to me, and you have my blessing, or whatever, to package this however you think is appropriate."

I do mean that. I've never wanted to have much control over my film adaptations—I have no training as a screenwriter, and besides, social media is always abuzz with gossip about this or that novelist who had a falling-out with the director. I don't want to be a creative diva. And maybe they have a point. Who wants to go to the theater and watch a bunch of people speaking in Chinese for two hours? I mean, wouldn't you go see a Chinese film instead? We're talking about a blockbuster made with an American audience in mind. Accessibility matters.

"Thanks for understanding." Justin beams. "We talk to authors sometimes, and they—you know . . ."

"They're very picky," says Harvey. "They want every scene in the movie to match the book, word for word."

"And they don't get that film is a totally different medium, and requires different storytelling skills," says Justin. "It's a translation, really. And translation across mediums is inherently unfaithful to some extent. Roland Barthes. An act of translation is an act of betrayal."

"*Belles infidèles*," says Harvey. "Beautiful and unfaithful."

"You get it, though," says Justin. "Which is awesome."

And that's the end of it. This is awesome. I am awesome. We are all so, so excited to make things work. I keep waiting for them to offer more substantive details. How much money is on the table? What's their timeline? Are they going to start reaching out to this Danny Baker kid, like, tomorrow? (Harvey made it sound like he would DM him right away.) But all they're giving me are vagaries, and I get the sense that this is perhaps not the right context to press. So I sit back and let them buy me some overpriced strudel (named the "Inglourious Pastry") and chat at me about how gorgeous the waterfront is. Justin handles the check, and both of them hug me tightly before we part ways.

I stroll until they've turned around the opposite corner, and then I dash back into the café and pee for a full minute.

THAT WENT OKAY. I EMAIL BRETT A SUMMARY OF THE MEETING AS I stroll back over the bridge to Rosslyn. I think they liked me, but it seems like they're still feeling out some things before there's cash on the table. I don't think Jasmine Zhang is attached, which is weird?

Pretty standard as far as Hollywood meetings go, Brett responds. They were just getting a sense of you as a person. Hard offers don't come until later. Not sure what's going on with Jasmine, though it does seem like the main interest is coming from Justin. I'll keep you updated if there's any news.

I'm impatient to hear more, but this is how things are. Publishing *crawls*. Gatekeepers sit on manuscripts for months, and meetings happen behind closed doors while you're dying from anticipation on the outside. Publishing means no news for weeks, until you're standing in line at Starbucks or waiting for the bus, and your phone pings with the email that will change your life.

So I head down into the metro, put my Hollywood dreams on hold, and wait for Brett to inform me that I'm about to become a millionaire.

I try to temper my expectations. After all, the vast majority of options deals go nowhere. All that an option means is that the production company has exclusive rights to package the story into something a studio might want to buy. The vast majority of projects linger in development hell, and very few ever get green-lit by studio executives. I learn this over the next few hours as I scour the internet for articles about this process, catching myself up on industry terminology and trying to gauge how excited I should be.

I'm probably not getting my Warner Bros. film. I probably won't be a millionaire. The hype could still help me, though—I could still make some tens of thousands of dollars from Greenhouse's option offer. I could sell a few thousand more copies based on the publicity from that deal alone.

And there's always that elusive, tempting "maybe." Maybe this *will* get picked up by Netflix, or HBO or Hulu. Maybe the film will be a massive hit, and they'll do another print run of my book with the movie poster on the cover, and I'll get to attend the premiere in a dress tailor-made for me, arm in arm with the handsome Asian actor they cast to play A Geng. Elle Fanning will star as Annie Waters, and we'll take a cute selfie together at the premiere like the one Athena once took with Anne Hathaway.

Why not dream big? I've found, as I keep hitting my publishing goalposts, that my ambitions get larger and larger. I got my embarrassingly large advance. I got my bestseller status, my major magazine profiles, my prizes and honors. Now, with the sickly sweet taste of the Miss Saigon lingering on my tongue, all that feels paltry in comparison to what true literary stardom looks like. I want what Stephen King has, what Neil Gaiman has. Why *not* a movie deal? Why not Hollywood stardom? Why not a multimedia empire? Why not the world?

Eleven

THE ATTACKS START ON TWITTER.

The first tweet comes from an account named @AthenaLiusGhost, created earlier this week; no profile picture, no words in the bio:

> Juniper Song, aka June Hayward, did not write The Last Front. I did. She stole my book, stole my voice, and stole my words. #SaveAthena.

Then, dated a few hours later, several sickening follow-ups in the thread.

> June Hayward befriended me a few years ago to get closer to my process and my work. She came over often to my apartment, and I would catch her rooting through my notebooks when she thought I wasn't looking.

The proof is in black and white. Read my previous novels. Compare them to the prose in The Last Front. Read June's debut novel, and ask yourself: is The Last Front a novel a white woman could have written?

For let's be clear: Juniper Song Hayward is a white woman.

She's using the pen name Juniper Song to pretend to be Chinese American. She's taken new author photos to look more tan and ethnic, but she's as white as they come. June Hayward, you are a thief and a liar. You've stolen my legacy, and now you spit on my grave.

Shame on June. Shame on Eden Press. Daniella Woodhouse must withdraw the current edition from bookstores and return the rights to Athena's mother, Patricia Liu. All future editions should be published under Athena's name alone.

Do not let injustice stand. #SaveAthena.

There's a penultimate tweet tagging over a dozen prominent Twitter accounts, begging them to RT for visibility.

Then a final tweet, tagging me.

My vision's gone fuzzy by the time I read to the end. I take a breath, and my bedroom tilts. I can't stand up; I can hardly move. My mind's fizzled out; I can't form coherent thoughts anymore, I can only click REFRESH on @AthenaLiusGhost's page, reading the tweets over and over again, watching as the thread slowly gains traction.

In the first several hours, it garnered no likes, and I had a wild hope that this, like all crazy fringe accounts, would just fade into the ether. But all those tags must have grabbed it some attention, because fifteen minutes after I first see it, people start responding to the thread. Some book blogger with six thousand followers retweets the first tweet, and then some aspiring author who's gone viral several times for their literary "hot takes" (which mostly have boiled down to "y'all need to take a critical reading course" and "not all villains are problematic") quote tweets it with the addition Sickening if true. Oh my god. And then the floodgates are open. People start replying:

> Are you fucking serious?
>
> Where's the proof?
>
> Always thought there was something off about Song. Hmm.
>
> Sounds like another Yalie "prodigy" is just a big, lying fraud.
>
> WTF!!! SEND HER ASS TO JAIL!

I can't move away from my laptop. Even when I finally get up to pee, my eyes remain glued to my phone. The healthy thing to do would be to shut down all my devices, but I can't step back. I have to watch the whole disaster unfold in real time, have to see exactly who has retweeted it and who is responding.

Then the DMs start coming. They're all from total strangers. I don't know why I even open them, but I'm too curious, or too masochistic, to simply delete them.

Die, bitch.

June, have you seen these tweets? Are they true? You need to defend yourself if not.

You should burn in hell for what you did. Racist thieving whore.

You owe Mrs. Liu every cent in your bank account!!!

I was a fan of The Last Front. This is incredibly disappointing. You owe the entire book community a public apology, immediately.

I'm going to come to DC and beat the living shit out of you. Racist bitch.

It's after that last one that I finally hurl my phone across my bed. *Holy shit.* My heartbeat is so loud in my eardrums that I stand up, pace around my apartment, wedge a chair under my front door (no, I don't think someone's about to barge in and murder me, it just *feels* that way), and then curl up on my bed, where I pull my knees up to my chest and rock back and forth.

Oh my God.

Oh my God.

It's all over. People know. The whole world is about to know. Daniella will find out, Eden will fire me, I'll lose all my money, Mrs. Liu will sue me, she'll decimate me in court, Brett will drop me as a client, my career will be over, and I'll go down in literary history as the bitch who stole Athena Liu's work. They'll make a Wikipedia page about me. They'll write endless think pieces about me. You won't be able to mention my name among industry professionals without knowing sneers and awkward laughter. I'll be a meme. And not a single word I write will ever be published again.

Why in God's name did I publish *The Last Front*? I want to kick my former self for being so stupid. I thought I was doing something good. Something noble—to bring Athena's work into the world the way it deserved. But how could I ever have imagined this wouldn't all come back to bite me in the ass?

I've been so stable up until now. I've done such a good job of managing my anxiety, of focusing on the *present* instead of all my terrors and insecurities, of compartmentalizing the horror of where and how I got my hands on that original manuscript, of moving *on*. And it all comes flooding back now—Athena's hands flying to her throat, her bluing face, her feet drumming against the ground.

Oh God, what have I *done*?

My phone, faceup on my bed, keeps flashing blue with new notifications. They look like alarm sirens.

I burst into wails, loud and ugly, wanton like a toddler's. My own volume frightens me; I'm scared my neighbors will hear, so I turn my face into my pillow, and that's how I stay, muffled and hysterical, for hours.

THE SUN GOES DOWN. THE ROOM GETS DARK. AT SOME POINT MY adrenaline rush subsides, my pulse slows, my throat goes hoarse from sobbing, and I have no tears left to cry. My panic attack ebbs, probably because I've obsessed over the worst-case scenarios so many times now that they can't scare me anymore. My social and professional implosion is now a familiar concept, and, paradoxically, that means I can think again.

I reach for my phone, and as I scroll through Twitter, I realize perhaps this situation isn't as bad as it first seemed. There's no way the person behind @AthenaLiusGhost knows what truly happened. They're right about the central thesis, but wrong about all the other details. I'd never been to Athena's apartment except for that first and final time. I met Athena in college, not in DC. And I certainly didn't befriend her intending to steal *The Last Front*. Until the night Athena died, I didn't even know it existed.

Whoever this person is, they've made a very lucky guess at the truth. But they've fabricated the rest. And that suggests they do not, in fact, have any concrete evidence.

Perhaps, if all they have are suspicions, there's a way to clear my name. Perhaps there's a way to exorcise this ghost.

My mind keeps wandering to the implications of that Twitter handle—Athena Liu's *ghost*—and the memory of Athena's face at Politics and Prose, her eyes glittering, her lips curled in a patronizing smile. I push it away. On that road lies madness. Athena is fucking dead. I saw her die. And this is a problem for the living.

I DON'T WANT BRETT TO HEAR ABOUT THIS FROM TWITTER, SO I SEND him a quick email: There's something weird going on. Do you have a moment to get on the phone?

He must have seen the tweets already, because he calls me not even five minutes later, though it's nearly nine in the evening. I pick up, trembling. "Hey, Brett."

"Hi, June." His voice sounds flat, though I can't tell if I'm projecting. "So what's going on?"

I clear my throat. "I'm guessing you've seen the tweets?"

"If you could clarify—"

"The ones that say I stole *The Last Front* from Athena Liu."

"Well." A long pause. "So, yeah. It's not *true*, is it?"

"No!" My voice flies up in pitch. "No, of course not. I don't know who's behind it, I don't know how this started . . ."

"Well, if it's not true, then don't make such a big deal of it." Brett doesn't sound nearly as upset as he should be. I thought he'd be angry, but he just seems mildly irritated. "It's just some troll; it'll blow over."

"No, it won't," I insist. "All sorts of people are going to see it. They're going to form opinions—"

"So let them form opinions. Eden's not going to take the book off the shelves on the basis of some internet gossip. And most consumers don't have their eyes glued to Twitter—trust me, it's a very small fraction of publishing that's going to care."

I make a gross whining noise. "My reputation with that fraction *matters*, though."

"Your reputation is intact," he says breezily. "It's all allegations, isn't it? Totally groundless, right? Don't issue a response. Don't get entangled. If they've got nothing, they've got nothing, and soon enough people will see it for the nasty character assassination that it is."

He sounds so confident, so wholly unconcerned, that I feel a flutter of relief. Maybe he's right. Maybe this will get construed as bullying—the Twitterati are always vehemently against bullying. Maybe it'll all be good press for me in the end.

Brett yammers on for a bit longer, citing examples of other famous authors who have been targets of online hate campaigns. "It never hurts sales, Junie. It never does. Just let the trolls say what they want. You're going to be fine."

I nod and bite back what I want to say. Brett's right—there's no point in escalating this, since any response only gives the allegations legitimacy. "Okay."

"Okay? Good." Brett sounds like he's ready to be done with this call. "Don't worry so much, all right?"

"Hey, wait . . ." The thought has just crossed my mind. "Have you heard anything from the Greenhouse people?"

"Hmm? Oh, nah. But it's only been a week, they're probably resting up from their trip. Give them some time."

I feel a niggling dread then, but I tell myself I'm being silly. It's not like these two things are connected. Justin and Harvey aren't necessarily glued to Twitter, following the latest book gossip. They've got better things to do. "Okay."

"Just relax, June. You're going to get some haters. It comes with the territory. If it's not true, then you have nothing to worry about." Brett pauses for a moment. "I mean, it's *not* true, is it?"

"No! God. Of course not."

"Then block and ignore them." Brett snorts. "Or better yet, block Twitter altogether. You writers are too online to begin with. This will blow over. These things always do."

BRETT'S WRONG. THIS WON'T BLOW OVER. TWITTER SCANDALS ARE like snowballs; the more people that see it, the more who feel it necessary to weigh in with their own opinions and agendas, creating an explosion of discourse branching off the instigating conversation.

Past a critical mass of visibility, everyone in the industry starts talking about it. And @AthenaLiusGhost, whoever they are, has nearly a thousand followers by now. They've reached that critical mass.

The Athena-June scandal, as it's being now referred to, has become the Discourse of the Moment. This is wholly different from the Lily Wu discourse, which involved a dozen people at most. This time, there's blood in the water. Silence isn't an option. Everyone has to declare a side, or they're accused of complicity. (SMH at so many supposed allies staying silent now that their friend's been exposed, tweet anonymous accounts happily stirring the pot.) A lot of high-profile writers straddle the line, trying to cover their asses but also establish loyalties at the same time.

Plagiarism is terrible, writes one author. If Hayward really did plagiarize—and we don't know yet if she did—then she owes her royalties back to Athena Liu's family.

It's awful if it's true, writes another. But until there's substantiated proof, I hesitate to join this lynch mob.

There's then a heated debate over whether it's appropriate to use the words "lynch mob" when describing a white woman, and it ends with dozens of people calling the above referenced author a racist. Said author's account is locked within hours.

It's the Twitter accounts that are non-notable public figures, who have nothing to lose and everything to gain by digging their claws into me, that are most vicious.

She used to write as June Hayward, tweets a user named rey1089. But she published her book about China as June Song. Fucked up, right?

The literal definition of yellowface, writes one reply. I don't think they know what "literal" means.

So pathetic, crows another.

And without fail, the evergreen Will white people ever stop whiting?

Someone else tweets a photo of me taken off my Instagram paired with a photo of Scarlett Johansson, captioned: Corporate wants you to find the differences between these two images LMAO.

The replies involve every mean-spirited observation about my appearance you can imagine:

I swear to God why do all white women look the same.

Ok aside from the fact that ScarJo could actually get it LOLLL

Is she squinting because she wants to look more Asian or cuz she's not used to being out in the sun?

I should have stopped looking once I'd glimpsed what I thought was the bottom of the pit of internet stupidity. But reading discourse about myself is like prodding at a sore tooth. I'm compelled to keep digging, just to see how far the rot goes.

I search Twitter, Reddit, YouTube (already three book bloggers have put up videos titled variations of "Spilling the tea on Juniper 'Song'!"), Google News, and even TikTok (yes, this has reached the infants on TikTok) by the hour. It's debilitating. I can't focus on anything else. I can't even leave my apartment; all I do is lie curled up in my bed, scrolling alternately on my laptop or my phone, reading and rereading the same updates across the same five websites.

People make up absurd rumors about me. Someone says my past reviews on Goodreads are racist. (All I did was write once that I couldn't relate to an Indian writer's romance novel, because all the characters were unlikable and way too obsessed with their family duties to the point of disbelief.) Someone says that I regularly harass and bully people who criticize my work. (I put out a snide subtweet about a particularly dumb review of *Over the Sycamore*, *once*, and that was three years ago!) Someone claims that I once hit on them at a convention by "complimenting their skin in a very racist way." (All I said was that their red dress really brought out the yellow undertones in their skin. Jesus, I was just being nice. I didn't even like the dress that much.) And yet the Twitterati have now spun that into a narrative about how I have a fetish for Asian people, which is proven by my recent BTS retweets and the fact that I played some Japanese video games once and tweeted about how hot the characters were, which means I obviously have a perverted obsession with emasculated and submissive Asian people. (Except I don't even like BTS that much, and the video game characters in question were designed to be European, so what gives?)

All the red flags are in the text itself, writes an anonymous Tumblr account, which I found by clicking through "citations" on a Reddit exposé. See on page 317, where she describes A Geng's almond eyes and smooth skin. Almond eyes? Really??? White women have been fantasizing about Asian men for decades. (But I didn't even write that description! Athena did!)

Someone who did a text comparison of *The Last Front* and Athena's other works using NLP programming on Python announces that there is a "stunning frequency in overlap of key words in both texts." But the words in question are things like "said," "fought," "he," "she," and "they." By that standard, couldn't one argue that I plagiarized from Hemingway?

My detractors scour every public statement I've ever made about *The Last Front* to cherry-pick them for further proof of my awfulness. Apparently it's not appropriate to call stories about Chinese people "romantic," "exotic," or "fascinating." Apparently my description of this book as a drama undercuts its potential critique of racial capitalism. "I object to the characterization of the laborers as indentured servants," I said once. "The Chinese government volunteered these troops for World War One in an attempt to win soft power with Western countries. The laborers went out of their own free will." (This perspective is "ignorant of the pressures of Western hegemony" and "totally clueless about the coercions of global capital.") "These men were largely illiterate," writes Adele Sparks-Sato. "They were recruited by promises of higher wages, yes, but many had no idea what awaited them in Europe. That Hayward/Song would characterize their employment as free and without coercion demonstrates, at best, scholarly dimness, and at worst, a malicious indifference to the conditions of the Global South's working class."

They call *The Last Front* a "white savior story." They don't like that I've shown valor and bravery by white soldiers and missionaries; they think it centers the white experience. (But those men did exist. One missionary, Robert Haden, drowned trying to save a Chinese man when the steamship *Athos* was torpedoed by German submarines. Doesn't his death matter, too?)

And they're calling me a racist for saying that the laborers were recruited from the north because the British thought southerners from warmer climates would be unsuitable for manual labor. But that's not *my* view, it's the view of British army officers. Why can't they sort out the difference? What happened to critical reading skills?

Also, is it even racist to say that people from the north are better suited for cold climates if it's *true*?

I want to issue a line-by-line rebuttal. I made the creative choices I did because I wanted to broaden the number of human experiences in the story, not to hew closely to stereotypes, good or bad. Similarly, I included depictions of racism in the text not because I agree with them, but because I wanted to remain faithful to the historical record.

But I know it won't matter. They've already decided on their narrative about me. Now they're just collecting "facts" to back it up.

They don't know me. They *can't* know me; they've never met me. They've taken bits of information about me strewn across the internet and pieced them together into an image that fits their imagined villain but has no bearing on reality.

I don't have yellow fever. I'm not one of those creepy dudes who write exclusively about Japanese folklore and wear kimonos and pronounce every loan word from Asian languages with a deliberate, constructed accent. *Matcha. Otaku.* I'm not obsessed with stealing Asian culture—I mean, before *The Last Front*, I had no interest in modern Chinese history whatsoever.

But the worst part is, sometimes the trolls have me doubting my own understanding of myself. Sometimes I wonder if *I'm* the one with a warped version of reality, whether I really am a sociopath who fetishizes Asian women, whether Athena did in fact feel terrified of me throughout our friendship, and whether my presence in her apartment that night was more nefarious than I thought. But I always nip those creeping worries in the bud. I stop my thoughts from spiraling out, just like Dr. Gaily taught me. It's the internet that's fucked, not me. It's this contingent of social justice warriors, these clout-chasing white "allies," and Asian activists seeking attention who are acting up. I am not the bad guy. I am the victim here.

AT LEAST SOME PEOPLE SPEAK OUT ON MY BEHALF. MOSTLY WHITE people, to be fair, but that doesn't necessarily mean we're in the wrong.

Brett, bless him, puts up the following statement: "The recently made allegations against my client Juniper Song are utterly groundless and ill-intentioned. The online attacks have been nothing short of character assassination." He waxes on a bit about my unimpeachable writing talent, about how hard I've worked at my craft since he signed me four years ago, and then finishes with, "I and the Lambert Agency stand firmly behind Juniper Song."

My team at Eden don't say a thing, which annoys me a bit. But given the sheer number of accounts tagging Eden urging them to drop my contract, Eden's indifference is a vote of confidence in and of itself. Daniella sent us a concerned email when the allegations first circulated, but when Brett assured her there was no truth to the accusations, she counseled us to keep our heads down. We don't want to legitimize the claims by responding. Our team has found that in the past, engaging with trolls only emboldens them. I'm sorry this is happening to June, but we do believe the best thing to do is to keep quiet.

"These are wild accusations to make without solid proof," tweets an internet personality who is largely famous for having reasonable and nuanced takes on unreasonable situations. "These are people's livelihoods at stake. I'm troubled by how eager this community is to delight in the suffering of others. We all need to do better."

A pop-culture blogger with conservative leanings and seventy thousand followers launches a hate campaign against Adele Sparks-Sato. ASS IS A CRAZY PERSON WITH A VENDETTA AGAINST MORE SUCCESSFUL WRITERS, he rants. NEWS FLASH: JEALOUSY LOOKS UGLY ON YOU, ADELE. (This is entertaining to witness, but to be clear, I do not condone such actions. I guess it's nice to have someone speak in your defense, but in a perfect world, they wouldn't be frequent commentators on Fox News.)

Eden's Angels, bless them, are firmly on my side.

From Jen: So normally I don't agree with fascists but he's right about ASS lmao.

Marnie: Well you don't need to be a fascist to know that!

Jen: You alright, though? Hanging in there?

Marnie: This is horrendous. I am so, so sorry you're going through this. Let me know if there's anything we can do. You are so brave.

Jen: It's tall poppy syndrome. They hate seeing young women succeed. That's all this is. I get shit like this all the time from male CEOS. They can't STAND us.

Marnie: They're dogpiling on you for clout and attention and they know it. It's not about you, it's about them.

Jen: Don't wrestle with pigs, and all that!! Block it out, Junie. Ignore the haters. RISE ABOVE!!

IF ONLY I COULD. I CANNOT UNGLUE MYSELF FROM MY DEVICES. WHENever I close my eyes, I still see that azure-blue screen. I still imagine the likes racking up on yet another takedown thread about me.

I do try a digital purge. Everyone keeps urging that I do this, as if pretending Twitter doesn't exist will solve all my problems. *Trolls feed on your attention!* Jen keeps reminding me. *What's on the internet can't hurt you if you don't look at it.* But it doesn't feel like a cleanse; it feels like sticking my head in the sand while everything is falling down around me. I can't ignore the damage. I have to track the exact trajectory of the hurricane, because knowing the precise moment it'll hit and where will make things hurt less. At least, my brain is convinced this is so.

I try taking a walk, to lose myself in details like birdsong and splattered sunlight and the wet patches left by the rain on the cement, but the world outside feels so insubstantial, irrelevant, like a video game environment that's still buffering. Sometimes I do manage to forget it all for a moment, but then my focus slips and I think back to my phone lying on my bed, buzzing with more and more notifications. And then my breathing quickens, and my head swims, and I know I'm on the verge of an anxiety attack, so I double back to my apartment and curl up on my bed and whip out my phone for another hour of doom-scrolling, because that is paradoxically the only thing that calms things down.

I can't eat. I *want* to eat—I'm starving all the time, and I keep ordering huge, hot, greasy delivery meals of pizza or pasta bowls, but the moment I start to chew, my thoughts begin to spiral again about my impending professional implosion and then I can't take another bite without gagging.

I can't sleep. I lie awake every night until the sun comes up, feverishly refreshing various threads and accounts to see who's retweeted or responded to what, composing imaginary responses in my head, then composing imaginary rebuttals to the backlash to those responses.

I wish I had an exit strategy. I wish there were some magical apology I could make, or defense I could offer, that would make everything stop. But there is no point, I know, in getting embroiled in the mess. Anything I post will become further evidence that people can use against me. And what would an online victory even look like? There's no way to reverse the exposure, to make the internet forget about me. I'm marked forever. Every time someone Googles my name, or brings me up at a literary conference, the association with this plagiarism scandal will foul the air like a persistent fart.

I know some authors who have been able to jump from scandal to scandal with their reputations perfectly intact. Mostly white. Mostly male. Isaac Asimov was a serial sexual harasser; so was Harlan Ellison. David Foster Wallace abused, harassed, and stalked Mary Karr. They are still hailed as geniuses.

Sometimes, I think ruefully to myself that maybe this is just something I have to get through. An online raking over the coals feels like a rite of passage every notable author must now undergo. Last year, a YA writer was driven off social media for encouraging her fans to leave one-star reviews on another writer's debut (afterward, it transpired the debut writer had stolen her fiancé). In any case, both writers involved just signed new, six-figure deals for their follow-up trilogies. And Marnie Kimball, Daniella's favorite author, has gotten in hot water at least a dozen times, always for tweeting something edgy and indefensible, like The classics are just better and if you don't get them, you don't know how to read. Sorry. Her sales are doing fine. Maybe Daniella's right. Maybe silence is the best response.

Even Athena suffered her own period of online vitriol, though in her case she really had done nothing wrong. Two years ago, she'd tweeted some uncontroversial, bleeding-heart thread about the recent rise of hate crimes against Asian Americans. I've never been so nervous to be in my own skin, she'd said. Until now, I never felt so much like this country was not my own. It read as a little cheesy and narcissistic, but whatever; it was a cause close to her heart, and you couldn't exactly hate on someone who was afraid of being attacked on the street.

But then some anonymous account with an emoji of the Chinese flag in the bio asked her, If you care about Asians so much, why are you dating white?

I don't know why Athena responded. One never argues a racist troll into submission. But she must have been feeling defensive, or raring for a fight, because she quote tweeted the reply and said: Who I date has nothing to do with my politics. Hating on interracial couples? Is this 2018?

Then the floodgates opened. Hateful messages inundated her replies and DMs. She showed some of them to me when we met up for coffee later that week, and they were utterly vile:

> Shut up and go suck white cock

> WAMF couples are unnatural. WAMF is how you get Eliot Rodger. You want me to come shoot you up like Eliot Rodger?

> The whites will never love you LOL stop trying honey

> Don't you dare speak for Asians. You lost that right when you let a white man colonize your cunt.

By the time she took her account private, the AMRAs (the Asian Men's Rights Activists, she called them) had already found her author account and email address. She started getting death threats. Screenshots of the initial Twitter encounter started circulating on Reddit, on which the main thread eventually acquired over a thousand posts, many of them screenshotted photos of Athena and her then-boyfriend, Geoff, pulled from their respective Instagram accounts, with captions like RACE TRAITOR and Some Asians have no loyalty for their race. They only want white cock, white money, white baby. But some day they will wake up and learn that white supremacy will not save them. Pray that this girl learns before it is too late.

Someone hacked her author website so that when you clicked on the home page, all you found was a cartoon of an Asian woman with slants for eyes prostrating herself to a crowd of slobbering white johns.

Here for you, I'd texted her, because it seemed like the appropriate thing to say. People are such assholes.

Thanks, she answered. Then: I'll be okay, I think. It's just so fucking scary. Like, I don't feel safe in my own home.

I'd thought she was exaggerating back then. Athena was good at that, playing up her fear for sympathy, the way she played up her vulnerability for attention at barcons all the time. Anyhow, the internet was just the internet. What, was some Reddit lowlife living in his mother's basement really going to drive hundreds of miles to DC to accost her outside her apartment? Back then, I'd thought this ugly thought: Why couldn't she just stay offline for a while and focus on the fact that she was rich, pretty, and successful?

But now I know exactly what Athena meant. You can't shut it out. You lose all sense of security, because at every moment—when you're sleeping, when you're awake, when you've just put your phone down for a few minutes because you've hopped in the shower—dozens, maybe hundreds, maybe *thousands* of strangers are out there, mining your personal information, worming their ways into your life, looking for ways to mock, humiliate, or worse, endanger you. You come to regret everything you've ever shared about yourself: every photo, every meme, every comment on a YouTube video, every offhand tweet. Because the trolls *will* find them. I deleted as much of my digital footprint as I could in those first twenty-four hours, but the Wayback Machine still exists. Someone mocks my enthusiastic review of *Wonder Woman* from 2018: Of fucking course Hayward loves white woman savior narratives. How much do you want to bet she loves the IDF, too? Someone pulls up a photo of me at my high school prom: This dress is Juniper Song's villain origin story. Someone posts information about the test prep company where I used to work: Parents, if you're using this service, BEWARE of Juniper Song! If I hadn't quit Veritas already, I truly believe that these people could have gotten me fired.

You all need to get outside, a prominent writer had complained once on Twitter. Get some fresh air. Twitter is not real life.

But Twitter *is* real life; it's realer than real life, because that is the realm that the social economy of publishing exists on, because the industry has no alternative. Offline, writers are all faceless, hypothetical creatures pounding out words in isolation from one another. You can't peek over anyone's shoulder. You can't tell if everyone else is really doing as dandy as they pretend they are. But online, you can tune into all the hot gossip, even if you're not nearly important enough to have a seat in the room where it happens. Online, you can tell Stephen King to go fuck himself. Online, you can discover that the current literary star of the moment is actually so problematic that all of her works should be canceled, forever. Reputations in publishing are built and destroyed, constantly, online.

I imagine a crowd of angry voices and pointed fingers, converging on me to rip pieces of flesh from my body like the naiads did to Orpheus, until all that's left is the prurient, whispered question, "Did you hear about Juniper Song?" and fragments of rumors growing darker and more distorted; bloody, decomposing shreds of my virtual identity; until there is nothing left but the statement, justified or not, that Juniper Song Is Canceled.

Twelve

All I want is to hibernate in my apartment for the indefinite future, but I have two prior commitments for the month—a library visit with students in DC, and a panel at a Virginia literary festival about writing East Asia–inspired stories. I've also been emailing back and forth with some woman from the French Embassy about a visit to the CLC memorial in Noyelles-sur-Mer next month to coincide with the release of the French edition of *The Last Front.* But she stopped answering my emails around the same time that the smear campaign went viral, which is fine with me; the last thing I want is to sit seven hours on a plane just for obnoxious French people to snub me on the other end. But neither the library nor the literary festival has sent me any updates since the news broke, which I take to mean they still want me to come. To cancel may as well be admitting guilt.

The library visit goes okay. The students turn out to be third graders, instead of the high schoolers I'd expected. They won't be old enough to tackle *The Last Front* for years, and they certainly have no interest in Chinese laborers in World War I. Thankfully, this means that they're too young to care about Twitter drama as well—though they're not especially excited to see me, they don't greet me with revulsion, either. They sit, fidgeting but silent, in the lobby of the MLK Jr. Memorial Library while I read for twenty minutes from the first chapter, and then they ask some cute, inane questions on what it's like to be a published author ("Do you get to see the factories where the books are made?" "Do you get paid millions of dollars?"). I tell them some bland truisms about how literacy is important because it opens doors to other worlds, and how maybe they'll want to become storytellers as well. Then their teacher thanks me, we take a group picture, and we all part ways without fuss.

The panel is a disaster.

I've already pissed everyone off by arriving late. I misread the schedule—my panel is in the Oak Room, not the Cedar Room, which means I have to haul ass all the way across the conference center. The room is packed by the time I arrive. All the other panelists are huddled at the far end of the table, talking to one another with their hands over their mics. They hush when I approach.

"I'm so sorry," I pant as I find my seat. I'm nearly ten minutes late. "This place is so confusing, huh?"

No one responds. Two of them glance my way, and then at each other; the last one stares down at her phone. The hostility is adamant.

"All right!" Annie Brosch, our moderator, says cheerily. "Now we're all here, so let's begin—shall we do names first, and our most recent publications?"

We go down the table, left to right. There's Diana Qiu, a poet and visual artist; Noor Rishi, a writer of young adult contemporaries who daylights as a civil rights lawyer; and Ailin Zhou, a critically acclaimed author of historical romances set in a "race-bended" (her words) Victorian England. Then there's me. I lean toward my mic. "Um, hi, I'm June Hayward, also writing as Juniper Song. I wrote *The Last Front.*"

This gets bland stares, but no boos. Right now, that's the best I can hope for.

"I'd love for everyone to discuss what inspired their books," says Annie. "Juniper, why don't you kick us off?"

My mouth has gone dry; my voice cracks, and I cough before I continue. "So I'm very inspired by history, like Ailing. I actually first learned about the CLC—"

Ailin interrupts me. "My name is pronounced 'Ai-*lin*.'"

"Oh, Ailin, sorry." I feel a twinge of irritation. I was copying Annie's pronunciation, and Ailin hadn't interrupted *her.*

"I just think it's very important that we get our names right," Ailin says to a smattering of applause. "I used to be afraid of telling people they'd gotten my name wrong, but I've now made it a part of my praxis. It matters that we defy white supremacy, every day, bit by bit. It matters that we demand respect."

More applause. I lean back from my mic, cheeks red. Seriously? *Praxis?*

"Of course," Annie says smoothly. "Sorry about that, Ailin. I should have asked for pronunciation guides before the panel."

"Ai-*lin,*" I say, slowly and correctly, since I feel obligated to say *something.* "Like you're ailing, but in Texas." I'm trying to be funny, but apparently this comes off the wrong way as well, because the audience visibly tenses.

Ailin says nothing. There's a long, awkward pause, and then Annie asks, "And, um, Noor? What inspires your work?"

We go on like this for a while. Annie, at least, is good at keeping the conversation moving. She addresses questions to each one of us in turn, instead of letting the panelists lead the conversation, which means I can stay in my lane and avoid talking to Ailin directly for the entire hour. The other panelists cross-reference and riff off of one another's answers often, but no one responds to what I'm saying. The audience doesn't seem to care about me, either; I might as well be talking into thin air. But that's fine. I just need to get through this hour.

Annie must notice that I've been giving rather curt answers, because she turns to me and asks, "And Juniper? Did you want to elaborate further on what narrative fiction can do for underrepresented groups?"

"Um, sure." I clear my throat again. "Yeah. So, um, here's an anecdote that always comes to mind when I think about why I wrote *The Last Front*. So in the early twentieth century, Canada was so hostile to Chinese immigrants that there was a five-hundred-dollar head tax imposed on every Chinese person to enter the country. When the CLC laborers were brought to Canada, the head tax for their immigration was waived since that was part of the war effort, but that meant that they weren't allowed to get out of the trains during their trip, and that they were closely guarded the whole time they were in Canada."

Usually when I tell this story, I get riveted stares. But maybe this audience has simply decided to hate me, or maybe they're overheated and tired and bored of my moralizing, because people keep fidgeting, glancing around, or checking their phones. No one looks at my face.

There's nothing I can do but soldier on. "They stayed in those railway cars for days in the heat. They couldn't get medical treatment, even when some fainted from dehydration. They couldn't speak to a single person on the outside, because the Canadian government had issued a total press blackout on the presence of the Chinese laborers. And I think that's a good metaphor for the central argument of the book, which is that Chinese labor was used, then hidden and discredited like it was something shameful."

"Oh, really?" Diana Qiu cuts in suddenly. "So you have a problem with unacknowledged Asian labor?"

I'm so startled by this interruption that for a moment I just stare at her. Diana Qiu is a lean, artsy type with sharp, dark eyes, finely plucked brows, and red lipstick so boldly scarlet it looks like an open scar in her face. Her edgy-chic aesthetic reminds me a bit of Athena, actually, and the resemblance makes me shiver.

From the corner of my eye, I see a flash. Someone's taken a photo. Several audience members lift their phones—they're recording this exchange.

"What kind of question is that?" I know I shouldn't escalate, but the indignance slips out before I can stop it. "I mean, obviously that's wrong; that's the whole point—"

"So is stealing words from a dead woman," Diana says.

Several audience members literally gasp.

"Let's keep the discussion to the prepared questions," Annie says ineffectually. "Noor, what do you think about—"

"Someone has to say it." Diana raises her voice. "There's good evidence now that June Hayward did not write *The Last Front*. We've all seen the allegations. Let's not pretend. And I'm sorry, but I'm not going to sit around on this panel and pretend like she's a colleague who deserves my respect, when Athena's legacy is at stake—"

"Please," Annie says, more loudly this time. "This is not an appropriate venue for that discussion, and we need to respect all of our invited panelists."

Diana looks like she wants to say something more. But then Noor touches her on the arm, and Diana leans back from her mic, arms crossed.

I say nothing. I don't know what I *could* say. Diana and the audience have already judged my guilt, and nothing I utter could redeem me in their eyes. I can only sit there, heart racing, awash in the humiliation.

"All right?" Annie asks. "Please. Could we move on?"

"All right," Diana says curtly.

Annie, audibly relieved, goes on to ask Ailin for her thoughts on *Bridgerton*.

It's too late. There's no salvaging this panel. We continue to the end of the hour, but no one cares anymore about Annie's prepared questions. The audience members that haven't left the room are typing furiously into their phones, no doubt recapping the whole thing for their followers. Noor and Ailin valiantly play along with Annie's prompts, as if anyone is still remotely interested in prehistoric Chinese writing systems or Islamic mysticism. Diana doesn't speak for the rest of the hour, and neither do I. I sit as still as I can, cheeks flaming, chin wobbling, trying my hardest to keep from breaking into tears. I'm sure that people are already creating memes using photos of my stunned face as we speak.

When we're finally free, I gather my things and walk out as quickly as I can without breaking into a full sprint. Annie calls after me, perhaps trying to offer an apology, but I don't stop until I've turned the corner. Right then, all I want is to disappear from sight.

Marnie: WOW WHAT A BITCH

Jen: Is she ill? Like, is she mentally ill?

Marnie: I mean, it doesn't matter what she thinks she knows. Confronting you like that in public is the Opposite of Classy. She clearly wasn't looking for a resolution, she just wanted Attention.

Jen: RIGHT. Exactly. This performative outrage is disgusting. It's such a clear ploy for self-enrichment. She's probably trying to hawk some art deals out of this.

Marnie: If you can call that art . . .

I chuckle. I'm curled up in bed, my covers pulled up to my chin. *God bless the Eden's Angels*, I think. Elsewhere on the internet, Diana's rant is circulating among gleeful mobs of Juniper Song haters, but for now, I'm happy to watch Jen and Marnie shit all over Diana's portfolio.

Marnie: Maybe I don't get performance art

Marnie: But in this video she's just giving herself a haircut

Marnie: It's not even a good haircut

Marnie: Also her nose ring is ugly

Jen: Since when did we start calling psychotic breakdowns visual art lmao this girl needs help

Marnie: Omg you can't say that

Marnie: Lmao

I snort. I switch screens back to Diana Qiu's website, where her latest exhibit, titled *Mukbang*, features her chewing hard-boiled eggs painted to look like Asian faces for thirteen minutes straight while staring into the camera wearing an unchanging, deadpan expression.

The Eden's Angels are right. As I take in Diana's face—her flat, angry eyes; the bits of yolk dribbling from her thin-lipped mouth—I can't believe I ever let this small, petty person with her cringey, try-hard art bring me down. She's jealous. They're all just jealous; that's where this vitriol is coming from. And maybe I've taken some hits, but I will not let deranged, vicious internet celebrity wannabes like Diana destroy my career.

Thirteen

THAT WEEKEND, I TAKE THE SUBWAY OUT TO ALEXANDRIA FOR A backyard grill with my sister and her husband.

Rory and I aren't terribly close, but we have the easy intimacy of two sisters who can't fathom what the other finds attractive about their lifestyle, and have long given up trying to convert them. Rory thinks I'm itinerant, badly prepared for the future, wasting an Ivy League degree, and getting a little too old to keep chasing the publishing pipe dream instead of a stable career with benefits and a retirement plan. And I think Rory, who studied accounting at UT Austin and now does precisely that, has such a boring, cookie-cutter, picket-fence life that I'd rather claw out my eyeballs than live it.

Rory is married to her college sweetheart, Tom, an IT technician who has always struck me as having the appearance and personality of wet dough. Neither of them knows a thing about publishing. They aren't, as Rory puts it, "bookish people." They like browsing the airport store for the latest John Grisham paperbacks, and Rory takes out the occasional Jodi Picoult title from their local library over the holidays, but otherwise they haven't a clue about the vicissitudes of my world, nor are they dying to learn. I don't think Rory even has a Twitter account.

Tonight, that's a blessing.

Rory and Tom live far enough out in the suburbs that they can afford a spacious backyard with a deck, where they host family grills the last Saturday of every month. The weather tonight is perfect: humid and hot, but breezy enough that it's not a bother. Rory is making corn bread, and it smells so good, I think this might be the first meal I stomach this week that doesn't come roiling back up from anxiety.

They're bickering on the patio when I arrive. The argument, I gather, is whether it was fair of HR to reprimand Rory's desk mate for telling a colleague that her hair looked gorgeous that day.

"I just don't think you should touch people without their permission," says Tom. "Like, that's an etiquette thing, not a race thing."

"Oh, come on, it wasn't like she was, like, assaulting her," says Rory. "It was a compliment. And it's so crazy to call Chelsea a racist—I mean, she's a Democrat. She voted for *Obama*—oh, hey, honey." Rory squeezes me from the side as I walk up. Usually I cringe from Rory's big-sisterly affectations—it's always struck me as a bit fake, overcompensating for her distance when we were younger—but tonight I lean into her touch. "Have a beer. I'm going to go check on the oven."

"How's tricks?" Tom gestures to the picnic table, and I sit down across from him. He's been growing his beard out. It's nearly two inches long now, and it emphasizes his solid, unbothered lumberjack's aesthetic. Every time I see Tom, I wonder what it would be like to go through life with the easy contentment of a rock.

"Just the usual," I say, accepting a Corona Light. "Could be better."

"Rory told me you published another book, right? Congrats!"

I wince. I hope they haven't Googled me recently. "Well, thanks."

"What's it about?"

"Oh, uh, World War One. Just, like, narratives of laborers on the front." I always feel awkward explaining the Chinese Labour Corps to people who don't already know about my book, because the inevitable follow-up is always a nose scrunch and a flat, awkward *I didn't know the Chinese were in World War One* or *Huh, why the Chinese?* "It's told like a mosaic, kind of like that movie *Dunkirk*. A broader story told through the amalgamation of a lot of little stories."

"Very cool." Tom nods. "Great subject for a novel. It seems like all the books and movies are obsessed with World War Two. You know? Like *Captain America*, and all those Holocaust movies. We don't get enough stuff about World War One."

"*Wonder Woman* is about World War One," Rory calls from inside the kitchen. "The movie."

"Well, sure. But that's just *Wonder Woman*; that's not serious literature." Tom turns to me for backup. "Right?"

Jesus Christ, I think. This is why I don't talk to family about publishing. "How's Allie?"

Allie is my eight-year-old niece. I see plastic animals strewn all over the yard, but no bite-size, peanut-breathed hurricane of destruction, so I assume I'm free from auntie duties for the evening. I'm not opposed to children in theory, but I think I would have liked Allie better if she were a shy, bookish type I could have taken on shopping sprees at indie bookstores instead of an iPhone-addicted, TikTok-obsessed basic bitch in training.

"Oh, she's great. She's at a sleepover with her friends tonight. They're reading *Charlotte's Web* in class, which means she's refusing to eat meat this month. Veggie burgers only."

"I'm sure that'll last."

"Ha. Tell me about it."

We both sip our beers, having exhausted our range of routine conversation topics. Often I feel like talking to Rory and Tom is like making conversation with a pollster's hypothetical Average American, or with a blank Facebook profile. *What are your thoughts on movies? On music?* I've tried asking Tom about work, but it seems there is nothing interesting to say about the duties of an IT technician.

Or is there? A thought occurs to me. "Hey, Tom? Could you trace the IP address of, like, any random Twitter account?"

His brows furrow. "What do you need an IP address for?"

"Um, there's this account that's been harassing me." I pause, wondering how much to explain, or whether I could even explain things in a way that makes sense to people not keyed deeply into publishing. "Like, spreading lies about me and stuff."

"Couldn't you report the account to Twitter?"

"I did that." Brett's been encouraging people to report and block accounts that are flinging vitriol my way, but Twitter is notoriously bad about enforcing its antiharassment policies, and as far as I can tell it hasn't made a difference. "I don't think they're going to do anything about it, though."

"I see. Well, I don't think you're going to be able to find them using a Twitter handle."

"Don't websites store the IP addresses of visitors?"

"Yes, but Twitter's data is protected. All major social media sites protect their data; they have to by law."

"You couldn't, like, break into it? Aren't you a hacker?"

He chuckles. "Not that kind of hacker. And a data breach like that would make headlines. That's a huge privacy violation. Not trying to go to prison here, Junie."

"But if I owned and ran my own website, I could see the IP addresses of anyone who visited?"

Tom considers this, then shrugs. "Well, I guess, yeah. There are plug-ins for that sort of thing. You could even do it on WordPress. But the problem is that an IP address doesn't tell you all that much. You can find out what city they live in, maybe. Or even what neighborhood. But it's not like in TV shows, where it magically pinpoints their exact GPS location. And it makes a difference whether they're accessing a website from their cell phone, or from their home internet router . . ."

"But you could tell me a broad geographical range," I say. "That is, if I got you the address?"

Tom hesitates. "You're not doing anything illegal, are you?"

"Of course not. Jesus. I'm not going to like, throw a Molotov cocktail through their window."

I'm trying to be funny, but the specificity of this scenario puts him off. He fiddles with the rim of his beer bottle. "Then could you tell me a bit more about what you need? Because if they really are harassing you, then maybe it's not safe—"

"I just want to know who it is," I say. "Or just generally, where they are, and if they're nearby—you know, so I can make sure they're not a physical threat. Like, whether I should be worried about them stalking me, or—"

"Stalking? What's going on?" Rory pops up, balancing a platter of corn bread in one hand and a bowl of watermelon chunks in the other. She sets the food down, slides onto the bench next to me, and gives me another side hug. "Everything okay, Junie?"

"No, yeah, it's just this stupid thing. Just asking for Tom's help finding this person who's been bullying me on Twitter."

Rory frowns. "Bullying?"

I know what she's thinking. I put up with a lot of bullying in middle school, back when our home life was going off the rails. I withdrew into books then. I spent all my waking hours in fantasy worlds, which I guess made me come off as nonverbal and antisocial. I'd show up at school carrying chunky volumes of Lord of the Rings or The Spiderwick Chronicles, and I'd hunch over them all day, oblivious to everything around me.

The other kids didn't like that. Some of my classmates made a game of making faces behind me while I was reading to see if I'd notice. Some spread the rumor that I didn't know how to talk. *Loony Junie*, they'd call me, as if "loony" weren't a word we left back in the nineties.

"No, it's not like that; it's more like . . . creepy internet people," I say. I don't think Rory will understand the concept of trolling. "It's just, like, they think I'm a famous writer now, so they can say whatever shit they want to me. Death threats and stuff. I was just asking Tom to help me find out who's doing it, or at least, like, vaguely where they're located."

Rory looks to her husband. "You can do that, right? This sounds serious."

Tom sighs, hapless. "Again, I can't get IP addresses from Twitter—"

"I'll get you the IP address," I say. "I just need you to look it up for me."

Between my pleading face and Rory's expectant glare, I imagine Tom doesn't feel like he has a choice.

"Sure." He reaches for another beer. "Happy to help out."

He doesn't ask any more questions. Tom, bless him, takes everything at face value. So does Rory. I feel a deep pang of affection for them right then. There's no guile in this family; just open, loving trust, and the best corn bread with kale chili I've ever tasted.

WHEN I GET HOME THAT NIGHT, I SETTLE DOWN AT MY DESK TO TEACH myself some basic web design.

It's not too difficult. I participated in a four-week HTML boot camp in undergrad, back when I had the half-baked idea that if I couldn't make it as a writer then at least I'd have a steady income as a programmer, until I realized that the programming market is also quickly becoming too saturated for anyone who isn't a natural talent. I couldn't get a job with the skills I retained, but I do know enough to throw together a half-decent website that doesn't immediately appear like a Russian hacker's trap.

The design of the site isn't too important—it's supposed to look like a janky homegrown blog. I spend about fifteen minutes copying, pasting, and formatting some of the more vicious "proof" of my alleged plagiarism onto the homepage. I also make sure to keep this website hidden from any SEO searches—I don't want random users Googling the scandal to stumble on my website.

Finally I make my own fake Twitter account. No profile picture, no header. Just the handle @LazarusAthena—that'll catch the eye.

When that's all set up, I send a DM to the @AthenaLiusGhost account:

Hey. I don't know who you are, but thank you for doing all this work to expose June Hayward. I have some additional proof documented here, if you're interested.

Then I paste the link to my honey trap.

THE @ATHENALIUSGHOST ACCOUNT DOESN'T RESPOND IMMEDIATELY. I lie in bed for ten minutes or so, constantly refreshing my Twitter app, but it looks like @AthenaLiusGhost isn't even online. In the meantime, on my real account, I get three new DMs from strangers encouraging me to kill myself, so I stop checking my messages for the time being.

Still, I can't help but browse my timeline to check on the rest of the conversation. The flurry of accusations has died down, though some prominent bloggers are still calling for my head. (Why hasn't @EdenPress responded to these allegations yet? demands Adele Sparks-Sato. This is a terrible look for your imprint, @DaniellaWoodhouse. Says a lot about how much you care about marginalized voices.)

The discourse has taken an unpredicted turn, though: rumors have begun swirling about Athena, too. From what I can tell, it started with a long thread by another new, anonymous account with the handle @NoHeroesNoGods. June Song's actions are indeed sickening, if true, reads their first tweet. But we shouldn't act as if Athena Liu was the paragon of good Asian American rep. Thread. [1/?]

> We in the Chinese American community have been uncomfortable with the way she's chosen to write about racialization and Chinese history for years. [2/?]

> Her treatment of the Kuomintang, for instance, is a stunning example of Western imperialist brainwashing. She frames the Nationalists as the obvious choice for Chinese democratization, but ignores the atrocities carried out by the KMT after their move to Taiwan. What would Taiwanese aboriginals say to these claims? [3/?]

> Moreover, in her short story "My Father's Escape," Athena refers to the dissidents from Tiananmen Square as heroes. Many of these same dissidents, however, became fervent Trump supporters when they escaped to the West. [4/?]

> Does Athena Liu's support of democracy extend only to PRC bashing? What's more, many of Athena's statements about her father's experiences are inconsistent. Her representation of her entire family history is inconsistent, for that matter. [5/?]

And on and on for sixteen tweets, culminating in a linked Google Doc with more evidence of Athena's crimes. Athena, @NoHeroesNoGods concludes, was out of touch with most radical Asian diaspora movements. Athena was not a real Marxist; she was a champagne socialist at best. Athena lied about her family history to make it seem more tragic than it was—for convenience, for claims to authenticity, for attention. Athena, like Maxine Hong Kingston, always presented the worst of Chinese history and culture to milk sympathy from her white audience. Athena was a race traitor.

Most people on Twitter have no fucking clue what's going on, because no one is that deep into Chinese history or politics, nor have they read Athena's work closely enough to make a smart judgment. But what they see, and what they latch on to, is "Athena Liu = Problematic."

Then the second wave of the shitstorm starts, this time with Athena at the center. Most of the accounts that participate so clearly do not care about the truth. They're here for the entertainment. These people love to have a target, and they'll tear apart anything you put in front of them.

> What a piece of shit!!!

> I always knew she was fake.

> Glad this bitch has finally been exposed. I've been iffy on Athena for years.

A TikTok of someone ripping all the pages out of Athena's books and throwing them on a bonfire goes viral. (This sparks another debate about Nazis and book burning, but I won't drag you down that corner of the internet.) Kimberly Deng, the YouTuber at UCLA, posts an hour-long video dissecting "problematic" lines in each one of Athena's books. (Athena once wrote about a love interest's "almond-shaped eyes," which buys into Western standards of beauty and the objectification of Asian women.)

There's something disturbing, almost *gleeful*, about the way they rip into her. It's like they've been waiting for this opportunity all along, like they've been preparing these barbs for years. I'm not surprised, to be honest. Athena is such a perfect target. She was too pretty, too successful, too suspiciously clean to have nothing on her ledger. She had it coming for her, and I'm sure some blowback like this would have happened sooner or later, even if she hadn't choked to death on a pandan pancake.

Marnie: Wow, are you guys seeing this stuff about Athena Liu?
Jen: Yeah, wild . . . sorry, what's a Han supremacist?
Marnie: I think like a white supremacist, but for Chinese ethnic groups. I mean, her lack of inclusion of other Chinese minorities in her work is CONSPICUOUS.
Jen: I didn't know you liked her books
Marnie: Oh I only read one. Lol. Couldn't get past the first page. Very try-hard litfic, if you know what I mean.
Marnie: But here are some threads that break it down.

Someone threads a story eerily similar to my memory of Athena at the American History Museum: I went to an event where she interviewed Korean War vets and recorded everything they said in a little dictaphone. Her story "Parasails Over Choson" came out six months later. It's been praised as one of the more faithful depictions of POWs in Korea, but it's always sat wrong with me. It felt like she was pulling the words straight from the veterans' mouths, putting them on paper, and passing them off as her own. There was no credit, no acknowledgment. She made it sound like she'd come up with it all by herself. I've kept this to myself for years because I didn't want to come off as attacking another Asian writer. But if we're talking about literary legacies, I think this is important to bring up.

I'll confess, I'm enjoying this a bit. It feels good to know that someone out there also knows as well as I do that Athena was a thief.

Though it doesn't matter what the truth is. No one spreading these rumors cares about fact-checking or due diligence. They'll use phrases like "I think it's important to know" and "I just found out" and "sharing this so my followers are aware," but deep down they're all so fucking delighted, gorging themselves on this hot gossip, thrilled at the chance to take Athena Liu down. *She was mortal after all*, they're thinking. *She was just like us. And in destroying her, we create an audience; we create moral authority for ourselves.*

In a perverse way, this is very good for me. The more Athena gets dragged into the mud, the more confusing this whole thing seems, which undercuts the righteous authority of my detractors. Two wrongs don't make a right, obviously, but the internet is very bad at recognizing this. Now that the story's been complicated, it's not so satisfying to lambast me for stealing from a lovely, innocent victim. Now Athena is a pretentious snob, a maybe-racist (no one can really make up their minds on that one), a definite Han Chinese supremacist, and a thief in her own right for her representations of Korean and Vietnamese characters. Athena is the liar, the hypocrite. Athena Liu Is Posthumously Canceled.

I don't bring it up with Brett or Daniella. I'm over it; we all know how these things end up. I saw this same cycle happen once with a debut writer in her twenties who accused a much older and established writer of grooming and creeping on her, only for others to accuse her of grooming and creeping on even younger writers in return. Still today no one knows the truth, but she hasn't gotten another book deal in years. Such is the nature of a Twitter dustup. Allegations get flung left and right, everyone's reputations are torn down, and when the dust clears, everything remains exactly as it was.

I GET THE DM I WAS WAITING FOR THAT EVENING.

Thanks, says @AthenaLiusGhost. Have linked to most of that stuff already, though. If you come up with any new proof please let me know. Let's get justice for Athena.

I dash over to my desk and open WordPress on my laptop. Just as I'd hoped, my website has received its first, and only, visitor. I copy the nine-digit IP address and text it to Tom. Here you go. Any shred of information would be amazing.

I have a few theories on who the account is. Adele Sparks-Sato, maybe. Lily Wu and Kimberly Deng are contenders. Or Diana Qiu, that deranged visual artist. Though I'm not sure what I'd do if they were the culprits—Adele and Diana are based in NYC, and Lily in Boston, and an IP address from either would be circumstantial at best.

Tom texts me back a few hours later.

> You're in luck. Tried a couple of different IP geolocation services, and they all spit out the same city. You don't know anyone in Fairfax, do you?
>
> Sorry . . . I'm guessing that's a little close for comfort. Probably you should go to the police if you think they might try anything serious?
>
> Also, sorry I can't be more specific.
>
> You can usually get within a couple of miles, but you'd need to do some heavy duty hacking to pin down a physical address.

But I don't need a physical address. I know exactly who this is. There's only one person Athena and I both know who lives in Fairfax, and I wouldn't put this past him at all.

Heart hammering, I pull up Twitter and search "Geoffrey Carlino" to see what Athena's ex-boyfriend has been up to lately.

Fourteen

AH, GEOFF.

Where does one even start with Geoff?

Athena and I weren't close when they started dating. I was still in NYC, struggling through my underpaid, understimulating Teach for America year, but I know as well as anyone the story of their disastrous implosion, a messy affair that played out on Twitter and Instagram for the entire world to see. From what I understand, Geoff and Athena met at a writers' residency in Oregon, back when both were young, up-and-coming hotshots. She was months away from the launch of her first novel; he was fresh off signing his first deal with a small but prestigious genre publishing house. Their coupling was foreordained; they were both hot and for the most part straight, both prodigies on the verge of taking the publishing world by storm. I suppose Geoff's study-abroad year in Beijing was part of the attraction (though after they broke up, Athena would complain to me how "Geoff's Chinese name was Jie Fu, and he wanted me to call him that when we were alone, and isn't that just so fucking weird? Like, his name is fucking Geoff").

After the residency, Athena moved into Geoff's parents' second house in Fairfax. I know this because for the next six months, both their Instagram feeds constantly churned out sickeningly cute photos of the two of them: close-ups with their bright smiles pressed side to side, skin clear and freckles radiant; black-and-white shots taken at coffee shops, captioned with things like writer at work; and full body pics of them hiking up and down the East Coast, their tall, lithe forms dripping with sweat. There was a time it seemed that they would join the ranks of famous literary couples like Jean Paul Sartre and Simone de Beauvoir, Anaïs Nin and Henry Miller, and F. Scott and Zelda Fitzgerald if Zelda had published more.

But Geoff . . . How does one put this kindly? Geoff simply isn't that talented. We might even compare Geoff's publication history to mine. He started out strong with dozens of award-winning publications in prestigious short-story magazines. But his first novel, a self-proclaimed "genre-bending thriller" about "race-hopping" androids in a near-future society, failed to make the expected splash. A reviewer at *Locus* called it "a confused and ultimately misguided, possibly malicious, exploration of postraciality and racial fluidity." My debut novel didn't sell very well, but at least no reviewers ever said that I should "keep the ill-considered and shallow philosophizing to undergraduate bars and off the page where grown adults can see."

Geoff was very miffed by this particular review, and he wrote up some long and embarrassing blog post about how he'd been misread, and how the *Locus* reviewer didn't have the "intellectual range" to appreciate the complexity and radicalness of his racial critique. Twitter, predictably, dunked hard on this. Athena broke up with him shortly after (this we plebeians inferred from the fact that all of her "working from home" Instagram posts were suddenly shot from a new location).

The breakup might sound sudden, but we all saw it coming. One should also mention that before his debut flopped, Geoff published a series of short stories about an android girl named Xiao Li who puts up with a number of abuses from lecherous human clients before self-destructing in a blast that destroys over half of New Beijing. The stories, Geoff argued, were a scorching interrogation of colonial misogyny, AI rights, and Chinese patriarchy. Someone on Twitter asked him how he had researched all the Chinese phrases he'd littered through the text; Geoff blithely responded that he was dating a "long-haired dictionary." (That made the Twitter rounds for days.) There were also allegations of drunk groping at bars and an account that looks suspiciously like Geoff's on a well-known porn site with "got that yellow FEVER!" in the bio, but we're all too polite to bring that up in company.

So Geoff's book flopped. Athena did what everyone expected and distanced herself from that mess, and publishing's most attractive young couple was reduced to publishing's most attractive young author and a white boy whose career was over before it started.

At that point, Geoff should have licked his wounds and moved on. He still had a powerhouse literary agent, a second book under contract, and a chance to salvage his career. But then his Twitter presence took a savage turn. He started positing long screeds about how he'd been unjustly made a villain, how in fact it was Athena who had encouraged him to write that original post about *Locus* but had failed to stand up for him.

I got secondhand embarrassment from watching it all go down.

Athena did the smart thing, which was to deactivate her Twitter and say nothing until the internet found something else in which to invest their prurient fascination disguised as care. Geoff kept pointlessly responding to scathing replies until his follower count dwindled to the double digits, at which point he, too, deactivated his account. His agent dropped him for "personal and private reasons." The sequel to his first book remains under contract, but it's unclear whether that will ever see the light of day, assuming Geoff is still trying to finish it.

Who really knows what happened? Twitter makes unqualified yet eager judges of us all. Depending on who you talk to, Geoff is either a manipulative, abusive, gaslighting, insecure leech, or a victim himself. Athena came out pretty clean, but mostly because no one could believe that dating the beautiful and talented Athena Liu was as awful as Geoff made it sound, and because it's always easier to make the cishet white guy the punching bag.

As far as I know, Athena and Geoff hadn't spoken for months.

So what on earth is he targeting me for?

After some more sleuthing, I'm certain he's the one behind all this. His account has faithfully retweeted everything that the @AthenaLiusGhost account has ever tweeted. Sometimes he adds his own quote tweets: Can't believe no one is talking about this. Eden, and Juniper Song, should be ashamed.

Before that, the only thing he's tweeted was from over a month ago: Does anyone get weird looks when they ask for "real spicy, not just white people spicy" at Indian restaurants? (This got three likes, and the following response from one RichardBurns08: Me too. Been with my Thai wife for three years now, and they still think this gaijin can't handle it. Love to prove them wrong!) The timing is too convenient.

I have to act fast. Geoff is an idiot, but he's an unstable, unpredictable idiot. Best to nip this in the bud. I think I can hold my own against him, but I'd like to know exactly what he has up his sleeve.

I still have Geoff's number from back when Athena invited us and several others on a writers' retreat by the Potomac. The retreat never happened; we started bickering about the cost of the cabins, and whether it was heteronormative and regressive to insist on gender-separated cabins or if the people who weren't in relationships would have to awkwardly share, and then suddenly everyone had scheduling errors and had to cancel at the last minute. But I meticulously saved everyone's contact information, if only to differentiate from all the 202 and 401 area codes.

I send Geoff a screenshot of @AthenaLiusGhost's first tweet, and then add: I know.

He's one of those assholes who leaves read receipts on. He sees it right away. He doesn't answer.

My heart's pounding so hard I can feel it in my boobs. I type: Tomorrow, outside Coco's in Tyson's Corner, 3:30. Only chance. Show up or I'll tell everyone it's you.

Then I turn off my phone, hurl it across my bed, and scream.

I SHOW UP EARLY TO COCO'S COFFEE. I GET AN ICED LATTE, BUT I ONLY allow myself tiny sips; I don't want to have to pee in the middle of this. It's unseasonably hot, so I have the outdoor seating area to myself. I pick a two-seater table near the corner, which gives me a full view of the patio and easy escape routes in all directions. I don't know why I'm scanning for possible exits like I'm a KGB agent in enemy territory, but that's not a bad description of our situation: two people who've been trading lies on the internet, trying to decide how to ruin the other's reputation.

I'm shocked when Geoff shows up. I see him coming from across the square, head down like he's afraid of being recognized. He's wearing a baseball cap and a massive pair of sunglasses. He looks ridiculous.

"Hi, Junie." He yanks out the chair across from me, sits down, and removes his sunglasses. "Nice to see you again."

I can see why Athena once adored him. Geoff is, superficially, very handsome. I know from his author photos how sharp his jawline is, how intensely green his eyes are. In person, these features are all so pronounced it's a bit overwhelming. He looks like the love interest from some dark and steamy YA novel come to life, all mussed dark hair and rough stubble.

Only I've read his tweets, so I find him too pathetic to be sexy.

I take another sip of my latte. I've decided not to give him control of the agenda—I don't want to let him think for a moment that he has the upper hand. I'm coming out the gate as aggressively as I can. "So what's this nonsense about stealing Athena's manuscript?"

He leans back and folds his arms across his barrel chest. (So this, I realize, is what people mean when they write "barrel chest.") "I think we both know what I'm talking about."

"I don't," I say angrily. It's not hard to conjure outrage. His relaxed superiority makes me want to hit him. "It's ludicrous."

"Then why'd you call this meeting?"

"Because what you're doing is vile," I snap. "It's sickening, disrespectful—not only to me but to Athena. And if you were anyone else, I'd tell you to fuck right off, but given you—your history with my best friend, I thought I might as well do that in person."

He rolls his eyes. "Really, Junie? We're going to pretend?"

I smack my hand against the metal table. It's dramatic, but I like that it makes him flinch. "The only one pretending is you. And I'm going to give you one chance to explain yourself before I sue you for defamation."

His confidence slips, just for a moment. Did that work? Did I scare him off?

"We spoke about the manuscript," he blurts. "Athena and I."

My gut twists.

"She told me about it while we were dating. I saw her researching it. The migrant laborers, the forgotten voices at the front. I saw those Wikipedia pages." He leans forward and holds my gaze with narrowed eyes. "And it strikes me as very convenient that shortly after her death, you come out with a book about the very same subject."

"More than one person can write a World War One story," I say drily. "There's no copyright on history, Geoffrey."

"Don't bullshit me."

"I suppose you're going to whip out all your folders of evidence now?" My strategy is to make him show his cards from the start. If he *does* have proof, I'm finished anyways, and I'd like to at least see it coming. But if he doesn't, there's room to maneuver.

His face tightens. "I know what you did. We all do. You can't lie your way out of this one."

Could I have guessed right? Is it possible he has nothing at all?

I decide to push him a bit further, just to see how he reacts. "I see you're still delusional."

"*I'm* delusional?" He snorts. "At least I'm not running around parading a friendship that never was. I know you two weren't close.

Best friends since college? Please. Athena never even mentioned you the entire time we were dating. I saw you at a convention once before, you know. I saw your bio in the program—it said where you'd gone to school, and I asked Athena if she knew you. You know what she said?"

I don't want to hear it. There's no reason why this should bother me so much, but it does, and clearly Geoff notices, because he grins, bares his fangs like a hound that's sniffed blood. "She called you some loser from school. Said she didn't know why you were still hacking at it, that your debut was thoroughly mediocre, and that you'd be better off calling it quits before this industry chewed you up entirely." He chuckles. "You know how Athena did that over-the-top fake sympathy, when she was trying to convince us she had human emotions? *Boohoo. Poor thing. Come on, let's go before she sees us.*"

My eyes feel wet. I blink in irritation. "Clearly you didn't know her as well as you think you did."

"Sweetheart, I've seen the stains on her G-strings. She's an open book. And so are you."

I'm tempted then to storm off, or even to reach over the table and smack him across his smug, cruel face. But then I'd have accomplished none of what I came for.

Focus. I'm so close to the finish. I just need to make this all go away.

"Suppose . . ." I tap my fingernails on the table and blink nervously for effect. "Suppose I did take it."

His eyes widen. "I fucking knew it, you fucking liar—"

"Okay, stop, please." I feign terror, lifting my hands up as if to show him I have no claws. I let my voice tremble. "What do you *want*, Geoff?"

His face settles back into a smug grin. He's getting cocky; he knows he's in control. "So you really thought you could get away with it."

"Can we just make this go away?" I plead. It's not hard to sound scared. All I have to do is imagine I'm walking home alone at night, and Geoff is on the other side of the road, and that there are none of the usual social mores against violence separating his fists from my face. He's huge and jacked; he could crush me, and I bat my eyelids frantically to remind him of that. I want him to feel like he's got me in a corner. "Please, if you leak this, I'll—I'll lose everything . . ."

"Or maybe you won't." He leans forward, palms flat against the table. "Maybe we can come to some sort of agreement."

I fight to keep my face still. "What . . . what do you mean?"

"You must be making bank from that book, right?" His eyes dart around, checking for eavesdroppers. "Don't lie. I saw that advance announcement. Mid–six figures, wasn't it? And I know you've already earned out."

My throat bobs. "You . . . you're blackmailing me?"

"I just think it could be a profitable arrangement for the both of us," he says. "You keep selling your books. I keep your secret. Win-win, no? Shall we discuss my rates?"

Jesus Christ. How stupid is he? Does he hear the words coming out of his mouth? I imagine leaking this sound bite all over Twitter, and the rage that would follow. Geoff would never make a cent from writing again. He'd have to go into hiding. He'd never be able to exist again, publicly, as himself.

But such an implosion would be messy, and I'd likely be caught in the blast radius. What I need is to make this all quietly disappear.

"Hmm . . . no." I make a big show of tapping my lip, and then pouting. "No, I don't think I'll do that."

Geoff's eyes narrow. "You don't really get a choice here."

"Don't I?"

"What do you think will happen when everyone finds out?"

"They're not going to find out." I shrug. "Because it's not true. You're full of shit, Geoffrey, and we both know it."

"I know you stole the book—"

"But you *don't* know. You don't have a shred of proof; you're just making things up to get a reaction." I tap my side pocket, where my iPhone sits secure behind a zipper, recording this whole conversation. "What I do have, though, is a record of you trying to *blackmail me* for a cut of the royalties on a book you claim was stolen. You're not doing this for Athena. You're trying to leech off her legacy. And when this leaks, Geoff, do you think you're ever going to get another publishing deal in your life?"

Geoff looks like he wants to strangle me. His eyes have gone so wide I can see the whites around his pupils. His lips curl back, revealing canines. For a moment I'm nervous I've overplayed my hand, that I've pushed him off the edge. I think of all those films about nice-seeming young white men who snap. Chris Evans in *Knives Out*. That rapist in *Promising Young Woman*. Maybe Geoff will jump across the table and stab me in the collarbone. Maybe he'll tamp down his anger now, watch me walk away, and then hit me with his car on the way home.

But this isn't a movie, it's real life, and Geoffrey Carlino isn't an alpha male whose fury can't be tamed. He's a pathetic, insecure little boy who's all bluster, who has no more cards up his sleeve.

He doesn't have the drive to take this any further. Rage shrinks to defeat. I watch his shoulders deflate.

"You're a horrible person," he spits.

"I am a brilliant writer and a good friend," I say. "You, on the other hand, are on record trying to mooch off the supposedly stolen words of your ex."

"Go to hell, bitch."

"Oh, fuck off." I stand up. I once saw a video of a hunter who shot a lion between the eyes right as it sprang. I wonder if the hunter felt like I do now: breathless, victorious, just this side of safe. I wonder if he, too, looked at his victim and marveled at all that power, that potential, wasted. "Don't contact me again."

ONCE I KNOW GEOFF HAS NOTHING UP HIS SLEEVE, I HAVE NO TROUBLE crafting my response narrative. After running some drafts by Jen and Marnie, I post my official statement about the whole fiasco on my author website, which I link to on Twitter. (I thought about posting a phone screenshot of my statement drafted in the Notes app, but Notes app apologies have become a genre in and of themselves, and not a very respectable one.)

> Hi everyone,
>
> I've of course been aware of the recent allegations circulating about the authorship of *The Last Front*. I apologize for not speaking up sooner. Please understand that this has been a

difficult time for me and that I am still struggling to cope with my best friend's tragic death.

In short, the allegations are completely false. *The Last Front* is my original creation. I was inspired by Athena to look into this forgotten chapter of global history, and it's no surprise that her voice shines through in my work.

I understand this whole situation is racially fraught. It upsets me to see arguments that only Athena could have written *The Last Front*, because Athena's work was so concerned with Asian diaspora issues. This pigeonholes both of us, and flattens our identities as writers.

I don't know the motives of the people behind this rumor, but I can only take it as a hurtful, malicious attack on my relationship with someone I miss very much, and whose death was one of the most traumatic experiences of my life.

My agent and editor have conducted their own independent investigations and have found no wrongdoing. I won't be speaking on this again.

Thank you,
Juniper

THE INITIAL RESPONSES AND QUOTE TWEETS ARE, OF COURSE, VICIOUS.

Fucking liar.

So you just happened to write a book that your dead friend would have been working on? Seems convenient to me.

LOL she's not even good at writing apologies.

Ugh, so June Song came out with her non-apology, and I bet white people will be jumping over themselves to defend her. I hate this industry.

Don't believe a word from your mouth, racist bitch.

If that's the truth, why did it take you so long to say anything?

Though once I get through the initial flurry of fuck-yous, it's apparent that my statement has gone over quite well. I can actually *see* the needle of public opinion shifting from skepticism to sympathy overnight.

This has been one of the most vicious and malicious campaigns I've ever seen, tweets a prominent blogger who's been neutral on the debacle so far. Shame on you all for the damage done to Juniper Song, and to Athena Liu's legacy.

Twitter, this is why we can't have nice things, says a BookTuber with fifty thousand subscribers. When will we learn not to dog pile on situations we know nothing about?

There's also this statement from Xiao Chen, which, honestly, I'll take: This book is so racist that it's obvious only a white person could have written it.

By the next morning, the @AthenaLiusGhost account has disappeared. There's nothing to point back to now; no original claim to bolster. The citation links are broken; the quote tweets lead to nothing. Some people are still making a stink, lambasting the publishing industry's haste to believe young white women over everyone else, but elsewhere it seems people would like to pretend this all never happened. I'm sure there are still angry detractors out there who believe I did it, but there's not a shred of concrete proof—they don't have enough to escalate this to legal action. Besides, the only one who could act on behalf of Athena's literary estate is Mrs. Liu, and she hasn't made a statement or reached out to me. There is nothing solid to this smoke monster; only the fleeting memory of lots of people yelling over nothing.

BRETT EMAILS ME WITH SOME GOOD NEWS THE FOLLOWING MONDAY.

> Greenhouse Productions made an offer of fifteen thousand for the option. Eighteen months, with the option to renew, and more money for you if they do. I'm going to try to talk them up to eighteen thousand, which I think I can get. We'll have our film agent look over the contract and make sure everything's up front, and then we'll send it to you to sign. Sound good?

Fifteen thousand is a bit lower than what I'd hoped for given all the hype, but I guess the fact that Greenhouse is making any offer at all signals their continued faith in me.

Just like that? I write back. What was the holdup?

Oh, Hollywood moves slow, Brett replies. Trust me, this counts as quick. I'll get the paperwork to you by the end of the week.

Everything goes back to normal. *Deadline* runs a nice press release on the option deal, and lots of people congratulate it for me online (they all seem to be under the impression that it's Jasmine Zhang directing, but I don't correct them). The publishing news cycle moves on to the next juicy scandal, which involves a YA writer who sent anonymous death threats to a rival for months before slipping up and sending one from her own email address. (She's trying to pass it off as a joke, but no one believes her, and the affected writer has started a GoFundMe to raise money to sue for emotional damages.)

The death threats dwindle to only one or two a day, and then none at all. I feel safe opening my DMs again. Within a week, all I get in my notifications are the normal slew of "congratulations" posts, tags in book stacks and reviews, and the occasional creep asking if I'll personally review their five-hundred-page manuscript. All the mean tweets about me are lost to the black hole of Twitter's memory. I start sleeping through the night again. I can eat without dry heaving again.

I am innocent in the court of public opinion. And at least for now, Athena's ghost has been banished.

Fifteen

I SHOULD HAVE LEFT THINGS THERE.

The Discourse has finally blown over, just as Brett had promised. I no longer need to mute my notifications for fear they'll crash my phone. I'm no longer Twitter's main character. But that's precisely the problem—I'm now trending toward irrelevance.

Such is the life cycle of every book that doesn't become a classic. *The Last Front* has been out for nearly a year at this point. It finally dropped off bestseller lists after four months. It didn't win any of the awards it was short-listed for, in no small part due to the @AthenaLiusGhost scandal. The fan mail, good and bad, is all starting to dry up. The school and library invitations have ground to a halt. I've heard no news from Greenhouse Productions since I signed the contract—which is common, apparently; most optioned properties sit untouched on the shelf until the option period is up. People have stopped soliciting me for op-eds and essays. Nowadays, when I tweet something funny, I get fifty or sixty likes at most.

I've been an internet nobody before, clinging to one or two

weekly Twitter mentions for a boost of serotonin. But I hadn't realized that even if you capture the entire literary world in the palm of your hand, it can still forget about you in the blink of the eye. Out with the old; in with the hot new thing, which is from what I can tell a pretty, fit, twentysomething debut writer named Kimmy Kai who spent her childhood doing acrobatics for a traveling circus in Hawaii and has now published a memoir about spending her childhood doing acrobatics for a traveling circus in Hawaii.

I'm not starving. I've done the math. If I live modestly—"modestly" defined as staying in my current apartment and ordering takeout every other day instead of every day—I could survive the next ten, even fifteen years on my earnings from *The Last Front* alone. The hardcover of *The Last Front* has gone back for its eleventh printing. The paperback edition just came out, which has generated a nice sales bump—paperbacks are cheaper, so they sell a bit better. I truly don't need the money. I could walk away from all of this and be perfectly fine.

But, my God, I want to be back in the spotlight.

You enjoy this delightful waterfall of attention when your book is the latest breakout success. You dominate the cultural conversation. You possess the literary equivalent of the hot hand. Everyone wants to interview you. Everyone wants you to blurb their book, or host their launch event. Everything you say matters. If you utter a hot take about the writing process, about other books, or even about life itself, people take your word as gospel. If you recommend a book on social media, people actually drive out that day to go buy it.

But your time in the spotlight never lasts. I've seen people who were massive bestsellers not even six years ago, sitting alone and forlorn at neglected signing tables while lines stretched around the corner for their younger, hotter peers. It's hard to reach such a pinnacle of literary prominence that you remain a household name for years, decades past your latest release. Only a handful of Nobel Prize winners can get away with that. The rest of us have to keep racing along the hamster wheel of relevance.

I've just learned from Twitter that my mentee, Emmy Cho, has signed with Athena's former literary agent, Jared, a hotshot shark known for six- and seven-figure deals. As her mentor I'm happy for her, but I also feel a spike of anxiety every time Emmy shares her good news. I'm afraid she'll catch up to me, that her inevitable book deal will involve an advance bigger than mine, that she'll sell film rights to a production company that will actually sell it to a studio, that her fame will then overshoot mine, and that the next time we see each other at some literary event she will merely greet me with a cool, superior nod.

The only way to get ahead, of course, is to dazzle the world with my next project.

But I've no clue what that might be.

BRETT CALLS ONE MORNING, OSTENSIBLY TO CATCH UP. WE TRADE pleasantries for a while, and then he asks, "So, how are things going in writing land?"

I know what he's really asking. Everyone's clamoring for my next pitch, and it's not only because publishing has such a short attention span. What he's thinking, and what Daniella is thinking, is that if I can put out a follow-up to *The Last Front* soon, something clearly not plagiarized or so intimately linked to Athena, but that still retains the ineffable Juniper Song spark, then we can dispel the rumors once and for all.

I sigh. "I've got to be honest: I have nothing. I'm out of ideas. I've been toying with a few concepts, but nothing really sticks."

"Well, that's all right." I can't tell if he's irritated or not. This is the third time we've had this conversation, and I know that time is running out. There's no hard deadline—I only signed a one-book contract with Eden, but that contract stipulates that Daniella has the right to a first look on my next work. Brett wants to show her something very soon, while we're still in her good graces, otherwise who knows what other publishers would want to pick me up next? "You have to let creativity come when it comes; I know that. It's just that you've got social capital right now, and it's best to strike when the iron's hot—"

"I know, I know." I press my fingers against my temples. "I just can't think of anything that hooks me. I have to really *care* about something, you know? It's got to have the heft, the importance—"

"It doesn't have to be great, Junie. We're not trying to win the Pulitzer. We don't even need something like *The Last Front*." Brett pauses. "You just have to publish, you know, something. Anything."

"Okay, Brett."

"You get what I'm saying, though?"

I roll my eyes. "Loud and clear."

We say our goodbyes. Brett hangs up. I groan and turn back to my laptop, where I've been staring at the same blank, accusing Word document for weeks.

THE PROBLEM ISN'T THAT I'M OUT OF IDEAS. I'VE GOT PLENTY OF IDEAS, and even more time to turn those ideas into full drafts. Now that publicity commitments for *The Last Front* have died down, I have no excuse not to be productive. Brett's right to be impatient—I've been making vague promises about forthcoming projects for over a year now, and nothing has materialized.

The problem is that every time I sit down to write, all I hear is Athena's voice.

The Last Front was supposed to be a onetime collaboration. Athena's research and brainstorming, my prose and polish. I felt a wonderful, mysterious alchemy during those fevered weeks, when I conjured her writing voice from beyond the grave and harmonized my own against it. I wasn't dependent on her—I've never *needed* her to write—but the joint exercise gave me confidence at a time when I had none. It made my pen so *sure*, knowing I was writing across her footsteps.

But now that I'm trying to move on, she won't leave me alone. Most authors will confess they hear an "inner editor," an internal naysayer that nitpicks and hampers their attempts at first drafts. Mine has taken the form of Athena. Haughtily, she peruses and dismisses every story idea I attempt. Too trite. Too formulaic. Too *white*. She's even harsher at the sentence level. *The rhythm's off. That imagery doesn't work. Seriously? Another em dash?*

I've tried to block her out and push through, to write in spite of and to spite her. But it's in those moments that her laughing grows louder, her taunts meaner. My doubts only ever intensify. Who am I to imagine I can achieve anything without her?

I've put on a stiff upper lip in public, but Geoff's Twitter antics rattled me more than I let on. Athena Liu's Ghost. A grotesque choice of name; surely chosen to surprise and provoke, but there's more truth to it than even Geoff knew. Athena's ghost has anchored itself to me; it hovers over my shoulder, whispering in my ear every waking moment of my day.

It's maddening. These days I've started dreading the thought of trying to write, because I can't write without thinking of *her.* Then, of course, my thoughts inevitably spiral beyond the writing to the memories: the final night, the pancakes, the gurgling sounds she made as she thrashed against the floor.

I thought I'd gotten over her death. I was doing so well mentally. I was in a *good space.* I was *fine.*

Until she returned.

But isn't that what ghosts do? Howl, moan, make themselves into spectacles? That's the whole point of a ghost, is it not? Anything to remind you that they're still there. Anything to keep you from forgetting.

I MUST CONFESS: I DOUBLE-DIPPED.

That night in Athena's apartment, I didn't only take *The Last Front.* I also took a smattering of papers lying across her desk, some typewritten, some covered in Athena's looping, nearly illegible scrawl, accompanied by abstract line doodles whose significance I still haven't figured out.

I swear it was only out of curiosity. Athena was always so cagey about her creative process. The way she described it, it was like the gods dropped award-winning stories into her mind fully formed. I just wanted to get a look inside her head, to see if her early-stage brainstorming was anything like mine.

It turns out, we create in very similar ways. She starts with random words or phrases, some original, some clearly song lyrics or minor modifications of other, more famous lines of literature—*Rook was already dead when I arrived; the boy from nowhere; it was a dark yet brilliant night; if I hit you, would it feel like a kiss?*

I place them out on my desk now, staring at them, hunting for a shred of inspiration. I can't get Athena's voice out of my head, but maybe I can work with it. Maybe I can force her ghost back into service and resurrect that same unholy chemistry that fueled *The Last Front.*

There are only a few completed sentences and only one completed paragraph, written out by hand, which begins like this:

In my nightmares she walks into a dark and never-ending hallway, and as many times as I call her name, she never turns around. Her dress leaves wet streaks on the carpet. Her pale arms are bloody and scratched. I know she has slain the bear. I know she has escaped the forest. She moves now with that same urgency, abandoning the past like Orpheus, inverted, like if she never glances back over her shoulder, it will cease to exist. She forgets I am trapped here, unable to move, unable to make her see me. She forgets me entirely.

I don't know how to explain what happens next. It's like the story was already in my heart, waiting to be told, and Athena's voice is the spell to draw it out. Suddenly my writer's block dissipates, and the unlocked gates to my imagination swing wide open.

I can see the shape of the story in full: its opening hook, its underlying themes, its shocking yet inevitable ending. Our protagonist is a barefoot girl, a young witch chasing her immortal mother through eternity, uncovering her secrets only to form more questions about herself and where she's come from. It's a not-so-subtle exploration of my feelings toward my own mother: how she transformed so abruptly after my father's death; how the adventurous young girl she once was, who was perhaps not so different from me, has been locked entirely away. It's about wishing you knew who your parents were. It's about needing things from your parents you'll never get.

When you're in the zone, drafting doesn't feel like an effortful artifice. It feels like remembering, like putting down in written form something that has been locked inside you all along. The story pours out of me, paragraph by paragraph, until I look up and realize that it's nearly dawn, and that I've written almost ten thousand words in a manic sprint.

Athena's ghost has not bothered me once. At last, I've arrived at a project even she can't find fault with.

I sketch out an outline for the rest of the story and create a work schedule for myself: at a rate of two thousand words a day, and factoring in time for revisions and line edits, I can have this finished in less than a month. Then, before I crash into sleep, I type out a title at the top of the document:

Mother Witch.

No one in their right mind could call this stealing. That's what's most fucked up about this whole debacle. *Mother Witch* is my original creation. All Athena contributed was a couple of sentences, maybe some underlying imagery. She was the catalyst, nothing more. Who knows where she would have taken the rest of the story? I certainly don't—and I bet that, whatever it was, it's nothing like what I ultimately publish.

And yet it's this story that brings me down.

FIRST, LET ME TELL YOU ABOUT THE TIME ATHENA STOLE FROM ME.

We became friends at the start of our freshman year. We were both assigned to the same floor in our dorm, so naturally that became our default social circle those first few weeks. We ate all our meals together, went shopping for dorm goods together, took the Yale shuttle to Trader Joe's for pepper jack cheese and cookie butter, hung out late nights in the common room, and stalked the streets of downtown New Haven on Friday nights in short skirts and tight-fitting tops, watching like vultures for the noise and lights that signified a party, hoping that someone knew someone who would let us in.

Athena and I had bonded instantly over our love of the same book, Elif Batuman's *The Idiot*. "It is the perfect campus tale," Athena said, articulating clearly every feeling I'd ever had about the novel. "It describes precisely that gulf between wanting others to know you, and being terrified that they might understand, at a time when we're not sure who we are at all. It's not just about translating between Russian and English, it's also about translating an unformed identity. I love it." We would go together to open mic nights at bookstore cafés and apartment parties hosted by upperclassmen in our fiction seminars, and from late August through September I made myself believe I was the sort of person this impossibly cool goddess would be friends with.

The first weekend of October, I went on a date with a cute sophomore named Andrew: someone I'd noticed during my World History discussion sections but hadn't worked up the nerve to speak to until we crossed paths at a Delta Phi party, both falling-down drunk and just looking for a body to glue ourselves to. We hadn't exchanged two words before we started making out. I can't remember if it was good or not, only that it was very sticky, but it felt like we were doing the expected, and that in itself seemed like an achievement. Before my friends dragged me home, I put my number in his phone. Miraculously, he texted me the next day, invited me over to his room the following Friday to watch an episode of *Sherlock* while his roommate was at late-night Ultimate Frisbee practice.

What happened next is so mundane it almost doesn't feel worth describing. He had a handle of Burnett's on hand. Excited, I drank too much and too fast. We never got around to watching *Sherlock*. I woke up the next morning with my panties around my ankles and violent, purplish-black hickeys on my neck. My vagina, to be honest, felt fine—later I would poke and prod at it, trying to tell if I was sore or bleeding, but it all seemed normal. I was just dry-mouthed, hungover, and so nauseated that I kept leaning over the side of the bunk bed to dry heave. Everything was blurry; I'd fallen asleep with my contacts in, and my eyes were so dry I could barely keep them open. Beside me, Andrew was fully clothed and asleep. He didn't wake up when I climbed over him out of bed, for which I was desperately grateful.

I found my heels, pulled them on, and staggered back to my dorm.

I was fine throughout the weekend. I didn't go out again, even though half the girls I knew were getting pretty for a sorority open house night. I stayed in, enjoyed a popcorn and movie night with some girls on my floor, and attempted my course reading. It was getting colder outside; I wore turtlenecks and scarves to hide my hickeys. Back in my room, where I could not conceal my bare neck from my roommate, Michelle, I made jokes about having a wild weekend, and that was the last we spoke of it.

Andrew hadn't texted me since I left his room, which didn't bother me much. Mostly I felt blasé about the whole affair, and proud of being blasé. I felt grown-up, womanly, accomplished. I'd hooked up with a sophomore. A *cute* sophomore. The enormity of it delighted me. I'd crossed a bridge into adulthood; I'd "hooked up" with someone, as the youths say. And I was fine.

It was only the next week that I started suffering flashbacks. Andrew's face would pop up in my mind during lectures: vivid, up close, his chin prickly and his breath sour with cinnamon Burnett's. I'd find myself unable to breathe, unable to move without feeling waves of vertigo. My imagination would spiral out, imagining the worst possible scenarios. Could I be pregnant? Did I have HIV? HPV? Herpes? AIDS? Would my uterus rot out inside me? Should I see campus health? If I saw campus health, would it cost me hundreds of dollars I didn't have? Had my mom waived the student insurance plan? I couldn't remember. Was I going to die because of a stupid mistake I'd made, something I hadn't even been awake for?

Andrew didn't text me until two in the morning the following Saturday: Hey, u up? I saw it when I got up to pee and deleted it, hoping to spare my waking self the reminder of his existence.

But I couldn't get his face, his smell, his touch out of my mind. I started taking incredibly long showers, three or four times a day. I kept having nightmares in which I was pinned beneath him, trapped under his scratchy chin, unable to move or scream. Michelle would wake me up, shaking my shoulders gently, asking me apologetically and diplomatically if I had earplugs she could borrow, because she had discussion section at eight in the morning and I was interrupting her REM cycles. I found myself weeping randomly in the afternoons, overwhelmed with self-loathing. I even considered going to a student Bible study group, though I'd stopped going to church after Dad since the pastor told me he was going to hell as he'd never been baptized, just because I wanted something that could help me make sense of my very retrograde but still strong conviction that I was irreversibly tainted, used, and dirty.

"Hey, Juniper?" Athena stopped me one afternoon on my way back from the dining hall. Back then, Athena was the only one who used my full name, which was a habit she would sustain through adulthood, calling Tashas "Natasha" and Bills "William" as if this insistence on formality would elevate everyone in the conversation. (It did.) She touched my arm. Her fingers were smooth and cool. "Are you okay?"

And maybe it was because I'd been holding it all in for so long, or because she was the first person at Yale who'd really looked at me and noticed that something wasn't right, but I burst immediately into loud, ugly tears.

"Come on," she said, rubbing gentle circles on my back. "Let's go to my room."

Athena held my hand while I recounted the whole thing through hiccupping sobs. She talked me through my options, made me look through the campus resources list, and helped me decide if I wanted to seek counseling (yes) or report Andrew to the campus police to try and press charges (no). She walked with me to my first appointment with Dr. Gaily, where I got a diagnosis for my anxiety, unpacked all this shit I'd been carrying since my father's death, and learned coping mechanisms that I still use today. She left takeout meals from the cafeteria outside my door when she noticed I hadn't gone to dinner. She texted me puppy photos late at night captioned, Hope you dream of this!

For two weeks, Athena Liu was my guardian angel. I thought she was so kind. I thought we would be friends forever.

But freshman friendships don't last. By our second semester, I was running in my own circles, and she in hers. We still smiled and waved when we passed each other in the dining hall. We still liked each other's Facebook posts. But we weren't talking for hours on the floors of our rooms, trading stories about authors we hoped to meet and literary scandals we'd read about on Twitter. We weren't texting each other during class anymore. Perhaps, I thought, the enormity of what I'd shared had killed a proper friendship in the bud. There are appropriate levels to intimacy. You can't break out "I think I was raped, but I don't really know," until at least three months in.

We all moved on. I forgot about Andrew, or at least buried him so deep in the back of my mind that he wouldn't resurface until therapy sessions many years later. The freshman girl's brain is startlingly capable of selective amnesia; I believe it is a survival reaction. I made new, closer friends, none of whom would ever know what had happened. My hickeys faded. I settled into life at Yale, stopped going to parties where I made a fool of myself, and threw myself into my coursework.

But then Athena's first short story came out in one of Yale's alt literary magazines, a pretentious rag titled *Ouroboros*. This was a big deal—freshmen never got published in *Ouroboros*, or so I heard, and we all bought copies to support her. I took my print volume up to my room to read. I felt a snarl of jealousy—I'd submitted my own story months ago and had been resoundingly rejected within a day—but I wanted to look like a good sport, so I thought I'd read enough to find a few particularly witty lines, and then quote them back at Athena the next time I saw her.

I flipped the issue open to page twelve, Athena's story, and found my own words staring back at me.

But they weren't quite *my* words. Just my feelings, all of my confused and tangled thoughts, articulated in a clean, understated yet sophisticated style that I didn't then have the eloquence to achieve.

And the worst part was that I didn't know, narrated the protagonist. *I truly couldn't tell if I'd been raped, if I'd wanted it, if anything had happened at all, if I was glad that nothing had happened, or if I wanted something to happen just so I could make it out to be more important than I was. The place between my legs is a lacuna. There is no memory, no shame, no pain. It's all just gone. And I do not know what to do with the lack.*

I read the story from beginning to end, again and again, spotting more and more similarities every time, identifying personal details changed with either astounding laziness or indifference. The guy's name was Anthony. The girl's name was Jillian. They drank strawberry lemonade Svedka. They were in the same Ancient Philosophy section. He invited her over to watch *The Hobbit.*

"I liked your story," I told Athena at dinner; holding her gaze, daring her to deny it. *I know what you did.*

She met my eyes, and gave me a polite, nothing smile—the one she would later give regularly to fans at signing tables. "Thank you, Juniper. That's really kind of you to say."

We never spoke about that story, or what happened with Andrew, again.

Maybe it was a coincidence. We were small, fragile freshmen girls at a large university where such things are known to happen. My story isn't remarkable. It is, in fact, utterly mundane. Not every girl has a rape story. But almost every girl has an "I'm not sure, I didn't like it, but I can't quite call it rape" story.

I couldn't, however, overlook the similarity between the phrases I'd used when describing my pain and the phrases Athena used in her story. I couldn't unlink Athena's prose from the memory of her doe-like brown eyes, blinking in sympathy as I told her every black, ugly thing in my heart between choked sobs.

She'd stolen my story. I was convinced of it. She'd stolen my words right out of my mouth. She did the same to everyone around her for the entirety of her career, and honestly, if I'm supposed to feel bad about getting my revenge, then fuck that.

Mother Witch COMES OUT TO A MODERATELY WARM RECEPTION—plenty of critical acclaim, but modest sales. We expected as much. It's a novella, not a full-length novel—I couldn't think of a way to build it out longer than forty thousand words—and the market for those is always smaller. I do a three-city tour at bookstores in DC, Boston, and NYC, where it's easier to wrangle together an audience of book enthusiasts on any given Friday. These are well attended. No one asks any nasty questions about my racial bona fides. No one mentions the plagiarism scandal.

The critical reception is good, in a faintly surprised way. From *Kirkus*, a starred review: "A quiet, heartrending tale of betrayal and innocence lost." From *Library Journal*, also a starred review: "Juniper Song proves adept at handling mature themes in contexts entirely removed from World War One." And our greatest achievement, in the *New York Times*, which I know Daniella had to pull strings to get: "If there were any suspicions that Juniper Song does not produce her own work, let *Mother Witch* settle those fears: this girl can write."

There's something unsettling about all this calm. Things are too quiet, suffocatingly so, like the air before a thunderstorm. But I'm too relieved, too ready to believe I might have put all the trouble behind me. I'm already thinking about the next contract, about possible film options for current properties. Maybe *Mother Witch* isn't blockbuster material, but you could make a quiet prestige TV series with it. Something like *Big Little Lies*, or *Little Fires Everywhere.* Someone call Reese Witherspoon to produce. Someone tap Amy Adams to play the mother. Someone tap Anna Kendrick to play me.

I let myself relax. I fill my head with dreams. After all this time, I finally stop hearing Athena's ghost every time I sit down to write.

I should have known it wouldn't last.

Sixteen

TWO WEEKS AFTER *MOTHER WITCH* COMES OUT, ADELE SPARKS-Sato puts out a blog post titled "*Mother Witch* Is Also Plagiarized, and I've Fucking Had It with June Hayward."

I glimpse the Google Alert just as I'm about to step into the shower. I sit back on my bed, clutching my towel tight against my chest as I click the link.

> Like many of you, I was curious when Eden Press announced June Hayward, writing as Juniper Song, was releasing a standalone novella. After the allegations surrounding *The Last Front*, I had doubts whether she could write something of equal quality, especially now as there are no remaining works of Athena's to steal from—or so we all thought. I couldn't believe my eyes when I turned to the first page.
>
> *Mother Witch* opens with identical lines from a story that Athena Liu workshopped at the Asian American Writers' Collective sum-

mer workshop in 2018. Such overlap is not coincidental. Here's the proof.

Below, Adele has included screenshots of Google Docs and photographs of printed story outlines with handwritten notes in the comments, along with so many corroborating dates and accounts that such an accusation would be impossible to fake.

In case anyone thinks this is some elaborate hoax, I've reached out to eight different attendees of the workshop that year. Not everyone still has their printouts from that summer, but everyone has gone on record as remembering Athena's work. They've attached their names to this write-up as endorsements. If you won't take my word for it, consider the weight of our combined testimonies.

The debate over the authorship of *The Last Front* has been fraught and troubling for many in the Asian diaspora community. A lot of us, myself included, did not want to believe anyone could do something so vile or selfish. And a lot of us were willing to give June Hayward the benefit of the doubt.

With this evidence, there's no longer a question about Hayward's intentions. Hayward; her agent, Brett Adams; and her team at Eden Press have a choice now to make about accountability, transparency, and their supposed commitment to justice.

The rest of us will be watching.

I lower my phone. The water's been running for a good ten minutes, but I can't summon the willpower to go turn it off. All I can do is sit at the edge of my bed, breathing in and out as the world narrows to a pinprick around me.

When I first saw Geoff's @AthenaLiusGhost tweets, I spiraled into an hours-long anxiety attack. This time, my reaction feels strangely muted. I feel like I'm submerged underwater. Everything sounds and feels wrong, distorted. Somehow, I am both more calm and more terrified than before. Perhaps it's because this time, there is no question about what will happen next. This time the truth is incontrovertible, and it'll make no difference whether I scramble to control the public narrative or not. I don't have to wonder what my friends and colleagues are thinking about me, or whether they'll believe my denials. It's all there in black and white. What happens next will happen, no matter what I do or say.

I put my phone on "do not disturb" mode. I slide my iPad into a drawer. I shut down my laptop. I grab a bottle of whisky from atop my fridge—WhistlePig, a gift from Daniella for three consecutive months on the *NYT* bestseller list—and settle down in front of my couch, watching old episodes of *Friends* while I chug straight from the bottle, until I'm out for the night.

Let the internet do its work while I'm gone. When I face the noise, I'd rather it come all at once.

I WAKE UP THE NEXT MORNING TO SEE I'VE LOST A THOUSAND FOLlowers. The metric is still dropping; nines turning to eights before my eyes. This time, I don't have to search my name to track the conversation. It's right there, all over my timeline and in my mentions.

I fucking knew it about Juniper Song.

June Hayward strikes again!

Does this bitch never stop?

Wake up publishing, the White Witch is back.

Last time, I'd kept my social media accounts active—partly so that I could stay tuned to what was being said, and partly because I feared deactivation would be an admission of guilt. This time, my guilt is a foregone conclusion—all I can hope for now is damage control, by which I mean managing threats to my personal safety. I delete my Twitter account. I set my Instagram to private. I turn off notifications from my publicly available email address. Certainly I'm getting death threats, but at least this way I won't know about them the second they arrive.

Someone edits my Wikipedia page to read: "Juniper Song Hayward is a 'novelist,' serial plagiarizer, and flaming racist." That particular line is gone within an hour—Wikipedia has minimal civility requirements, I suppose—but the "Plagiarism" section of my biography remains as follows: "In March 2020, literary critic Adele Sparks-Sato published an essay alleging that the first paragraph of Hayward's novella, *Mother Witch*, is a word-for-word copy of the first paragraph of *Her*, an unpublished story by late novelist Athena Liu. This allegation compounds long-running suspicions that Hayward also stole *The Last Front* from Liu, though there remains no conclusive proof this is true. Hayward's editor, Daniella Woodhouse, has released a brief statement claiming Eden Press is aware of these allegations and is looking into the matter."

My phone rings six times that day—all calls from Brett. I don't pick up. I will eventually, when I trust myself to hear I've been fired without breaking into sobs.

For now, I take a kind of perverse pleasure in watching everything fall apart.

Over the next week, all of my publishing relationships disintegrate. I'm asked to leave two professional Facebook groups and three Slacks I've joined in the past year. My so-called writer friends ghost me without exception, even the ones who professed a few months ago to be on my side against the mob.

I have no one to turn to but Eden's Angels.

Oh god, I text. It's happening again. When no one responds—which is atypical; Jen is addicted to her phone—I follow up a few hours later with, I'm having a really hard time right now, is anyone possibly available to talk?

They ignore me for three days. Finally Marnie writes: Hi, Junie. Sorry; have been so busy these last few days. Moving house.

Jen never responds at all.

I'm supposed to have my monthly mentee check-in session with Emmy Cho on Friday. On Thursday afternoon, I receive an email from the mentor program coordinator:

> Hi Juniper, Emmy doesn't think that continuing with your mentor relationship is a good idea, and has asked us to pass the mes-

sage on to you. Thank you for everything you've done for Emmy and for our program.

Bitch. Emmy could have at least mustered the courage to say that to my face. It's probably ill-advised, but I write back to the program coordinator, Thanks for telling me. Do you know if Emmy has any feedback for my mentorship style, so I can take that into account in the future? What I really want to know is if Emmy's going around badmouthing me. I don't expect a response, but the reply lands in my email later that night: Emmy simply feels that you have very different perceptions of how the industry works. She also requests that you do not contact her, directly or indirectly, any further.

ON FRIDAY I DRAG MYSELF OUT OF BED AND MAKE MYSELF PRESENTable for a videoconference with my team at Eden. I finally picked up one of Brett's calls the night before, after Rory texted me asking if I was alive: Your agent just emailed me. He said you weren't responding, and he was worried about you. What's going on? Is everything okay?

"Daniella wants to talk to you ASAP," Brett told me when I called him back. He sounded tired. He didn't even ask me if the allegations were true. "We've scheduled a Zoom meeting for tomorrow at two."

Brett's on the line with me now. All the Eden people are on the same screen, sitting together around a conference table: Daniella, Jessica, and Emily, and a red-haired man I don't recognize. No one is smiling. No one waves hello when I join the call.

"Hello, June." Daniella's voice is cool and low, which is how I know she's pissed. "I'm here with Jessica and Emily, and Todd Byrne from legal."

"I'm here as well," says Brett, ineffectually.

"Hi, Todd," I say weakly. No one told me I was getting a lawyer. Todd merely nods at me. I realize then that Todd isn't here for me, he's here for them.

"Where's Candice?" I ask, trying to get my bearings through small talk.

"Oh, Candice isn't here anymore," says Daniella. "She left a while ago."

"Oh." I wait, but Daniella doesn't elaborate. I try not to overthink it. Editorial assistants come and go all the time. They're underpaid entry-level employees in the most expensive city in the world—ill-treated, overlooked, and overworked with minimal opportunities for advancement. It takes inhuman drive to hack it in publishing. Probably Candice just couldn't take it. "That's too bad."

"Let's cut to the chase, shall we?" Daniella clears her throat. "June, if there's anything we need to know, you need to tell us right now."

My nose prickles. To my horror, I realize I'm already close to tears.

"I didn't do it," I say. "I swear to God. It's not plagiarized, it's all my own work, especially *Mother Witch*—"

"Especially?" Todd cuts in. "What does that mean?"

"I mean, *The Last Front* was inspired by conversations with Athena," I say quickly. "But she's dead now, obviously, and I didn't have her to talk to while I was drafting *Mother Witch*, so the writing style doesn't resemble hers as much—"

"That's not what Adele Sparks-Sato is claiming," says Jessica. She pronounces Adele's last name like she's reading some exotic soup ingredient from a grocery list. *Sparks Sa-touuu.* "It appears that she's gone public with some rather conclusive proof—"

"Adele's full of shit," I burst out. "Sorry. No—I mean, I get where she's coming from; I can see why she's protective of Athena's work. And, like, yes, I was inspired by a line that Athena wrote once. I saw—um, she showed me, in her notebook. But the story is completely original—it's based on my own relationship with my mother, in fact, I mean, like, you can call her, even—"

"I don't think that will be necessary," says Daniella. "What about *The Last Front*, then? Is that completely original?"

"Guys." My voice hitches. "Come on. You know me."

"You can tell us," says Daniella. "We're on your team. If there was any sort of . . . collaboration, or anything that means you are not the sole author, we need to know. We can still make this work. We could set up a split royalties arrangement with Athena's estate, perhaps, and then out a press release about the shared authorship where you explain that you felt like you needed to do justice to your friend's work, and that you did not intend to deceive anyone. Then perhaps we can set up a foundation in Athena's name—"

She's talking like she's certain I'm guilty.

"Hold on," I cut in. "No, look, I swear to God—it's *mine*, the project is mine, I wrote out every single word myself." And that's true. Completely true. I made *The Last Front*. Athena's version was utterly unpublishable. That book exists because of *me*.

"Do you possibly have proof of that?" Todd asks. "Early drafts, perhaps—emails with time stamps that we could verify?"

"Well, *no*, because I'm not in the habit of emailing things to myself."

"Is there any proof that it *is* plagiarized?" Brett cuts in. "I mean, what, are we assuming Junie is guilty until proven innocent? This is ridiculous. Didn't you guys just put out a book about criminal justice reform?"

"We're not persecuting Junie," says Daniella. "We're just trying to protect her, for the sake of her reputation and Eden's—"

"So are we being sued?" Brett presses. "Has Athena's estate issued a cease and desist? Or is all this precautionary?"

"It's precautionary," Todd admits. "As it stands, the copyright issue is quite easily contained. Athena's next of kin—that would be her mother, Patricia Liu—has expressed no desire to sue for damages, and as long as we take out or rewrite the opening paragraph of *Mother Witch*, there's no problem with the bulk of the work . . ."

I feel a glimmer of hope. Mrs. Liu's decision not to sue is news to me—here I thought I'd be on the hook for thousands of dollars in payments. "So we're all right, then?"

"Well." Daniella clears her throat. "There remains a problem of perception. We need to be clear on what our story is. That's what we're trying to do here: get all the facts straight, so we're all on the same page. So if June could repeat, for clarity, precisely her account of how she wrote *The Last Front* and *Mother Witch* . . ."

"*The Last Front* is entirely my original work, inspired by my conversations with Athena." My voice keeps steady. I'm still terrified, but I feel like I'm on more solid footing, now that I know I'm not getting dropped by my publisher. They're trying to help me. I just have to give them the right spin, and we can make this work. "And *Mother Witch* takes the first paragraph from one of Athena's unpublished drafts, but otherwise it is entirely original to me as well. I write my own stuff, you guys. I promise."

A brief pause. Daniella glances at Todd, her left eyebrow arched high.

"All right, then," Todd says. "We'll want this in writing, of course, but if that's all you did, then . . . this is fairly containable."

"So can we make this go away?" Brett asks.

Todd hesitates. "That's really a question for publicity . . ."

"Maybe I could put out a statement," I say. "Or do, like, an interview. Clear everything up. Most of this is all misunderstandings—maybe if I just . . ."

"I think what's best for you right now is to focus on your next work," Daniella says crisply. "Eden will put out a statement on your behalf. We'll send it over for your approval this afternoon."

Emily chips in. "We all feel that in the meantime, it's best that you, personally, stay off social media. But if you wanted to announce a new project, something you're currently working on . . ." She trails off.

I get the idea. Shut up, stay out of the spotlight, and prove you're capable of writing your own books. Preferably something that has nothing to do with Athena fucking Liu.

"What *are* you working on now?" Daniella prods. "Brett, I know it's not under contract with us, but we do have the first look, so if there's anything you can share with us . . ."

"I'm working on it," I say hoarsely. "Obviously this whole thing has been very distressing, so I've been distracted . . ."

"But she'll have something new soon," Brett jumps in. "I'll be in touch when she does. Does that sound good, everyone? Junie will fix that first paragraph ASAP, and I'll circle back next week when we've got something shaped like a pitch?"

Todd shrugs; his part in this is over. Daniella nods. We all exchange some niceties about how it's good we could get on the line and clear all this up in person, and then Daniella kills the Zoom room.

Brett rings me right after for a follow-up.

"Do they hate me?" I ask miserably. "Is Daniella done with me?"

"No, no." He pauses. "Actually, it's not as bad as it seems. Controversy of any sort is pretty good for free marketing. We're expecting your royalties to go up in the next payment period."

"What, seriously?"

"Well—so here's the thing. We didn't want to tell you over Zoom, but it seems like this whole fiasco got picked up by a lot of, um, well, right-wing commentators. Probably not people you really want to associate with. I mean, let's be clear about that. But they're turning this into a culture war issue, and that always drives attention, so sales are . . . up. And it's always nice when sales are up."

I can't believe it. This is the first piece of good news I've gotten all week. "By how much?"

"Enough that you're going to get a bonus."

It seems like a weird time to celebrate, and perhaps this is wildly inappropriate, but in the back of my mind, I make a mental note to finally get that IKEA couch I've been eyeing. It'll look nice next to my bookshelves.

"It just seemed like Daniella wanted to kill me." A hysterical giggle escapes my throat. "I mean, she looked *so* mad—"

"Oh, Daniella doesn't really care," says Brett. "She has to do her job, you understand. But at the end of the day all that really matters is cash flow. Eden's going to stand with you. You're pulling in too much money for them to back out now. Feel better?"

"So much better." I exhale. "Wow. All right."

"So you're going to work on something new?"

"I guess I'd fucking better, huh?"

"That would be nice." Brett laughs. "Write up some pitches for me to show Daniella next week. You don't have to outline a whole project—just throw out some ideas so that she knows you've still got it. Just maybe something that isn't about a Chinese girl, okay?"

"Ha ha," I say, and hang up.

MY PHONE RINGS ONCE MORE THAT NIGHT, JUST AS I'VE ORDERED some pizza for dinner. I hit the green ANSWER button, assuming it's my DoorDash guy. "Hello?"

"June?" A pause. "It's Patricia Liu. Athena's mom."

Oh, Jesus Christ. I have the fleeting urge to hang up and hurl my phone across the room. But that will only make things worse—then she'll know I'm too afraid to talk to her, and she'll make assumptions why, and I'll be up all night panicking over what she would have said to me. Better to have it out now and get this over with. If she's changed her mind about suing for damages, Brett and the Eden team need to know.

I can't keep my voice from cracking. "Hi, Mrs. Liu."

"Hello." Her voice sounds muffled and nasal. I wonder if she's been crying. "I'm calling because . . . well, there's no easy way to say this."

"Mrs. Liu, I think I know—"

"A woman named Adele Sparks-Sato reached out to me this morning. She wanted to know if I still had Athena's drafting notebooks, and if she could have a look."

She doesn't elaborate, which forces me to ask, "Yes?"

"Well, she insinuated that you had stolen *The Last Front* from Athena. And she wanted to look through Athena's notebooks, to see if there was any evidence that Athena had been working on that project."

I press my hand against my forehead. This is it. It's all over. I thought she was calling about *Mother Witch*, but this is so much worse. "Mrs. Liu, I don't know what to say."

"I told her no, of course." My heart skips a beat. Mrs. Liu continues. "I don't like when strangers . . . Anyhow, I told her to give me some time to think about it. And I thought I would talk to you first." She pauses again. I know what she wants to ask; she's just not brave enough to say it. I imagine her standing in her kitchen, nails digging into her palm, trying to speak aloud the possibility that the last person who saw her daughter alive might have stolen her magnum opus as well. "June . . ." Her voice catches. I hear her sniffle. "As you know, June, I very much do not want to open those notebooks."

And the follow-up question, unspoken: *Do I have reason to?*

Believe me, in that moment, I want to confess.

This would have been the best time, the *right* time, to come clean. I think of our last conversation, two years ago, when I visited her home. "I so wish I had been able to read her last novel," Mrs. Liu told me as I stood up to leave. "Athena so rarely opened herself up to me. Reading her work wasn't like knowing her thoughts, but it was at least a part of her she'd decided to let me see."

I've torn that from her. I've denied a mother her daughter's final words. If I tell her the truth now, Mrs. Liu will at least get those words back. She'll see the effort that occupied the last years of Athena's life.

But I can't break.

That's been the key to staying sane throughout all of this: holding the line, maintaining my innocence. In the face of it all, I've never once cracked, never admitted the theft to anyone. By now, I mostly believe the lie myself—that it was my efforts that made *The Last Front* the success that it was, that when it comes down to it, it is *my* book. I've contorted the truth into such ways that I can, in fact, make peace with it. If I tell Mrs. Liu otherwise, all of this unravels. I drive the nail in my own coffin. And the world may be crumbling around me regardless, but I can't let it all slip away if there's even the slightest hope of salvaging it.

"Mrs. Liu." I take a deep breath. "I worked very, very hard on *The Last Front*. My blood and sweat are in that book."

"I see."

"Your daughter was an exceptional writer. And so am I. And I think it hurts both her legacy, and my future, to overlook either truth."

I'm skilled with words. I know how to lie without lying. And I know, on some level, that Mrs. Liu must know what I'm really telling her. I'm sure she knows, if she gives Adele Sparks-Sato permission, what they will find in Athena's notebooks.

But she is terrified of what lies inside those Moleskines. That is clearer now than ever. I'm speaking to a mother who, when it comes down to it, would really rather not confront what dark things lay buried in her daughter's soul. No mother wants to know her child that well. Here, then, are the terms of our bargain—she'll keep my secrets, as long as she never has to confront Athena's.

"Very well," says Mrs. Liu. "Thank you, June."

Before she hangs up, I blurt, "And Mrs. Liu, about *Mother Witch* . . ." I trail off. I'm not sure what I want to say, or if it's prudent to say anything at all. Todd told me that Mrs. Liu isn't suing for damages, but I hate to have this hanging over me. I want confirmation from Mrs. Liu's own mouth that this is going away. "I mean, so I don't know if you've heard, but I'm going to rewrite the opening . . ."

"Oh, June." She sighs. "I don't care about that."

"It really is original work," I say. "I did—I did take the first paragraph—I don't know how, I think we were just trading excerpts, and it wound up in my notebook somehow, and it's been so long that I forgot . . . but anyways, the rest of the story . . ."

"I know," says Mrs. Liu, and now there's a hard edge in her voice. "I know, June. Athena never would have written something like that."

Before I can ask her what she means, she hangs up.

Seventeen

BY THE END OF THE MONTH, THE DUST HAS SETTLED AND ALL RELevant parties have made up their minds. I am hated by the internet, an embarrassment to the industry, and hanging on to my relationship with my publisher by a thread.

At least I'm not broke. Indeed, by most external measures, I am still quite a success. I occupy that curious space where the fraction of the reading population that's constantly online hates me, but the rest of America's book buyers don't. People are still picking my books off the sale racks at Target and Books-A-Million. Despite a petition circled by Adele Sparks-Sato and Diana Qiu to have Eden pull all my titles from shelves until they've conducted a third-party investigation (delusional), my sales haven't dropped.

In fact, they're doing better. Brett was right about scandals generating free marketing. Unofficial until your royalty statement, reads his latest email, but your sales are nearly double this month what they were this time a year ago.

It only takes a little exploring around the seedier corners of the internet to learn what's going on. Alt-right free-speech proponents have made me their cause célèbre. I and my pretty, Anglo-Saxon face have become the perfect victim of the left-wing fascist cancel-culture mob. (It appears the alt-right cares a lot about due process, but only when the accused has done something like sexual assault or racially motivated plagiarism.) A popular Fox News cohost encourages all of his millions of viewers to support me so that Eden doesn't drop me from their list, which has created a strange situation in which thousands of Trump voters are buying a book about mistreated Chinese laborers. My publicist passes on an interview request from a popular young YouTuber, but I decline when I discover that most of her viral videos are titled things like "WATCH ME SNEAK A GUN INTO MY ECON LECTURE LOL" and "LIB SNOWFLAKE GETS OWNED BY THE FACTS ON ABORTION."

Okay, yes, I know how bad this looks. Like Taylor Swift, I had no intention of becoming a white supremacist Barbie. Obviously I'm not a Trumper—I voted for Biden! But if these people are hurling money at me, is it so wrong of me to accept? Should we not celebrate scamming cash from racist rednecks whenever we get the chance?

So here's how things have shaken out. I've lost my reputation, but I'm far from canceled, and I have a steady income for the foreseeable future. Things could be worse. Maybe I've burned all my bridges in publishing, but that doesn't mean my life is over. I still have more savings than most people my age. Maybe it's time to stop while I'm ahead.

In those following weeks, I do think often about quitting writing altogether. Maybe my mother was right all along; maybe a lengthy career just isn't in the cards for me. Maybe I should treat *The Last Front* as the launchpad to get myself set up somewhere else. I have enough money to pay for any preprofessional graduate degree, and a suitably high GPA from an Ivy League school to get into most top-ten law or business programs. Maybe I'll study for the LSAT. Maybe I'll enroll in some online quant boot camps and then go into consulting.

It's attractive, the prospect of a stable job with clearly defined hours and benefits, where being white does not make you boring and redundant but rather a perfectly average and desirable hire. No more panic-scrolling; no more dick-measuring competitions; no more reading emails a thousand times over to figure out if my marketing person hates me or not.

But I can't quit the one thing that gives meaning to my life.

Writing is the closest thing we have to real magic. Writing is creating something out of nothing, is opening doors to other lands. Writing gives you power to shape your own world when the real one hurts too much. To stop writing would kill me. I'd never be able to walk through a bookstore without fingering the spines with longing, wondering at the lengthy editorial process that got these titles on shelves and reminiscing about my own. And I'd spend the rest of life curdling with jealousy every time someone like Emmy Cho gets a book deal, every time I learn that some young up-and-comer is living the life I should be living.

Writing has formed the core of my identity since I was a child. After Dad died, after Mom withdrew into herself, and after Rory decided to forge a life without me, writing gave me a reason to stay alive. And as miserable as it makes me, I'll cling to that magic for as long as I live.

THE PROBLEM IS THAT I HAVE NOTHING TO WRITE FOR DANIELLA. None of my old pitches will do. I've pulled a few of my former project drafts from the metaphorical trunk, but their premises all now strike me as dull, derivative, or plain stupid:

A YA rom-com about a girl in love with a boy who's been dead for a hundred years. (This one is all vibes and no plot, and based largely on my undergraduate crush on Nathan Hale's statue on campus.)

A pair of lovers who are reincarnated century after century into the same iteration of their tragic story until they can find a way to break the cycle. (The premise is cool, but it's too daunting to research so many different historical periods. I mean, what's cute about the 1700s?)

A girl murdered by an ex-boyfriend who comes back as a ghost and who tries to save his next victim, but she keeps failing, and eventually the murdered girls form this ghost posse that at last succeeds in putting the guy in jail. (Okay, that one has promise, but Netflix just aired a modern Bluebeard retelling, and I don't want to be accused of plagiarism again.)

I browse through Wikipedia and Encyclopedia Britannica, looking for promising nuggets of history to expand on. Maybe I could write about the missing Chinese survivors of the *Titanic*. Or the panhandlers of Gold Mountain. Or the NYPD Oriental Gang Unit—they were called the Jade Squad, and that'd be a fucking cool name for a title, wouldn't it? Or the Chinese mafia—Patrick Radden Keefe wrote a great nonfiction book about a Chinese snakehead who operated out of New York City for years. What if I did a fictionalized version of her life?

Why the obsession with China, though? Why am I limiting myself? Shouldn't it be equally viable to write about Russian immigrants, or African refugees? I never wanted to pigeonhole my writing brand to China; it only happened that way by accident. I think one of my grandparents or great-grandparents might have been Jewish; I could call up one of my aunts to ask, use that as a bridge to Jewish history and mythology. And I know for a fact that my mother's spoken about having some Cherokee heritage before. Maybe that's worth interrogating—maybe there's a story here about discovering connections I didn't even know I had.

Truth be told, I'm intimidated by the work involved. Since I've already done all that research for *The Last Front*, Chinese-inspired stories seem a bit easier. I already know so much about the history, about the current political touchpoints involved. I already speak the critical vocabulary; all I need is a hook.

I once met a poet who carried a tiny notebook everywhere she went and wrote down at least one quippy observation about every encounter she had throughout the day. *The barista's hair was a desperate shade of purple. The woman at the table beside her drew out the word "yes" like a stalling tactic. The boss's name slid off the doorman's tongue like rusty pennies.*

"I don't create so much as I collect," explained the poet. "The world is already so rich. All I do is distill the messiness of human life into a concentrated reading experience."

I try the same thing on a day running errands around DC. I record some thoughts on the dry cleaner—*crowded, efficient, owner is either Greek or Russian and is it racist that I can't tell which?*—and in the K Street Trader Joe's—*every time she came here, the shelves seemed full of organic promise, but she always inevitably left with the same bag of ginger snaps and microwave fettuccini.* I feel very Scholarly and Observant while I'm scribbling at the checkout counter, but when I get home,

I can't find the spark in anything I've produced. It's all so bland. No one wants to read about the culinary politics of Trader Ming's.

I need to go further. I need to write about things that white people don't see on a daily basis.

The next afternoon, I take the green line out to Chinatown, which—despite having lived in DC for nearly five years—I've actually never been to. I'm a bit apprehensive because I saw on Reddit that DC's Chinatown has the highest crime rates in the city, and when I get out of the metro station, the whole place does carry a menacing air of neglect. I walk with my hands shoved into my pockets, fingers tightly wrapped around my phone and wallet. I wish I'd brought pepper spray.

Stop being such a nervous white girl, I scold myself. *Real people live here; it's not a war zone.* I can't learn their stories if I'm acting like a jumpy tourist.

I stroll past the Calvary Baptist Church and snap a photo of the Friendship Archway, which welcomes me to Chinatown in resplendent shades of turquoise and gold. I don't know what the characters on the middle placard say; I'll have to look that up later.

Otherwise, Chinatown doesn't have much to offer in the cultural sphere. I stroll past a Starbucks, a Ruby Tuesday, a Rita's, and a Bed Bath & Beyond. These stores all have Chinese names hanging over their doorways in proud gold or red calligraphy, but on the inside, they carry the same stuff you'd find anywhere else. Weirdly, I don't see a lot of Chinese people around. I'd read an article a while back arguing that DC Chinatown had been viciously gentrified, but I hadn't expected it to look so much like any DC block.

I'm starving, so I duck into the first casual eatery I see—a shop called Mr. Shen's Dumplings, its English name barely visible among the Chinese signs and TripAdvisor clippings that crowd the display window. The place feels a little run-down. The tables are chipped, the windows greasy. But isn't that the mark of an authentic Chinese restaurant? I remember reading this on Twitter once. If a Chinese food joint expends no effort on its aesthetic, that's a sign the food is amazing. Or that the owners don't give a shit.

I'm the only person inside. That's not necessarily a bad sign. It's four in the afternoon; too late for lunch, too early for dinner. A waitress wordlessly places a dirty-looking cup of water and a plastic menu before me, then walks off.

I glance around, feeling stupid. I'm clearly intruding on the employees' off hours between meals, and I feel awkward taking up so much space. There's nothing I want to eat here. The menu consists entirely of different kinds of soup dumplings. I don't know what a soup dumpling is, but it sounds gross. The strong, musty, dumpster-like smell wafting from the kitchen doors is killing my appetite.

"Are you ready?" The waitress pops up at my side, pen and pad in hand.

"Oh—sorry, yeah." I pause, then point to the first thing I see on the menu. I guess it'd be rude to walk out at this point. "Can I get, um, the pork-and-leek dumplings?"

"Six or twelve?"

"Six."

"Boiled or pan-fried?"

"Uh—boiled?"

"Got it." She grabs my menu and heads back off behind the kitchen without another word.

What a bitch, I think, but then I remember that bad service is one of the hallmarks of good Chinese food, according to that one tweet. These soup dumplings had better be out of this world.

I try to focus on the positives. I can find some good narrative potential here, if I pay attention. Maybe this is the heartwarming story of a Chinatown restaurant going out of business, until the owner's daughter quits her soulless corporate job to turn the family business around with the help of the community, social media, and a magic, talking dragon. Maybe I can give my bitchy waitress a sympathetic backstory and a personality makeover. Or maybe not. The more I think about it, the more this sounds like the plots of *Ratatouille* and *Mulan* combined.

Stop looking through the white gaze, I caution myself. I can't make up stories about these people without knowing a thing about them. I have to talk to the locals. Make friends, understand where they're coming from, learn the quirky details that only Chinese Americans could know.

The only other person in sight is a middle-aged man wiping down the tables behind me. I figure he's as good a place to start as any.

I clear my throat and wave him over.

"What's your name?" My voice sounds artificially bright and cheery, and I try to rearrange my features into something neutral, or at least less creepy. I took an investigative journalism class back in high school, and I remember some of the tips: establish a friendly relationship, listen and watch attentively, maintain direct eye contact, and ask clear and open-ended questions. I wish I'd remembered to start an iPhone recording. I'm supposed to take down quotes as we're talking, but I don't want to have my pen and notebook out in case that intimidates him.

"Sorry, ma'am." He puts down the rag and walks toward me. "Is there a problem?"

"Oh no, no, I just, um, wanted to chat for a little, if you have the time."

I wince as the words leave my mouth. Why is this so uncomfortable? I feel like I'm doing something naughty, like speaking without permission to someone else's child. But that's ridiculous. What's wrong with a friendly conversation?

The waiter just stands there, watching me expectantly, so I blurt, "So, do you like living in Chinatown?"

"DC Chinatown?" He shrugs. "It's not really a Chinatown. Perhaps a simulacrum of Chinatown. I live out in Maryland, actually."

His English is a lot better than I expected. His accent is heavy, but what kind of new English speaker uses the word "simulacrum"? I wonder briefly if these accents are put on to convey authenticity to white customers. I wonder also if he's one of those professors or doctors who immigrated to the United States because he offended his home government. Either could be a fun plot twist. "So how long have you worked here?"

He pauses a moment to think. "Oh, maybe nine years now. Ten. My wife wanted to go to California, but I wanted to be near our daughter. Maybe we will move when she graduates."

"Oh, cool," I say. "Does your daughter go to Georgetown?"

"George Washington. Studying economics." He picks up his rag and turns halfway back to the other tables. I don't want to lose him, so I blurt, "So, how do you like working in this restaurant? Do you have any interesting stories—about, um, working in this restaurant?"

"Excuse me, can I help you?"

The waitress strides out from the kitchen. She glances between us, eyes narrowed, and then tells the older man something quick and terse in Chinese. His response sounds lackadaisical—I think maybe he's saying something like *take it easy*, but her tone grows higher, more urgent. Finally, shrugging, he tosses the rag on the table and retreats behind the kitchen doors.

The waitress turns to me. "If there's a problem, I'm happy to help."

"Oh, no, it's okay, I'm just trying to make conversation." I wave my hands in apology. "Sorry, I realize he's probably busy."

"Yes, we're all quite busy. I am sorry it's a bit quiet in here, but you're going to have to let the waitstaff do their jobs."

I roll my eyes. I'm the only customer here; how overworked could they be? "Okay," I say, as dismissively as possible.

She doesn't leave. "Any other questions?"

Her voice wobbles. She's *scared*. I realize suddenly what this looks like—she must think that I'm police or ICE, that I'm trying to bust the old guy. "Oh my God." I flap my hands in front of me to—to what, to prove I don't have a gun, or a badge? "No, it's not like that—"

"Then what's it like?" She looks me up and down, then cocks her head. "Wait, aren't you that writer?"

My heart skips a beat. I've never been recognized before in a place that wasn't a bookstore or a speaking event. I'm momentarily flattered, and some part of me thinks she's about to ask for my autograph. "I—um, yeah, I'm Juniper—"

"You're that girl who stole Athena Liu's work." Her face hardens. "I knew it—I've seen your photo online. Juniper Song, right? Or Hayward, or whatever. What do you want?"

"I'm just trying to make conversation," I say weakly. "I promise, I'm not out to—"

"I don't care," she says curtly. "I don't know what you're trying to do here, but we want no part of it. Actually, I'm going to have to ask you to leave."

She probably doesn't have the right to kick me out. I'm not causing a public disturbance; I haven't done anything illegal. All I did was make casual conversation with a waiter. I consider standing my ground, enforcing my rights as a customer, insisting that they call the police if they want to remove me. But I'd rather not go viral for yet another reason. I can imagine the YouTube title: "Chinatown Karen Insists She's Not ICE."

"Fine." I stand up. "Don't bother with my dumplings, then."

"You sure?" asks the waitress. "We don't do refunds. That's eight ninety-five, plus tax."

My face burns. My mind races to come up with some quippy response, but I can't think of anything that isn't pathetic or plain racist. Instead I dig a twenty out of my wallet, sling my bag over my shoulder, and push past her to the door, pretending not to hear the amused snorts behind me as I storm out.

BRETT STARTS BUGGING ME ABOUT A MONTH INTO MY CREATIVE DESert. I can tell he's been trying to give me space—all his emails so far have been gentle, tactfully worded nudges—but clearly, he's running out of patience.

Want to run a new opportunity by you, reads his latest missive. Call when convenient.

I groan, then reach for my phone.

He picks up on the first ring. "June! Good to hear from you. How've you been?"

"All right. The hate mail has stopped, mostly. Not getting death threats anymore."

"Well, that's good. I told you it would blow over." He pauses. "And, uh, regarding what we last discussed—"

"There's nothing." I figure it's best to just spit it out. "I've got nothing, not a single idea. I don't even know where to start. Sorry, I know that's not what you want to hear."

I feel a twinge of guilt. It's not about the money for Brett. His reputation is on the line, too; he doesn't want to burn bridges with the Eden editorial team by bringing them their most embarrassing client by far. But I can't give false hope where there is none.

I brace myself for Brett's disappointment. Instead he asks promptly, "Then what about IP work?"

I suppress a scoff. IP—intellectual property—work is for mediocre writers, or so I've always been told. It's cheap, work-for-hire labor for people who couldn't manage to sell their original projects. "What about it?"

"All I mean is, if you're having trouble coming up with your own concept, what about writing to an outline?"

"What, like a superhero novel? No thanks, Brett, I still have *standards*—"

"It's just—it's been a while, June. People are getting impatient."

"Donna Tartt spends a decade in between novels," I sniff.

"Well." Brett doesn't state the obvious: that I'm not Donna Tartt. "Circumstances are different."

I sigh. "What's the IP? Marvel? Disney?" I could go for a *Star*

Wars novel, maybe. I mean, it sounds very difficult, and I'd have to really dig deep into my nerd past to make myself care about whatever bit character they fling my way, but I could make something work. At least well enough to fool the average, undiscerning fanboy who buys those books.

"Actually, it wouldn't be for an existing franchise. Have you ever heard of Snowglobe?"

The name rings a bell. I've seen that word floating around Twitter—perhaps their account followed me recently—but otherwise I can't connect it with anything important. "Are they some kind of book packaging company? Like, a vanity press?"

"Well, they do all sorts of things. The founders have connections with both publishing houses and film studios. They work with editors to develop ideas that suit the market's current needs, and then they work with writers to create them. It takes the guesswork out of what editors at big publishers are looking for. And you'd have plenty of creative flexibility to really take on the idea, you know, and make it your own."

"I wouldn't own the copyright, though?" I don't know much about IP, but from what I've read online, it's usually a rough deal for the creator. Unlike original properties, for which you own the copyright and receive royalties, IP writers are typically only paid a flat fee up front. A novel for a popular video game franchise, for example, might sell tens of thousands of copies. But even if it was a runaway bestseller, the hired writer might never see more than ten thousand dollars. That's not incredible pay for six to eight months of work. "And people don't take IP seriously, do they? Like, it's not *serious* literary work."

"Many beloved titles are IP," says Brett. "It's just not common knowledge that they are. And anyways, it wouldn't be a permanent career move, just something to help you get over this slump. It seems like you might do better if you have . . . some preexisting scaffold."

I hate the way he puts that. Like it's a joke between us, like he knows the truth about *The Last Front. Wink wink, hint hint, Junie. We know you can paint by the numbers. Let's find you a new coloring book.*

To be fair, it's not the worst idea in the world. But my pride rankles at the thought. I've been in the running for some of the top literary prizes in the country; I can't imagine going from that to doing work for hire. "I'm assuming the pay would be awful."

"Well, they're willing to negotiate, especially for such a high-profile author. But yes, the royalties wouldn't be as high as you're used to."

"Then what's the point?"

"Well, you'd have a new book out. So you'd have something new to talk about. Something to move the conversation along."

Well played, Brett. Fair point. I can't help but ask: "And what's the pitch?"

He can't tell me right away. I have to sign an NDA first, but fortunately he has one ready, and he just needs to send me a DocuSign link. While he's getting that sorted, I look up Snowglobe and browse through their company website. The founders are all young, sleek-looking white women; the kind I see prowling around industry functions all the time, chardonnay in hand. On their "Current Projects" page, I see production deals listed with Amazon, Hulu, and Netflix. I've actually heard of a few of their titles—Brett was right, I really had no idea how many popular projects were actually IP. Maybe this wouldn't be so bad. Maybe it *would* be easier to let someone come up with what the market wants, so that I can focus on what I'm good at, which is writing beautifully.

"Okay." The NDA is signed; Brett is back on the line. "So they're really interested in tapping into your expertise on Chinese social issues, right?"

I feel an inkling of dread. "Okay . . ."

"And you know about the one-child policy, right?"

"Uh, the one where they forced women to have abortions?"

"No, I mean the population control policy in China introduced in 1978." He's reading this off of Wikipedia. I know, because I've just pulled up the same Wikipedia page.

"That's what I said, though. They were forcing women to have abortions." I do a quick search for the word "abortion" to check that I'm right, and I am, sort of. "They want a novel about *that*?"

"Well, they want a sort of modern twist on it. So the problem with the one-child policy is that there are way too many men in China, right? Because of selective abortions. Parents preferred to have boys, because it's a patriarchal culture, and all that, so there are lots of missing girls and women. Therefore it's hard for Chinese men to find wives, or to have children of their own. See the stakes so far?"

"Uh, sure."

"That's where the dystopian twist comes in. Imagine a world similar to *The Handmaid's Tale*. Women are raised in institutions, born and bred to be baby-makers, and they're sold to their husbands as house slaves." Brett gives a nervous chuckle. "Pretty sharp commentary, right? You could even broaden out the themes to make it a subtle critique of Western patriarchy, if you wanted to. Up to you.

Like I said, you'd have lots of flexibility to play with the concept. What do you think?"

I'm silent for a long time. Then, because one of us has to say it out loud, "Brett, that's idiotic. No one in their right mind is going to want to work on that."

(I'm wrong, in fact. Two weeks after this conversation, I will open Twitter in my browser to read the following announcement: "Simon & Schuster in partnership with Snowglobe, Inc., is so excited to have signed with renowned author Heidi Steel for the publication of *The Last Woman in China*, a thrilling romance set in a dystopian world inspired by the one-child policy!")

"I mean, I really think this could work," says Brett. "It's a cool concept. It gets you the feminist crowd. That's your book club market. And there's a lot of film potential here—I'm sure networks will be hunting for the next big thing once *The Handmaid's Tale* wraps up."

"But the *story* idea—I mean, that's conflating so many different . . . like, are they serious? The one-child policy meets *The Handmaid's Tale*? They're not worried we're going to offend, like, all of China?"

"Well, the book's going to be published in the West, Junie. So who really cares?"

I can see Adele Sparks-Sato and Xiao Chen sharpening their claws. I'm not that up to date with Chinese politics, but even I can spot the land mines just *glowing* around this thing. If I write this, I'll be eviscerated for hating the PRC, or Chinese people, or men, or all three.

"Absolutely not," I say. "This is a nonstarter. Don't they have any other ideas? Like, I'm not opposed to working with Snowglobe per se, I just really hate this one pitch."

"Well, they do, but they're tailoring their pitches to authors of the right . . . backgrounds. They're making a big pivot toward diversity this year."

I snort. "Baffling that they want me, then."

"Come on," says Brett. "At least take a look at the treatment. I've just sent it over. And you did get your start in speculative fiction, so you already have a built-in fan base . . ."

I'm not sure that Brett understands that the people who are into magical realism are so not into near-future science fiction of this sort. "Okay, but you've got to admit a dystopia set in Beijing is pretty far out of my wheelhouse."

"A few years ago, I would have said a project like *The Last Front* was pretty far out of your wheelhouse. It's never too late to broaden your horizons. Just think about it, Junie. This could rescue your career."

"No, it won't." I'm not sure whether I want to laugh or cry. "No, Brett, I'm pretty sure this is the sort of thing that ends careers."

"June. Come on. We might not get an opportunity like this again."

"Call me if, like, Lucasfilm gets on the line," I say. "But I'm sorry, Brett. Even I'm not stooping that low."

Eighteen

IN JULY, I PACK MY BAGS AND FLY UP NORTH TO TEACH AT THE Young AAPI Writers' Workshop in Massachusetts. It's the only program that's invited me back for the season, and likely only because I'm still paying for that stupid annual scholarship in Athena's name (the workshop is funded and hosted by the Asian American Writers' Collective, and Peggy Chan is the coordinator of both). My other regular engagements have dried up since the Adele Sparks-Sato blog hit. Last summer, I was booked week to week with keynote talks and guest lectureships; this summer, there's nothing on my calendar between May and August.

I strongly considered canceling on the YAWW, but ultimately I couldn't face an otherwise endless, monotonous summer. Any distraction seemed better than pacing my apartment all day, trying and failing to write a single word. Besides, I'm hoping this might be good for me. Teaching is an unassailably noble calling, and even if this doesn't redeem me in the public eye, it might at the very least build bridges with a group of students who haven't decided yet that I'm a public enemy. It might make writing fun again.

I'm assigned to lead a daily, four-hour critique session with the select class: all high school upperclassmen I handpicked on the strength of their writing samples. It's fascinating to meet them in person. I spot the big personalities in the group immediately: there's Christina Yee, a tiny goth girl with very pronounced black eyeliner whose writing sample involved lots of body horror and teeth; Johnson Chen, who sports gelled-up hair and eighties-style overcoats like some K-pop singer, and whose navel-gazing writing sample had led me to believe he was an ugly duckling but he is actually quite clearly a chick magnet; and Skylar Zhao, a tall and leggy rising senior who, during introductions, declares her intentions to be her generation's Athena Liu.

They slouch casually like they don't care how they're perceived, but I can tell how badly they want to impress me. They've got the classic fledgling talent mentality—they know they're good, or could be good, but they crave acknowledgment of this fact, and they're terrified of rejection. I remember this mix of feelings well: unbridled ambition, a growing pride that one's own work might in fact be *that* remarkable, paired with staggering, incurable insecurity. The resulting personality is astoundingly annoying, but I sympathize with these kids. They're just like myself, ten years ago. A well-phrased barb right now could irreparably destroy their confidence. But the right words of encouragement could help them fly.

This summer, I've decided I'll try to be that for them. I'll put the rest of the world aside. I'll stop checking Twitter, stop browsing Reddit, and stop agonizing over my own writing. I'll focus on doing this one thing that I might be good at.

The introductions go well. I use the same icebreakers I've picked up over years of creative writing classes: What's your favorite book? ("*Voice and Echo*," declares Skylar Zhao, citing Athena's debut. "*Lolita*," Christina responds, chin jutted out as if in challenge. "By Nabokov?") What's a book that would be perfect if you could rewrite the ending? ("*Anna Karenina*," declares Johnson. "Only Anna wouldn't kill herself.") We construct a short story by going around the room, each adding a sentence to the one that came before. We speed-revise that story in under five minutes. We play with different interpretations of the same line of dialogue: "I *never* said that we should kill *him*!"

By the end of the hour, we're all laughing and making inside jokes. We are no longer quite so scared of one another. I round out the session by hosting an AMA about the publishing industry—they're all eager to know what it's like to query agents, to have a book go to auction, and to work with a real, actual editor. The clock strikes four. I give them some homework—rewrite a passage by Dickens using no adverbs or adjectives—and they cheerfully slide their laptops into their backpacks as they stand up to leave.

"Thanks, Junie," they tell me on their way out the door. "You're the best." I smile and nod at each one of them as they depart, feeling like a wise, kind mentor.

THAT NIGHT I SCARF DOWN A SALAD FROM THE DINING HALL, THEN head to the nearest coffee shop and scribble out a half-dozen story ideas—descriptive paragraphs, experimental structures, crucial bits of dialogue, whatever comes to mind. I write so fast my hand cramps. I'm buzzing with creative energy. My students made stories seem so rich, elastic, full of infinite variations. Maybe my gears aren't irreparably jammed. Maybe I only needed to remember how good it feels to create.

After an hour of scribbling, I sit back to survey my work, scanning the pages for anything I might expand into an outline. On second glance, though, these ideas don't seem quite as fresh or scintillating. They are, in fact, slightly modified versions of my students' writing samples. A girl who can't get her mother's approval no matter how well she does at school. A boy who hates his aloof, taciturn father, until he learns the sort of war trauma that shaped his father's past. A pair of siblings who travel to Taiwan for the first time and reconnect with their heritage, even though they can't pronounce anything right and they don't like the food.

I snap my notebook shut in disgust. Is this all I can manage now? Stealing from fucking children?

It's fine, I tell myself. *Calm down.* All that matters is that I'm greasing the gears; I'm getting back into the zone. I've sparked a flame that I haven't felt in a very long time. I have to be patient with myself, to give that flame time and space to grow.

On my way back to the dormitory, I glimpse my students through the window of Mimi's, one of the many bubble tea cafés near campus. The twelve of them are crowded around a table meant for six; so many chairs pulled up that they each get only a little bit of table space. They seem totally comfortable around one another, hunched over their laptops and notebooks. They're writing—perhaps working on my homework assignment. I watch as they show one another snippets of work, laughing at funny turns of phrase, nodding appreciatively as they take turns reading out loud.

God, I miss that.

It has been so long since I thought of writing as a communal activity. All the published writers I know are so cagey about their writing schedules, their advances, and their sales numbers. They hate divulging information about their career trajectories, just in case someone else shows them up. They hate even more to share details about their works in progress, terrified that someone will scoop their ideas and publish before they can. It's a world of difference from my undergraduate days, when Athena and I would crowd around a library table late at night with our classmates, talking over metaphors and character development and plot twists until I couldn't tell anymore where my stories ended and theirs began.

Perhaps that's the price of professional success: isolation from jealous peers. Perhaps, once writing becomes a matter of individual advancement, it's impossible to share with anyone else.

I stand by the window of Mimi's perhaps longer than I ought to, watching wistfully as my students joke around. One of them—Skylar—glances up and almost sees me, but I duck my head down and stride quickly off toward the dorms.

I'M A FEW MINUTES LATE TO CLASS THE NEXT MORNING. THE LINE AT the campus Starbucks was moving at a glacial pace, and I discovered why when I got to the counter, where a girl with pink hair and two nose piercings struggled for nearly five minutes to input my very simple order. When I finally reach the classroom, all my students are crowded around Skylar's laptop, giggling. They don't notice as I walk in.

"Look," says Skylar. "There's even a sentence-by-sentence comparison of the first few paragraphs of both stories."

Christina leans forward. *"Noooo."*

"And there's an NLP comparison—look, here."

I know without asking: they've found Adele Sparks-Sato's blog report.

"They think all of *The Last Front* is stolen, too," says Johnson. "Look, the paragraph right after. There's a quote from a former editorial assistant at Eden; she says it always felt fishy—"

"You think she took it right out of her apartment? Like, the night she died?"

"Oh my God," says Skylar, delighted and horrified. "That's diabolical."

"Do you think she killed her?"

"Oh my God, don't—"

I clear my throat. "Good morning."

Their heads pop up. They look like startled rabbits. Skylar slams her laptop shut. I stride cheerfully to the front of the room, Starbucks in hand, trying my hardest to keep from trembling.

"How's everyone doing?" I don't know why I'm doing this oblivious bit. They all know I heard them. Their faces have turned a uniform scarlet; none of them will meet my eye. Skylar sits with her hand pressed against her mouth, exchanging panicked looks with a girl named Celeste.

"That bad, huh?" I nod to Johnson. "How was your evening, Johnson? How'd the homework go?"

He stammers out something about Dickens's verbosity, which gives me time to decide how I want to handle this. There's the honest route, which is to explain to them the details of the controversy, tell them the same thing I told my editors, and let them make up their own minds. It'll be an object lesson in the social economy of publishing, in how social media distorts and inflames the truth. Maybe they'll walk away with more respect for me.

Or I could make them regret this.

"Skylar?" My voice sounds more like a bark than I intended. Skylar flinches like she's been shot. "It's your story we're critiquing today, isn't it?"

"I—uh, yeah."

"So where are your printouts?"

Skylar blinks. "I mean, I emailed it to everyone."

I requested in the workshop guidelines that the subject of critique bring printed copies of their story to class. We've been using laptops since last year, though, and I know it's unfair to rip Skylar for it, but it's the first knock I can think of. "I made my expectations very clear in the handouts. Perhaps you don't think the rules apply to you, Skylar, but that attitude won't get you very far in publishing. Keep thinking you're the exception, and you'll end up like one of those creeps who corner editors in bathrooms and slide manuscripts under doors into hotel rooms because they don't think the industry guidelines apply."

This wins me a couple of snickers. Skylar's face goes white as paper.

"Are you going to corner editors in bathrooms, Skylar?"

"No," she drawls, rolling her eyes. She's trying to play it cool, but I can hear her voice quiver. "Obviously not."

"Good. So print your manuscript next time. That goes for all of you." I take a long, satisfying sip of my Very Berry Hibiscus Refresher. My knees are still trembling, but this verbal putdown gives me a rush of hot, spiteful confidence. "Well, let's get to it. Rexy, what did you think of Skylar's story?"

Rexy swallows. "I, uh, liked it."

"On what grounds?"

"Well, it's interesting."

" 'Interesting' is a word people use when they can't think of anything better to say. Be specific, Rexy."

That sets the tone for the rest of the morning. I used to think that mean teachers were a special kind of monster, but it turns out that cruelty comes naturally. Also, it's fun. Teenagers, after all, are unformed identities with undeveloped brains. No matter how clever they are, they still don't know much about anything, and it's easy to embarrass them for their ill-prepared remarks.

Skylar gets the worst of it. Technically her story—a whodunnit set in San Francisco's Chinatown, in which none of the witnesses will cooperate with the police because they have their own secrets and community codes of honor—is not bad. The writing is strong, the conceit is interesting, and there's even a clever twist at the end that makes you reevaluate every previous word uttered by the characters. It's very impressive for a high schooler. Still, her inexperience shows. Skylar's exposition is clumsy in parts, she makes use of quite a few contrived coincidences to move the story along, and she hasn't figured out how to toe the line between tense and histrionic dialogue.

I could gently correct these tendencies while encouraging Skylar to think up the solutions herself.

"And then, again, there's a lawyer on the scene out of nowhere." I tap the page. "Do lawyers grow on trees, Skylar? Maybe they have a spidey sense for marital discomfort?"

Then: "Do Chloe and Christopher have a weird incest thing going on, or is that just how you've chosen to portray all of their sibling interactions?"

Then: "Does every single Chinese person in this neighborhood know each other, or did you just find that convenient for the plot?"

Then: "I wonder if there's any better imagery you can use for sexual tension than literally biting into a strawberry."

Then: " 'She let out a breath she didn't know she was holding.' *Really?*"

By the end of it I've convinced most of the class that Skylar's story is horrible—whether they agree, or whether they're scared of invoking my ire, I don't care. We've picked her voice and style to shreds. Her metaphors are unoriginal, her dialogue is wooden (at one point I even make Johnson and Celeste act out a scene, just to highlight how cringey it sounds out loud), her plot twists are all borrowed from readily recognizable pop-culture sources, and she overuses her em dashes and semicolons to the extreme. By the end of our session, Skylar is close to tears. She has stopped nodding, frowning, or reacting to any bits of criticism whatsoever. She merely stares out the window, lower lip trembling, fingers twisting the top page of her notebook into tiny pieces.

I've won. It's a pathetic victory, sure, but it's better than sitting here and suffering their mocking glares.

That hot, vicious satisfaction stays with me through the rest of the morning. I conclude the critique circle, assign homework, and watch them flee wordlessly out the door.

I've only made things worse, I know. Now I'll have to sit before their resentful, condescending faces for another week and a half. I'm sure that, behind the scenes, they'll bitch about me endlessly until this workshop is over. I'm sure they'll join the chorus of Juniper Song haters online. But I've at least made myself into a terror rather than a punch line, and for now, I'm all right with that.

Once they've left the classroom, I pull out my phone and Google "Candice Lee Juniper Song Athena Liu." Johnson's words have been stuck in my mind all morning: *There's a quote from a former editorial assistant at Eden; she says it always felt fishy.*

My breath quickens with fear as the results load. What does Candice have on me?

But the relevant article—another tiresome Adele Sparks-Sato hit piece—contains nothing new. Candice offers no damning evidence, no new shreds of proof that haven't been overanalyzed to bits by the internet already. Just a vague quote that means nothing much at all.

I close the article and scroll through her social media accounts. Candice's Instagram is private; her Twitter has been inactive since last March. Her LinkedIn, however, announces she's recently taken on a new job as an editorial assistant at a small press based in Oregon.

My fear dissipates. No new developments, then. My line of careful deniability still holds, and Candice's quote is just the vague finger-pointing of a jealous ex–publishing insider.

Also, *Oregon*? I can't help but do some petty Googling. Candice's new employer puts out maybe ten litfic titles a year, none of which I've ever heard of, and none of which have broken even a hundred reviews on Goodreads. Half of them aren't even proper novels; they're *chapbooks*. They can't possibly be selling enough copies to stay afloat—she might as well be working at a vanity press. It's a drastic step down from her former job at Eden. I doubt she's even making a full-time salary.

Well, at least there's some cosmic justice in the world. It's a tiny victory, but it's the only thing just then that helps this rage in my chest cool down.

PEGGY CHAN GIVES ME A RING LATER THAT AFTERNOON.

"Several students complained about your behavior in workshop today," she says. "And, June, based on some of the reports, I'm concerned—"

"It was a heated workshop," I say. "Skylar Zhao is a talented writer, but she doesn't know how to take criticism. I wonder, actually, if this is the first time she's had to confront the fact that her writing isn't as wonderful as she thinks it is."

"You didn't say anything untoward to the students?"

"Not that I recall."

"A few of the students said it seemed you were bullying Skylar. June, we have a very strict antibullying policy in this workshop. There are things you can say to adults that you can't say to high school students. They are fragile—"

"Oh, they're certainly fragile."

"If you're available, June, I'd like you to come to the office—"

"Actually, Peggy . . ." I pause, then sigh. A few possible explanations flash through my mind. Skylar is oversensitive, she's making things up, she's the one who provoked me in the first place, she's turned the class against me. But then I take stock of the whole situation, and it's astoundingly pathetic. I don't need to engage in a she-said, she-said battle with a seventeen-year-old. I'm too big for this.

"I think I'm going to have to leave," I blurt. "Sorry, that's probably not the news you were expecting. But my mother—I've just heard that she's not doing so well—"

"Oh, June. I am very sorry to hear that."

"—and she's been asking if I can come visit, but I keep putting it off for work, and I thought, *Well, she's not always going to be around . . .*" I trail off, rather astounded by my brazen lie. My mother isn't sick at all. She's doing fine. "So perhaps it's the stress of that situation that is affecting my conduct, and for that I truly apologize . . ."

"I understand." Peggy doesn't seem the least bit suspicious. If anything, she sounds eager. Perhaps she, too, has been secretly hoping I would quit on my own.

I egg her along. "I'm sorry to leave the class . . ."

"Oh, we'll figure it out. There are some local writers in the area. We'll have to find a substitute for tomorrow, so I might ask Rachel from the office to step in . . ." She trails off. "Anyhow, we'll deal with it. We'll tell the class you had a family emergency. I'm sure they'll be disappointed, but they'll understand."

"Thank you, Peggy. That means a lot. I'm sorry for the inconvenience."

"You take care, June. I'm sorry again."

I hang up, then flop back onto my bed and groan in relief.

That was agonizing, but at least I'm free. I once read somewhere that Asian people are so polite because they have this cultural concept of letting each other save face. They might be judging the shit out of you on the inside, but on the outside, at least, they'll let you walk away with your pride intact.

Nineteen

AS IT TURNS OUT, I DO GO TO SEE MY MOTHER.

Mom lives in a suburb outside Philly—near enough to Boston that I can get on the Amtrak and be there by lunchtime the next day. I have to root around my phone for her street address—I haven't been to the Philly house in years, and I never see Mom outside of our yearly Christmas and Thanksgiving gatherings at Rory's. I'm sure this spur-of-the-moment visit is a product of vulnerability, motivated by fear and childlike regression. I'm also sure, past the initial hugs and tenderness, that I'll regret coming at all; that once the "I've missed you" and "You look good!" chatter turns to the same overcontrolling, patronizing comments that have spiraled into blowout fights in the past, I'll hop on the train and hurtle back to DC.

Right now, though, I just want to be near someone who doesn't hate me on principle.

Mom's waiting for me on the front porch when I pull up. I called a few hours ago to ask if I could come stay for a bit. She agreed without even asking what was going on. I wonder how much she knows; if she's seen my name smeared all over the internet.

"Hey, Junie." She envelops me in a hug, and the touch alone makes my eyes sting with tears. No one's hugged me in so long. "Is everything all right?"

"Yeah, of course—I was teaching a workshop in Boston, and it's just finished, so I thought I'd make a pit stop here before I head back home."

"Well, you're always welcome here." Mom turns, and I follow her into the house. She doesn't ask how the workshop went. Her blatant disinterest in anything that has to do with writing always stung when I was younger, but today, it's a comfort. "Watch your step, though—sorry about the mess."

The path to the kitchen is covered in half-empty cardboard boxes; blankets, bunched-up newspapers, and towels are strewn across the tiles. "What's going on?"

"I'm just putting some of the clutter in storage—careful around those vases. The Realtor said it'll look nicer without all this stuff in the way."

I pick my way around an array of white ceramic cats. "You're selling the house?"

"I've been getting it ready for a while," says Mom. "I'm headed back to Melbourne. Wanted to be closer to my girls. Cheryl's closing on a condo for me this week—there's plenty of guest rooms, you'll be able to visit. Rory didn't tell you?"

No, she didn't. I've known that Mom has wanted to go back to Florida ever since Dad died, that Philadelphia was only ever a compromise because my grandparents lived close by, but I never connected that with the real possibility that we might not call this place home anymore.

I suppose Rory never felt such a deep connection to this house, though. I was the one obsessed with the sycamore trees in the backyard, with hiding out among their roots and spinning stories long after Rory decided it was time to return to the real world.

"Did you pack my room up yet?"

"I've just gotten started," says Mom. "I was going to put most of your things in storage, but why don't you go see if there's anything you want? Give me some time to wrap up this porcelain, and then we'll meet back down here for dinner."

"I—oh, sure, okay." I pause on the staircase before I go up. I keep waiting for Mom to ask me what's going on, for her to intuit with her motherly senses that I'm deeply not all right. But she's already turned back toward those stupid ceramic cats.

MY NOTEBOOKS ARE RIGHT WHERE I LEFT THEM: STACKED AT THE TOP of my bookshelves in neat rows of five. They're each labeled with my name, the year, my phone number, and a ten-dollar reward offer if returned to the owner. No Moleskines here—my notebooks were always those college-ruled, black-and-white-splattered composition notebooks that you buy for ninety-nine cents at Walmart while your parents are doing back-to-school shopping. My dream worlds.

I pull them out and set them on the floor.

I used to live my entire life out of these notebooks. They're crammed with doodles I scribbled instead of listening during class; full-scale drawings I sketched out after school; half-finished scenes or story ideas or even fragments of lines of dialogue that came to me throughout the day. Nothing in these dream worlds ever became a fully formed product—I didn't have the discipline or craft skills then to write a complete novel. They're more like a smorgasbord of creative churning, half-formed doors to other worlds, worlds in which I lingered for hours when I didn't want to be in my own.

I flip through the pages, smiling. It's cute to see how derivative my story ideas were of whatever fandoms I was in at the time. Sixth grade: my *Twilight* phase, and I was clearly infatuated with Alice Cullen because I kept describing a protagonist with the same gravity-defying pixie cut. Ninth grade: my emo phase, and everything was Evanescence and Linkin Park lyrics. By then I'd begun sketching out some gothic, futuristic dystopian cityscape where kids flew around on skateboards and everyone had floppy, skunk-tail bangs and arm warmers. I guess Ayn Rand was an influence at some point in tenth grade, because by then I was writing paragraphs on paragraphs about a male lead named Howard Sharp, who bowed to no one, who had an unassailable sense of pride, who was a "lone believer in truth in a world of lies."

I spend the rest of the afternoon going through those notebooks. I don't notice the time slipping by until Mom calls upstairs asking if I want takeout for dinner, and it's only then that I realize the sun has set. I've lost myself for hours in those worlds.

I call down to Mom that takeout sounds fine. Then I root around for a cardboard box to load my notebooks into. I'll bring them back to my apartment and let them linger in the closet, maybe take them out whenever I'm feeling particularly nostalgic. They won't suit my current purposes—there's nothing there that I could turn into a sellable manuscript now. But they'll remind me, whenever I need it, that writing didn't used to be so miserable.

God, I miss my high school days, when I could flip my notebook open to an empty page and see possibility instead of frustration. When I took real pleasure in stringing words and sentences together just to see how they sounded. When writing was an act of sheer imagination, of taking myself away somewhere else, of creating something that was only for me.

I miss writing before I met Athena Liu.

But enter professional publishing, and suddenly writing is a matter of professional jealousies, obscure marketing budgets, and advances that don't measure up to those of your peers. Editors go in and mess around with your words, your vision. Marketing and publicity make you distill hundreds of pages of careful, nuanced reflection into cute, tweet-size talking points. Readers inflict their own expectations, not just on the story, but on your politics, your philosophy, your stance on all things ethical. You, not your writing, become the product—your looks, your wit, your quippy clapbacks and factional alignments with online beefs that no one in the real world gives a shit about.

And once you're writing for the market, it doesn't matter what stories are burning inside you. It matters what audiences want to see, and no one cares about the inner musings of a plain, straight white girl from Philly. They want the new and exotic, the *diverse*, and if I want to stay afloat, that's what I have to give them.

MOM ORDERS DINNER FROM GREAT WALL, THE LOCAL CHINESE PLACE.

"They're new," she informs me as I sit down. "Horrible service; I wouldn't go back there in person. It took me three tries just to get some water. But delivery is fast, and I like their orange chicken."

She opens a carton of rice and sets it before me. "You like Chinese food, right?"

I don't have the heart to tell her that it was Rory who liked Chinese, and that Chinese food makes my stomach roil, especially now, since that horrible club meeting in Rockville.

"Yeah, it's fine."

"I got you the Triple Buddha. Are you still vegetarian?"

"Oh, only sort of, but that's fine." I split my chopsticks open. "Thanks."

Mom, nodding, spoons some pork fried rice onto her plate and begins to eat.

We don't talk much. It's always been like this between us—either placid silence, or vicious fighting. There's no casual in-between, no common interests we can shoot the shit about. Whatever wildness Mom once possessed seems to have evaporated back in the eighties, when she was smoking pot and following bands around and naming her children things like Juniper Song and Aurora Whisper. She went back to work after Dad died, and since then has molded herself entirely into the American ideal of a working single mother: perfect attendance at her office job, perfect attendance at our parent-teacher meetings, just enough savings to put Rory and me through good schools with minimal student debt and to set up a retirement account for herself. The demands of such a hustle, it seems, left no room for creativity. She's the kind of suburban white mother who buys home living magazines at the grocery checkout counter, who drinks crate upon crate of four-dollar wines from Trader Joe's, who refers to *Twilight* as "those vampire books," and who hasn't read anything other than Costco discount paperbacks for decades.

Mom always got along better with Rory. I always got the sense that she didn't quite know what to do with me. It was Dad who could always follow me wherever my imagination went. But we don't talk about Dad.

We sit in silence for a while, chewing on egg rolls and stir-fried chicken bits so sweet they taste like candy. At last, Mom asks, "How's your, well, book writing going?"

Mom has always had the particular ability to reduce all my aspirations to trivial obsessions with a simple disinterested question.

I set down my chopsticks. "It's, uh, fine."

"Oh, that's good."

"Well, actually, I'm sort of . . ." I want to tell her why I've been so miserable these past few months, but I don't know where to begin. "I'm in a difficult place. Creatively. Like, I can't think of anything to write about."

"You mean like writer's block?"

"Sort of like that. Only usually I have all these tricks to break out of it. Writing exercises, listening to music, going on long walks and whatnot. It's not working this time."

Mom shoves some bits of chicken aside to snag a candied pecan. "Well, maybe it's time to move on, then."

"Mom."

"I'm just saying. Rory's friend can always get you into that class. You just have to fill out the application."

Mom has suggested that I do a master's in tax and accounting at American University every time I've seen her in the last four years. She's even gone so far as to print and mail me the application the summer after my debut novel flopped and I resorted to tutoring kids for the SAT to make rent.

"For the last time, I don't want to be an accountant."

"What's so wrong with being an accountant?"

"I've told you, I don't want to work an office job like you and Rory—"

I know what she'll say next. We've been hurling these lines at each other for years. "You're too good for office jobs? Junie the Yalie won't put in a hard day's work like the rest of us?"

"Mom, stop."

"Rory puts food on the table. Rory has a retirement account—"

"I make more than enough to live on," I snap. "I'm renting a one-bedroom in Rosslyn. I have insurance. I bought a new laptop. I'm probably richer than Rory, even—"

"Then what's the problem? What's so important about this next book?"

"I can't rely on my old work," I say, though I know I can't make her understand. "I need to write the next best thing. And then another. Otherwise the sales will whittle down, and people will stop reading my work, and everyone will forget about me." Saying this out loud makes me want to cry. I hadn't realized how much this terrified me: being unknown, being forgotten. I sniffle. "And then when I die, I won't have left any mark on the world. It'll be like I was never here at all."

Mom watches me for a long while, and then places her hand on my arm.

"Writing isn't the whole world, Junie. And there's plenty of careers that won't give you such constant heartbreak. That's all I'm saying."

But writing *is* the whole world. How can I explain this to her?

Stopping isn't an option. I *need* to create. It is a physical urge, a craving, like breathing, like eating; when it's going well, it's better than sex, and when it's not, I can't take pleasure in anything else.

Dad played the guitar during his off time; he understood. A musician needs to be heard; a writer needs to be read. I want to move people's hearts. I want my books in stores all over the world. I couldn't stand to be like Mom and Rory, living their little and self-contained lives, with no great projects or prospects to propel them from one chapter to the next. I want the world to wait with bated breath for what I will say next. I want my words to last forever. I want to be eternal, permanent; when I'm gone, I want to leave behind a mountain of pages that scream, *Juniper Song was here, and she told us what was on her mind.*

Only I don't know what it is I want to say anymore. I don't know if I ever did. And I'm terrified that the only thing I'll ever be remembered for, and the only method by which I can produce good work, is slipping on someone else's skin.

I don't want to only be the vessel for Athena's ghost.

"You could work with Aunt Cheryl," Mom suggests, oblivious. "She's still looking for an assistant. You could move out of DC—it's too expensive anyhow. Come down to Melbourne with me—you could buy a whole house in Suntree with your earnings. Rory showed me—"

I gape at her. "You asked Rory for my tax returns?"

"We were just planning for your future." Mom shrugs, unbothered. "So with what you have in savings now, it's smart that you make some property investments. Cheryl has a few houses in mind—"

"Jesus, it's precisely this . . ." I take a deep breath, force myself to calm down. Mom's been like this since I was a child. Nothing short of a brain transplant will change her now. "I don't want to have this conversation anymore."

"You have to be practical, Junie. You're young; you have assets. You've got to take advantage of them—"

"Okay, stop, please," I snap. "I know you've never supported my writing—"

She blinks. "Of course I supported your writing."

"No, you didn't. You hated it. You've always thought it was stupid, I get it—"

"Oh, no, Junie. I know what the arts are like. Not everyone's going to make it big." She rubs the top of my head, the way she did when I was a child, only now it doesn't feel remotely comforting. A gesture like this, between adult women, can only be patronizing. "And I just didn't want to see you get hurt."

Twenty

TWO DAYS LATER, I'M BACK IN DC, WITHOUT A SINGLE BOOK IDEA or any clue what to do.

When you've got a project in your jaws, a full-time writing schedule feels like a blessing. But when you're struggling to come up with a concept, the hours feel suffocating, accusatory. Time should be flying by as you sit wild-eyed at your laptop, possessed by the muse, pouring out your magnum opus. Instead the seconds creep to a halt.

I have nothing to do. Nothing to write, nothing with which to distract myself. Most days I occupy myself with housework, counting down the minutes until the distraction of my next mealtime. I water my plants. I arrange my mugs. I can make the ritual of consuming a microwave lasagna last for half an hour. I envy the barista at Starbucks, the clerks at Kramers; at least they can while away the days with their dignified menial labor.

I keep winding up on admissions pages of various graduate school programs. I don't filter for degrees in any one field in particular. I consider them all—law, social work, education, even accounting—because they all promise a gateway into a wholly different life, after an appropriately long period of educational hand-holding in which I don't have to do any thinking for myself.

I even consider returning to the Veritas College Institute, if only for something to do, but my willpower evaporates every time I reach for my phone. I told my boss I was quitting to pursue my dreams; I can't bear explaining why I want to come back.

Most nights I end up curled up in bed, phone clutched inches away from my face, browsing the web for mentions of myself and my books just to feel an echo of that thrill from the time I was a literary darling. I read old press releases about myself: the *Publishers Weekly* profile calling me "incisive and sensitive," the *New Yorker* blurb calling me "publishing's most exciting new talent." I read and reread the most glowing reviews of *The Last Front* and *Mother Witch* on Goodreads, trying to remind myself that there was a time when people truly loved my work.

Whenever that starts to feel stale—usually when the clock creeps toward midnight—I venture into reading the negative shit.

In the past, whenever I trawled Goodreads, I would filter out everything but the five-star reviews, which I would skim over and over again whenever I needed a little ego boost. But now I go straight for the vitriol. It's like pressing a bleeding sore repeatedly, trying to see how far you can go with your tolerance for pain, because if you know the limits of it, you gain some sense of control over it.

The one-star reviews contain everything you'd expect:

If I stole a novel, I'd steal something better than this LOL!

Just here to say, fuck June Hayward.

Haven't read this book, but giving this one star because the writer is a plagiarizing, racist thief.

Took off three stars for the Annie Waters scene alone.

I lie there for hours every night, awash in every cruel thing the internet has ever said about me. It's cathartic, in a perverse way. I like to concentrate all the negativity, to take it all in at once. I take comfort in the fact that it could literally not get any worse than this.

I've entertained, occasionally, the question of what literary redemption might look like. What if I begged my haters for forgiveness? What if, instead of holding the line, I admitted everything and made an attempt at reparations?

Diana Qiu has an article up on Medium titled "June Hayward Must Make Amends, and Here's How." The twelve-item laundry list includes things like: "Provide public proof she's taken a training course in racial sensitivity," "Donate the entirety of her earnings from *The Last Front* and *Mother Witch* to a charity selected by an objective committee of Asian American writers," and "Post her tax returns from the last three years to confirm how much she profited from Athena Liu's work."

Tax returns. Is she fucking serious? Who does Diana think she is?

I can stand to be a pariah. But to bend, to throw away all my savings, to kowtow to the Twitterati and prostrate myself before the taunting, smug crowd—I would rather die.

One night, I see a surprisingly thoughtful take amidst the kiddie pool of filth. It's a review of *The Last Front* published two months ago, so verbose that it's nearly a full-length article.

Drama aside, I find the question of authorship so interesting, reads the penultimate paragraph.

> Unless Hayward releases a detailed and honest statement, we'll never quite know the truth behind its creation. But a close reading leads one to believe that this is indeed a text of mixed authorship, for it seems quite schizophrenic in its handling of its central themes. At times it is so outraged about the covering up of the CLC that the moralizing bleeds off the page. At others, it descends to the same romantic platitudes that the rest of the text criticizes. It's either a very clever manipulation of the reader, or it is what we think it might be—a work partially completed by one author, and finished by another.

I sit up, suddenly curious. Who *is* this person? I click on their profile, but the username is bland and innocuous—"daisychain453." There is no profile picture. The account has no friends or followers I recognize, and its previous review history—similarly thoughtful takes on much-hated books like *The Help* and *American Dirt*—is fascinating to skim through, but reveals no clues about the author.

I'm frightened by how well this reviewer seems to know me. The earlier portions of the review were so clever, so incisive about the techniques employed in the text, that I wonder if she somehow got access to my editor's emails, if she is perhaps someone who worked at Eden.

It's the last paragraph, however, that lingers in my mind:

> What no one's really touched on in this discourse, however, is the nature of Liu and Hayward's relationship. All the evidence suggests that they were indeed friends, though this seems a horrible thing to do to a friend. Was it a case of petty jealousy, then? Was Hayward—gasp—somehow responsible for Liu's

death? Was she, in some twisted way, trying to pay tribute to a friendly rival? Or is she in fact innocent in this whole affair? In any case, I'd pay to read a novel about that whole mess itself.

I'VE COME UP WITH MY NEXT PROJECT.

I wake up with the concept sitting in my mind, fully formed, welded together by my unconscious over hours of fitful, dreaming sleep. This is it: the path to literary redemption and blockbuster success at once. The answer has been so obvious this entire time, I can't believe I didn't see it until now.

I won't dodge the controversy anymore. That mindset has been holding me back—until now, I'd been convinced that my literary resurrection would have to be divorced from Athena's legacy.

But I can't move on and forget. Nobody will let me forget, least of all Athena's ghost. I cannot rid myself of her influence, or of the rumors surrounding her, surrounding us.

Instead I have to face them head-on.

I'll write about us. Well, no—a fictionalized version of us, a pseudo-autobiography in which I blur fact and fiction. I'll describe the night she died in all its heart-stopping, lurid detail. I'll describe how I stole her work and published it. I'll describe every step along my way to literary stardom, and then my horrifying fall. Academics and scholars will have a field day with this text. They'll write entire books about how I cleverly blended the truth with lies, how I reclaimed the rumors about me, subverted the ugly gossip about a treasured friendship into a tale that confronts the reader with their own sick desire for scandal and destruction. They'll call it radical. Groundbreaking. No one's ever refuted literary expectations like this before.

I'll play up the sapphic quality of it all, too. Readers will love that; queer love stories are all the rage now. Drop in a little hint of girl crushing and the TikTokers will go rabid. They could cast us in a movie together. Florence Pugh will play me. That girl from *Crazy Rich Asians* will play Athena. The score will consist entirely of classical music. It'll win all the awards.

And once this scandal has been transformed and preserved in novel form, once all the ugly, unconfirmed rumors about me have been relegated safely to the realm of fiction, I'll be free.

I'm so excited that I almost email Daniella right then with the pitch. But Daniella's dealing with her own shitstorm right now. An unnamed former editorial assistant has testified to *Publishers Weekly* that Daniella had a habit of saying all sorts of bigoted things during meetings ("We already have a Muslim writer," she'd told the team once during acquisitions. "Any more and we'll be outnumbered."). Eden has gone into PR lockdown in response. I am firmly committed to promoting diversity, equity, inclusion in all areas of my work, Daniella assured us in an email sent to all her writers. These remarks were taken out of context, and leaked to the press by someone I believe has a personal vendetta against me. The last I heard, she'd made some donations to some bail fund in the Midwest, although it's not immediately obvious how this has anything to do with the original problem of Islamophobia.

I'm not terribly worried. The Daniella thing will blow over. Publishing professionals are accused of verbal gaffes all the time, but it's not like you can cancel the one female editor at an otherwise all-male imprint. But it's probably best not to wander into her inbox for now.

Instead, for the first time in weeks, I begin drafting in earnest. The words flow so easily from my fingertips, perhaps because there's nothing to make up, nothing to pause and wonder about. It's just the truth coming out of me, and this time I am in total control of the narrative. I start writing thousands of words a day, a level of productivity that I haven't hit since college. I actively look forward to sitting down with my laptop every morning. I don't stop writing until near midnight.

I can't help but feel that there is some greater, karmic reason why my writing flow has returned. This feels like redemption. No—like absolution. For if I can write this thing on my own, if I can turn this whole horrible mess into a beautiful story, then . . . well, it won't change what I've done. But it will assign artistic value to it all. It will be a way of revealing the truth without saying it. And beyond anything else, it will entertain. It will stay in readers' thoughts forever, like a catchy tune or a beautiful woman's face. This story will become eternal. Athena will be a part of that.

What more can we want as writers than such immortality? Don't ghosts just want to be remembered?

I THINK CONSTANTLY ABOUT ATHENA THESE DAYS.

Memories of her don't haunt me anymore. I don't force flashbacks of her out of my mind when they intrude. Instead I linger within them. I mine them for details, immerse myself in the feelings surrounding them, and imagine dozens of ways to reimagine and reframe them. I sit with her ghost. I invite her to speak.

My therapist taught me once that the best way to deal with panic-inducing flashbacks is to think of them as scenes from a horror movie. Jump scares are terrifying the first time you see them because they catch you off guard, and because you don't know what to expect. But once you watch them again and again, once you know exactly when the demon-possessed nun jumps out from behind the corner, they lose their power over you.

I do the same to every awful thought I've ever had about Athena. I delve deep into the horrible. I write out every excruciating detail of my evening at the Chinese American Social Club of Rockville. I describe how rotten I felt when the @AthenaLiusGhost account first went online, how the ensuing fallout wrecked my mental health. I capture Athena's specter and etch it out onto the page, where it is trapped in black-and-white immovable text, where it can do little more than say, "Boo!"

I write about how inadequate Athena has made me feel since college, how I swallowed back vinegary envy every time she achieved something I could not. The way I felt when Geoff told me how she'd mocked me at that convention. I recount the way she stole the story of my maybe-rape. I describe how, despite it all, I still loved her.

But as I dig into the past, I find myself lingering on good memories, too. There are more of them than I realized. I haven't let myself dwell on college for so long, but once I scratch the surface, it all comes bubbling to the fore. Starbucks every Tuesday after our Women in Victorian Lit seminar: an iced mocha for me, a Very

Berry Hibiscus Refresher for Athena. Nights at slam poetry events during which we'd sipped ginger beers and giggled at the performers, who were not *real* poets, and who would one day certainly grow out of this nonsense. A *Les Mis* sing-along party at a drama major's apartment, where we'd shrieked at the top of our lungs, "One day more!"

As I transcribe all this, I wonder if our friendship had indeed been as strained as I'd perceived it. Was that jealous tension always there? Were we rivals from the start? Or had I, in the throes of my insecurity, projected it all against Athena?

I remember the day during our senior year that Athena received the first offer on her debut novel, when her agent called and told her on her way to barre class that she would soon have her book on shelves. She called me first. *Me*. She hadn't even told her parents yet.

"Oh my God," she'd breathed. "June. You won't believe it. I can't believe it."

Then she told me about the offer, and I gasped, and we both screamed back and forth at each other for a good thirty seconds.

"Holy shit, Athena," I whispered. "It's *happening*. Everything you wanted—"

"I feel like I'm standing on a cliff, and my whole life is in front of me." I remember so clearly her breathy whisper; shocked and hopeful and vulnerable all at once. "I feel like everything is about to change."

"It will," I promised her. "Athena, you're going to be a fucking *star*."

And then we screamed back and forth a little more, relishing the other's presence at the other end of the line, for it was so nice to know someone who understood this exact dream, who knew how mere words can become sentences can become a completed masterpiece, how that masterpiece can rocket you into a wholly unrecognizable world where you have everything—a world you wrote for yourself.

I FALL IN LOVE WITH WRITING AGAIN. I START TO DREAM AGAIN. EVER since the @AthenaLiusGhost tweets broke, I've been operating from fear, defensiveness, and insecurity. But now I'm able to dwell once again on all of publishing's promises, the things this world could give me. Brett will sell this to Daniella for a much lower advance than *The Last Front* got, given the circumstances. But it'll be a surprise hit. It'll go into its second printing before launch day. Then the press cycle will kick up, and everyone will be unable to stop talking about the sheer audacity of it all. The frenzied discourse will drive sales, and I'll earn out my advance within weeks. I'll start making double the royalties I was before.

I'm feeling so good that I even log on to Instagram for the first time in weeks and—ignoring the slew of hateful comments on all my previous posts—put up a photo of myself from today's writing session. I'm sitting at a hardwood table near a café window during golden hour, freckles popping, hair falling in soft waves around my shoulders. One hand cups my cheek; the other skims my laptop keyboard, fingers ready to compose.

"Falling right into this manuscript," I write in the caption. "Blocking out the negativity, because when you're a writer, all that matters is the story within. We're overdue for the next chapter. I can't wait to share this one with you all."

ATHENA'S OLD INSTAGRAM ACCOUNT GOES ACTIVE THAT NIGHT.

I wouldn't have even seen the post if I hadn't been scrolling through my notifications, trawling for likes. Someone compliments my blemish-free skin and asks for my skin-care routine. Someone exclaims that they love the coffee shop I'm at. Someone else writes, New Juniper Song book? Can't wait!

But there's also a notification tag that simply reads: Thought you could get rid of me? I imagine it's just some shitpost, but the thumbnail image looks familiar, and the account has a blue verification check, so I click to view the post.

I almost drop my phone.

It's Athena's account, posting for the first time since the morning before her death. In the photo she's sitting at her writing desk, smiling sweetly, but everything is *off*—her eyes are a bit too wide, her toothy smile so stretched it looks painful, and her skin is ghost pale despite the sunlight streaming through her window. She looks like one of those CreepyPasta memes: an image that should look normal, but that makes your skin crawl with its deranged intensity. Lying open by her right hand is *The Last Front* in paperback. By her left, a slim hardcover of *Mother Witch.*

I click to expand the caption.

> Thought you could get rid of me? Sorry, Junie. I'm still kicking. Glad you had a good writing day! I had a good writing day too—here's me, flipping through some old works for inspiration. Heard you're a fan ☺

My dinner crawls up my throat. I run for the bathroom. It's nearly half an hour of panicked breathing and mental exercises before I'm near calm enough to approach my phone again.

I run some searches on Twitter: "Athena Liu Instagram," "Athena Instagram," "Athena Insta," "Ghost Athena," and all the other possible queries I can think of. No one's talking about this yet. The post didn't have any hashtags or tag any other accounts. What's more, the account, which once had nearly a million followers, now has zero. The person behind this has either blocked or soft-blocked all of Athena's followers. The only person seeing this post is me. Whoever this is, they're not trying to go viral—they just want to get my attention.

How is this even possible? Don't social media companies shut down accounts upon the owner's death?

This is so fucking stupid, but I Google "Athena Liu alive" to make sure she hasn't, like, resurrected thanks to some medical miracle without my knowing. But that search returns nothing useful; the most "relevant" result is an article about how a recent English department event at Yale was dedicated to keeping Athena's memory alive.

Athena is dead, gone, turned to ash. The only person who's convinced she's still around is me.

I ought to block the account and forget about this. It's likely just some troll, posting grotesque things to fuck with me. That's what Brett and Daniella would say. That's what Rory would say, if I tried to explain why I'm so upset. A troll is the obvious and rational explanation, and I repeat this over and over in my mind as I inhale and exhale into my fist, since the most annoying symptom of anxiety is refusing to believe the obvious and rational explanation.

Don't give it power, I urge myself. *Just let it alone.*

But I can't. It's like a splinter digging into my palm; even if it's tiny, I still can't rest easy, knowing that it's under my skin. I don't sleep a wink that night. I lie with my phone screen inches from my face, staring with aching eyes at Athena's forceful, mischievous smile.

A memory rises unbidden to my mind's eye, a memory that I'd hoped I'd drowned out or forgotten: Athena in her black boots and green shawl, sitting in the front row of the audience at Politics and Prose, beaming expectantly at me with bright, painted lips. Athena: inexplicably, impossibly alive.

It's late on a Friday night, so I can't get Brett or my publicity team on the line for another two days. But what good could they do? It's hardly a problem from a publicity perspective. Aside from me, who cares about this post? And it's not like I could explain why the account bothers me so much. *Yes, see, the thing is that I* did *steal* The Last Front, *and I'm riddled with guilt, so you understand why these posts give me such bad anxiety I want to puke?*

At last, because I have to do *something*, I reach for my phone.

I text Geoffrey Carlino. This isn't funny.

He doesn't respond. After five minutes, I follow up. Seriously. Stop.

Finally ellipses pop up at the bottom of my screen. He's typing.

I don't know what you're talking about.

I send him a screenshot of Athena's Instagram. Look familiar?

He types, stops typing, then finally sends the message. That isn't me.

Bullshit, I type furiously. I know that all this anger is misdirected, but I hit SEND anyways. I want to take this out on someone, anyone. I'm not even entirely sure that it's Geoff behind this—all I have are general vibes, and the fact that of everyone I know, Geoff is most likely to have access to Athena's passwords—but it doesn't matter. It's not about Geoff. I need to take control, to do *something* that feels like I'm fighting back, even if all I'm doing is firing blanks. Coco's, tomorrow. Or I'll post the recording.

Twenty-One

"Hey, June."

Geoff slides into the seat across from me, and I'm so startled I nearly knock over my tea. I didn't think he'd show. I straighten up. "Uh, hi."

An embarrassed confession: I sent him a barrage of texts last night, hurling wild accusations about his motives and cruel jabs about getting dumped by Athena. He didn't respond. I assumed he would delete them all and then block me.

But here he is, with heavy shadows under swollen eyes. He looks like he hasn't slept all night. "I don't suppose you still think I did it."

"No." I sigh. Part of me was hoping that he'd come off as somewhat guilty, but it's clear from glancing at him that he has nothing to do with this. "I'm sorry, I just . . ." I give my phone a shake. "It rattled me. And I thought, of all people who might have had access to her account . . ."

He extends a hand. "Can I see?"

"You didn't look?"

"She blocked me. Years ago."

"Ah." I unlock my phone, navigate to Athena's Instagram, and pass it over. Geoff scrolls up and down for a while, lingering on each photo, eyes scanning back and forth over the captions. I can't imagine what's going through his mind. This is his ex-girlfriend. This is someone he loved.

He lowers the phone. "No, this isn't her."

"What do you mean?"

"It's photoshopped from an old picture." He returns the phone. "Can't you see it? The lighting and shadows are all off. Also, she's blurred around the edges."

"Which old picture?" I ask. "I've been over all the photos I can find online. There's nothing in that exact pose."

"Maybe it's not public anymore? I don't know. I just know I've seen her looking like that before."

"Then who's behind it?" I press. "Who would know her password?"

"Who cares?" Geoff shrugs. "You've got plenty of haters, right? It could be anyone. Maybe Athena's passwords were easy to guess, or maybe someone's a very talented hacker, I don't know. It's just a joke."

I can't believe that, though. Something else is going on here. A random troll doesn't explain Athena showing up to my reading, or the fact that her specter haunts every professional move I make. Someone is pulling the strings.

"Does Athena have a sister?" I ask. "Any cousins?"

Mrs. Liu had told me Athena was an only child. But cousins can resemble each other, can't they? Or maybe Mrs. Liu was lying. All kinds of crazy plot twists fly through my head. A sister thought dead. A hidden twin, raised in Communist China, escaped to the free world and determined to step into her dead twin's life. Maybe that'd be a good idea for a novel. Maybe I should write that down, file it away for once I've finished my pseudo-memoir.

"I know what you're getting at." Geoff shakes his head. "It's not that, I promise."

"Are you sure?"

"Athena's folks lost touch with most of their relatives when they emigrated. I'm sure you've heard her talk about it. Seriously, there is some deeply fucked-up stuff in that family history. People were murdered, executed in firing squads, lost out at sea. And maybe it's all made-up, in which case that would be *supremely* fucked up, but I don't think it is. I've talked to Mrs. Liu about it a bit. That pain is real."

"You don't think . . ." I trail off.

"What? That it's *her*?" Geoff pauses. He's also had this suspicion, I can tell. It's crazy, but I wouldn't put it past Athena to fake her own death, to put the manuscript right where she knew I would find it. The funeral could have been staged. Her mom could be in on it. Maybe she's watching from the wings right now, laughing into her trench coat.

But Geoff shakes his head. "No. No, she was an odd one, but she wasn't, like, a crazy person. She's—she was a writer. Not a performance artist." He meets my gaze. "And didn't you—?"

Didn't I see her die?

Yes, I did. I saw the panic in her eyes, saw her thrashing and convulsing, trying to free her throat, saw her at last go still and blue in front of me. She couldn't have faked that. The best actress in the world couldn't have faked that.

"Then who's doing this to me?" I demand. "What do they *want*?"

"Does it matter?" Geoff shrugs. "Just ignore them. You've brushed it off every time before, haven't you? Where's your thick skin? Why start getting bothered now?"

"Because . . ." I swallow. "It hurts. I just—it hurts."

"Ah." He leans forward. "So are you going to tell me the truth now?"

I open my mouth, but nothing comes out. I can't do it. I've held the line for this long; I can't break it, even if, in some wretched way, it might set me free.

"I get it," says Geoff. "You say it once, you can never take it back."

He knows. I can tell from his face that he knows. I don't bother trying to convince him otherwise, or to explain the complexities involved—that I did put in the work, that *The Last Front* is just as much my accomplishment as it is Athena's, that it could not possibly exist in its current form without me. It doesn't matter. Geoff's made up his mind, and that's fine—there's nothing more he can do to me than what the internet already has.

I blink angrily down at the table, trying to collect my thoughts. I can't convince him that I'm innocent, but I need to make him understand.

"I just don't get why everyone's so obsessed with Athena's legacy," I say at last. "They all talk about her like she was this saint."

Geoff cocks his head, then settles into his chair, hands clasped in his lap like he's prepared to stay awhile. "So we're doing this."

"I've seen her writing process," I blurt out. I don't know why I'm saying this, especially to Geoff, of all people. I just can't keep it on my chest any longer, can't keep swallowing my resentment. "She was a thief. She took people's pain and made it her own to describe however she liked. She stole as much as I did—she stole from *me*. Back in college, she—" I choke. My nose stings, and I clamp my mouth shut. I've never told this story to anyone else before. If I keep talking, I'll burst into sobs.

"She stole from me, too," Geoff says. "Constantly."

I'm stunned. "You're saying that your stories—"

"No, I mean—look, it's complicated." His eyes dart around, like he's afraid that someone will overhear. He takes a deep breath. "It was more like—okay, look, here's an example. So we'd get into fights, right? Stupid stuff, like her dog allergy, or having joint finances—anyways, it felt so important at the time. And I'd yell something desperate, something vulnerable, only to find those same words published in a short story the very next month. Sometimes, when we fought, she would give me this very cool, narrow-eyed look. I knew that look, because it was the same look she got when she was drafting a scene. And I never knew if she was really *there* during our relationship, or if the whole thing for her was some kind of ongoing story, if she did what she did just to document my reaction. I felt like I was losing my mind." He presses his fingers against the bridge of his nose. "Sometimes she would say things that made me upset, or ask about things I'd been through—and as time went on all I could think was that she was *mining* me, using me as fodder."

It's hard for me to really feel sorry for Geoff. This is, after all, the same man who once threatened to leak nudes of Athena on Reddit if she didn't back him up against a *Locus* reviewer. But I can see the truth in his eyes, the pain. Athena always thought that what she did was a gift. A distillation of trauma into something eternal. *Give me your bruises and hurts*, she told us, *and I will return to you a diamond.*

Only she never cared that once the art was made, once the personal became spectacle, the pain was still there.

Suddenly my eyes flash up to the window. My breath halts and my hands clench before my brain catches up to what I'm seeing: Athena, dark curls loose over her shoulders, draped in that same emerald-green shawl she'd worn to my book launch. Her eyes glimmer with amusement. Her berry-red mouth forms a jagged hole in her face. She's laughing, *jeering*, at the sight of me with Geoff.

She lifts a hand to wave.

I blink, and then she's gone.

"You all right?" Geoff half turns toward what he thinks I'm looking at. "What were—?"

"Nothing," I say, rattled. "I just—sorry."

I take a deep breath. The window's empty. There's nothing I can point to, nothing that proves I'm not going mad. I have the fleeting urge to get up and sprint to the door, to chase this apparition around the block—but what if no one's there? What if I'm simply losing my mind?

Geoff gives me a sympathetic look. A silence passes, and then he says, leaning forward, "Look, June. You probably don't want to hear advice from me, but someone's got to say it. Go work on something else. Don't—I mean, just get out of her shadow. Leave this all behind."

It's decent advice. I imagine that's what he's been trying to do for the last two years. He's not on Twitter anymore, so I haven't heard much about what he's up to, but from what I gather from others he's making some decent money for himself writing for TV. He doesn't go to literary conventions anymore. His name isn't a punch line anymore, just a tired reference. He's freed himself from Athena's web.

But Athena is the reason for any modicum of success I've ever had. My career as an author does not exist without her.

Without Athena, who am I?

"I'm trying," I say in a very small voice. "I just—I don't think she'll let me go. Or these trolls, whoever they are—"

"Ignore them, June." Geoff looks so tired. "Just block them out."

"Do you—do you think I should respond? Try to get in touch?"

"What?" He sits up straight. "No, of course not, why would you—"

"Just to see what they want. To see if they want to talk, I mean—"

"There's nothing to say." Geoff seems inordinately angry; far angrier than this response justifies. It scares me a bit. I wonder what's going on in his mind, what ghosts of Athena's he's been struggling with himself. "All right, Junie? This road leads to nothing good. Just leave it alone, I swear to God. Don't encourage the crazies."

"All right." I exhale slowly. "You're right."

For lack of anything better to do, I finish my tea in silence. Geoff never orders a drink. He pays my bill without asking, then walks me out to the street. He gives me this long look as we stand waiting for my Uber, and I almost think he's going to ask me to come home with him. I imagine, for a fleeting moment, the act of sleeping with Geoffrey Carlino, the messy industry of clothing removal and frantic stimulation of parts. Shared trauma brings people together, doesn't it? Are we not both victims of the same narcissistic bitch? He's attractive, of course, but I feel no real twinge of desire. If I fucked Geoff, I'd only be doing it for the shock value, for the narrative wrench it would throw in this whole mess. And, though I can't quite articulate why, I know the only winner to come out of this would be Athena.

"I guess I'll see you, then," I say. "Around. Maybe."

"Maybe." Geoff glances down at me. "And June?"

"Yeah?"

"It's going to be fine," he says. "These things always feel like the end of the world when they're happening. But they're not. Social media is such a tiny, insular space. Once you close your screen, no one gives a fuck. And you shouldn't, either, all right?"

"I—all right, Geoff. Thanks."

He gives me a nod and walks off in the direction of the bus stop.

Maybe I've been too harsh. Maybe Geoffrey Carlino isn't such an asshole. Maybe he was just young, and insecure, and caught up in a relationship he wasn't ready for. Maybe Athena really did hurt him quite badly, and maybe we all judged him too quickly because he was a wealthy, cishet white guy and Athena was Athena.

What's more, Geoff is one of the few people on earth who also understands the unique pain of trying to love Athena Liu. The futility of it all. Like Echo looking at Narcissus. Like Icarus, hurtling straight at the sun, just to feel its warmth on his skin.

Twenty-Two

Athena's Instagram starts posting at least once a day. They're always impossible photos of Athena, alive and well, positioned near objects that are deliberately dated—newspapers, recent *New Yorker* issues, books released after her death. Sometimes she's winking or waving, taunting me with her insouciance. Sometimes her face is contorted in grotesque expressions; eyes wide, tongue wagging. Sometimes she's clutching her throat, eyes crossed in mockery of her death. She always tags me at the end of her captions.

How ya doing, @JuniperSong?

Miss me, @JuniperSong?

I try to take Geoff's advice. I mute the account, and then, since I still can't stop myself from scrolling through the photos on writing breaks, I buy a timed safe in which to lock my phone during the day. I try to take refuge in my work. But I can't lose myself in the words like I have before. All my happy memories with Athena are tinged now with niggling guilt, so all I can bear to dwell on are the bad ones—of awkward exchanges, of social snubbing, of constant stabs of jealousy in my gut. Of Athena, laughing obliviously as she asked about my floundering career. Of Athena, dying on the floor of her kitchen while I stood by, doing nothing.

I dream of Athena every night. I see her in her last moments: her wide panicked eyes, her fingernails tearing at her skin, her feet drumming against the floor. Powerless, helpless, literally voiceless. She works her mouth, desperate to make me understand. But no words come out, only a series of awful, strained gurgles, until her eyes roll up to the back of her head, until her convulsions dwindle to a faint twitch.

Those are the tame dreams. Worse are the dreams when she's reanimated. She comes magically to life, but this time she's not the same. There's a scarlet glinting energy in her eyes, all the fury of the underworld, and vengeful delight twists her lovely face as she leaps up, arms out, reaching for my neck to return the favor.

SOMETIMES MY IMAGINATION RUNS WILD IN THE MIDDLE OF THE DAY, and I convince myself of myriad ways that Athena might still be alive. The funeral was closed casket, wasn't it? She could have faked the choking. She could have hired those EMTs. This could all be one grand literary hoax, a deranged publicity campaign for her next project. Perhaps she'll jump out from behind the corner any minute. *Boo! Gotcha, Junie!*

But the living are burdened with bodies. They make shadows, footprints. I would prefer that Athena were alive and stalking me, because then she would leave traces—public spottings, narrative inconsistencies, breadcrumbs of proof. The living can't appear and disappear at will. The living can't haunt you at every turn. Athena's ghost has wormed its way into my every waking moment. Only the dead can be so constantly present.

I find myself typing "Chinese ghosts" into Google Scholar and diving deep into all the literature that comes up. The Chinese have so many different words for ghost—"*gui*," "*ling*," "*yao*," "*hunpo*." They are obsessed with death without peace. I learn that the most common word for ghost, "*gui*," is a homophone for a different "*gui*," which means to return. I learn that the female revenant is a common theme in early Chinese literature, a trope employed to explore the regrets of single, unmarried women who died violent and unnatural deaths. I learn about a trope called the "amorous ghost," in which all the female ghost needs to sate its haunted desire is a good fucking. I learn about something called *jiangshi*, which as far as I can tell is like a zombie, a corpse reanimated by a spell written on a slip of paper. Perhaps someone reanimated Athena. Perhaps I composed the spell myself, when I published her words against her will.

When the nonfiction sources turn up no helpful advice on exorcising the damn things, I start devouring Chinese ghost stories.

From the Southern Song dynasty: A grave robber breaks into the tomb of a girl recently passed away from heartache and is so taken by her beauty that he rapes her corpse. The infusion of his male energy to her body restores her to life, but since no one else knows she's alive, the grave robber imprisons her as his sex slave without any suspicions. The girl finally escapes and flees to the home of her former lover, but the lover, frightened by her presence and convinced she is a ghost, throws a cauldron at her head and kills her.

From the Six Dynasties period: A man's wife of ten years dies before she can bear him a son. Distraught, he weeps over her corpse. His grief reanimates her corpse, and she instructs him to come make love to her in the dark until she becomes pregnant. She hasn't come fully back to life, mind you—they keep her body in a side room, where she lies inert, waiting to be fucked. Ten months later, she gives birth to a baby boy, and then promptly becomes a limp corpse once again.

Also from the Six Dynasties period: A man's wife dies, so he marries her cousin. One day, his icy-cold, reanimated first wife comes to lie beside him. He asks her to leave. Later she rebukes her cousin for marrying her widower, and shortly after, the man and the cousin drop dead.

The cultural constructions are clear: so many Chinese ghosts are hungry, angry, voiceless women. In taking Athena's legacy, I've added one to their ranks.

But the normal methods of dispelling ghosts, the ones that work in all the stories, seem insufficient. I doubt Athena will be happy with offerings of food, incense, or burnt paper. Which isn't to say I don't try. Deep down I know it's stupid, but I'm desperate enough to hope the rituals might at least calm my mind. I order incense sticks on Amazon and kung pao chicken from Kitchen No. 1 and place both before a framed photo of Athena, but all it does is stink up my apartment. I print paper cutouts of all the things I imagine Athena could want in the underworld—stacks of money, a lavish apartment, the entire IKEA catalogue—and light them up with a match, but that only sets off the fire alarm, which pisses off my neighbors and lands me with a hefty fine.

I don't feel better. I feel like a meme of a clueless white person.

The wildest thing about all this is that even now I cannot stop composing. I'm trying to funnel this awfulness into something lovely. My salacious roman à clef will become a horror novel. My terror will become my readers' terror. I will take my fugue state of delirious panic and compost it into a fertile bed of creativity—for aren't all the best novels borne from some madness, which is borne from truth?

Perhaps, if I can capture all my fears and constrain them safely on the page, this will rob them of their power. Don't all the ancient myths tell us that we gain control over a thing once we name it? Dr. Gaily once made me write out by hand detailed descriptions of my encounter with Andrew, and then burn them. It felt good to translate those nebulous, nauseating feelings to concrete words. It felt good to see them crumple to ash, to nothing. Maybe I can't make Athena disappear, but perhaps I can trap her safely within the covers of a book.

But I'm losing track of the narrative. My thoughts spiral out beyond what the pages can contain. This has gone from a dark, literary coming-of-age story to a jumbled, frantic ghost story. My carefully constructed outline falls apart against the story Athena wants to see. I abandon my original plot. I furiously transcribe everything that comes to mind, which oscillates between my truth and the truth.

I've written myself into a corner. The first two-thirds of the book were a breeze to compose, but what do I do with the ending? Where do I leave my protagonist, now that there's a hungry ghost in the mix, and no clear resolution?

I stare at my screen for hours, trying out various endings, hoping to find one that will please Athena. The ghost devours me whole.

The ghost rips me apart limb from limb and bathes in my blood. The ghost sinks into my body and takes over my life for my remaining years as reparations. The ghost impels me to suicide, and I join her in the underworld: two miserable souls without justice.

But none of these produce the necessary catharsis. Athena is not satisfied.

Frustrated, I flop onto my bed and reach, as ever, for my phone.

Athena's account has updated again.

She's standing in front of a mirror. There's a long white paper taped to her forehead. *The Last Front*, it reads. *By Juniper Hayward.*

It's a multiphoto post. I swipe right.

Athena, lying prone on the floor, hands at her neck. *Swipe.*

Athena, my book on her chest, eyes open. *Swipe.*

Athena, reanimated, standing up. *Swipe.*

Athena, veins protruding in her neck and forearms, mascara leaking from her eyes, howling at the camera, grinning, claws out like she wants to rip me apart head to toe. *Swipe.*

Athena, a vicious blur, leaping toward the camera lens.

I turn off my phone and hurl it across the room.

I'M OVERSTATING MY BEWILDERMENT. THE CONDITIONS OF EXORCISM are no great mystery. I know what this ghost wants, what sort of ending could make this all go away. It's such a simple truth, loath as I am to admit it: that Athena wrote *The Last Front*, that I am at best a coauthor, that even though I deserve some credit for this novel, she does, too.

But I'm too deep into this now to confess. That is the only line

I cannot cross. If I confess now, I won't only lose everything I've gained, I'll lose any chance I have at a future. I won't just go back to square zero. I'll be sentenced to both literary and social hell.

Tell me, do I truly deserve that? Does anyone?

Athena's been dead for over two years. She's already left an impressive legacy. The literary world will remember her forever. She has nothing more to gain.

But I need to survive this, somehow. And the truth would destroy me.

So I simply must continue to live with this ghost, to grow accustomed to her face lingering on the backs of my eyelids. We must find some other equilibrium of coexistence that does not involve my giving her the only thing she wants.

I'M WRITING IN A BOOTH AT SAXBY'S ONE AFTERNOON WHEN A FLASH of emerald green catches my eye. I look up through the window and see her, windswept locks floating around her face, staring right back at me. She's wearing the same shawl, the same high-heeled boots. Is this not proof she is a ghost? The living change clothes, do they not? The dead stay the same.

Our eyes meet. She whirls about to flee.

I jump up and sprint out of the coffee shop. I don't have a plan; I only want to pin down this apparition, to shake its shoulders and demand answers. *What are you? What do you want?*

But by the time I weave around irritated patrons and out the door, she's already a block away. Her heels clack rapidly against the pavement; her shawl billows in the wind. No, she is no ghost. She's a *person*, flesh and blood, as mundane and solid as I am. I sprint as hard as I can—two strides and I've caught up to her. My hands reach out, grasp for her shoulders, and meet solid flesh—I *have* her—

She whirls around. "What the *fuck*?"

It's not Athena.

I take in her bright, hard eyes, razor-thin brows, the brilliant gash of red lipstick across thin, angry lips. My stomach drops.

It's Diana Qiu.

"June?" She flinches back as if I'm trying to bite her. Her hand flies to her purse, whips out a canister of pepper spray. "Holy shit—stay back—"

"I caught you," I breathe. "I caught you—"

"I don't know what you want," says Diana. "But stay the hell away from me—"

"Don't gaslight me." I can feel my heartbeat in my throat. My face feels terribly hot, tight; my head dizzy. Reality is careening away from me, and I'm only hanging on by a thread. All I know—all I can hold on to—is the revelation that Diana did this to me. It's been Diana all along. "I know what you're doing. I know it's you—"

"Jesus Christ." Diana's arm trembles, but she doesn't spray me. "What are you *talking* about?"

"Those are *her* boots. *Her* shawl." I almost choke, I'm so angry. Was it Diana that first night at Politics and Prose? Was it Diana at Coco's? Has she been fucking with me for *months*? I think back to that rant she gave at the panel in Virginia, to all those interviews and blog pieces she's put out about me since. The woman is obsessed with me. Is this all some perverse art project for her? The Haunting of Juniper Song?

"Hold on." Diana lowers the can. "Do you think I'm trying to dress up like *Athena Liu*?"

"You can't pretend," I insist. "You're dressed up like her; you're stalking me—"

"These are my boots," says Diana. "These are my clothes. And I'm walking by Saxby's because I fucking live here, you psycho."

"I'm not a psycho—"

"Not all Asian women look the same," Diana snarls. "Is that so hard to comprehend, you crazy bitch?"

I almost slap her then. "I'm not crazy."

But up close, all the resemblances fall apart. Those aren't Athena's boots—Athena's favorite Uggs were brown, with tassels. Diana's are black, with buckles and stiletto heels. Diana's hair is blunt and straight-edged, not loosely curled. She's wearing hoops, not emerald danglers. Her lipstick is far, far brighter than anything Athena would ever wear.

She doesn't look like Athena. She doesn't look like her at all.

What on earth did I see in that café window?

"I'm not crazy." But I can think of no evidence otherwise. I can't trust my eyes. I can't trust my memory. All the fight goes out of me then, and my chest sags; the air lets out. My voice cracks. "I'm not."

Diana watches me for a long moment, her face a mix of curiosity, pity, and disgust. At last, she places the pepper spray back in her bag.

"Jesus," she mutters, then hurries away from me, glancing over her shoulder with every other step as if making sure I don't follow. "You need help."

SOMEHOW I MANAGE TO COLLECT MY THINGS FROM SAXBY'S AND head home. My Uber driver must think I'm drunk—I'm breathing hard and I can't stop reeling, clutching the armrest like it's the only thing that will keep me from toppling over. My mind keeps replaying the encounter with Diana. My fingers digging into her shoulders. Her pepper spray. The disgust in her eyes, the fear.

For a moment there, she really thought I was going to attack her.

I can't believe I did that. There's no excuse. No explanation. I *accosted* someone in broad daylight.

I run for my bathroom and dry heave over the sink, shoulders quaking, until my breathing steadies. A thin stream of saliva trickles into the porcelain. I look up at the mirror, and what I see there makes me want to cry.

My cheeks are hollow. My hair's unwashed, my eyes bloodshot and sunken against dark, mottled bags. I haven't slept. I haven't talked to anyone who wasn't my doorman in days. I've been living a haunted existence from hour to hour, trying to distract myself with my manuscript so that my thoughts don't torture me, and I can't do this anymore. I'm so fucking tired of it all—the visions, the paranoia, the nightmares. I'm tired of seeing Athena around every corner, hearing her voice, her laughter. I didn't ask for this. I didn't ask to witness Athena's death in the first place. I didn't even want to be there that night, but she insisted, and there I was, and it's clearly fucked me up even more than I realized.

I'm tired.

I'm so tired.

I just want her to go away. I want to be okay.

I call Rory. She won't understand anything I'm talking about, but I'll explain it all from the beginning. It doesn't matter for her to know the details, it only matters that she listens, hears me, hears how much I'm hurting. I need someone to know that I'm not all right.

The phone rings and rings. I call a second time, and then a third, but Rory never picks up.

I search Dr. Gaily's name in my phone. I haven't had an appointment with her for years, not since I graduated, but I still have her number saved. She answers in two rings. "Hello?"

"Dr. Gaily?" My words spill out, too eager, too desperate. "I don't know if you remember me—I'm June Hayward, I was a patient of yours a few years ago, I was at Yale—I was the one who, um—"

"June, of course. Hello." Her voice is kind, if puzzled. "What can I do for you?"

"I know it's been a while—" I have to stop then, take a deep breath to keep my sobs from overwhelming me. "But you said to give you a call if I ever needed therapy again, and, um—I think I'm really not all right—a lot has happened recently, and I'm not dealing with it well, and I think it's bringing up a lot of, um, past trauma—"

"Slow down, June. One thing at a time." Dr. Gaily pauses for a moment. "Would you like to schedule an appointment with me? Is that what you're asking?"

"Oh—um, sorry, I know you're probably busy, but if you have any availability *now*—"

"We can look into that." She pauses. I hear a drawer open; I think she's just sat down at her desk. "But I need to know if you're still living in Connecticut."

"I'm in Rosslyn. Virginia." I sniffle. "But I have insurance—well, I guess you'd be out of network, but I can pay out of pocket—"

"It's not about that, June. I can't give you telehealth care if you're not in Connecticut. I'm not licensed to practice in Virginia."

"Oh." I wipe my nose. My hand comes away streaked with snot. My mind feels very blank right then. "I see."

"But I can set you up with some referrals." I think I hear papers shuffling. "You said you're in Rosslyn, right?"

I can't do this. "Actually, Dr. Gaily, it's all right—I can look up in-state therapists myself. I'm sorry for wasting your time—"

"Hold on," she says. "June, are you having any thoughts of harming yourself? Or anyone else? Because I can connect you to a hotline—"

"No—no, I'm okay." I'm suddenly so embarrassed. I didn't mean to take things so far; I didn't mean to be such a problem. "I'm not suicidal. I'm fine, I'm just—I'm having a really bad day. I just wanted someone to talk to."

"I understand, Junie." Her tone softens. "I can't offer you care in another state. But we're going to set you up with the help you need, all right? Can you be patient for me?"

"Okay," I croak. "Yeah. That sounds good."

"Then I'll email you some referrals tomorrow first thing in the morning. Are you still using the same address on file?"

"I—yeah. That one works."

"Then you'll have some contacts in the morning. Take care, Junie."

She hangs up. I sit cross-legged on my bed, my face pressed into my hands. I feel even worse than before. I want to disappear. Why did I fucking do that? It's past nine on a weekday. Long past work hours. Dr. Gaily must be bitching to her husband right now—*Sorry, dear, I had a former patient call; she was being a psycho—*

My phone lights up. I lunge at it, desperate—but it's not Rory. It's an Instagram notification.

It's from the ghost.

This time Athena is sitting in a booth at Saxby's, sticking her tongue mischievously out over her straw. She's wearing precisely the same outfit I saw her in at the reading, at Coco's Coffee—the outfit

I thought I saw at Saxby's this afternoon. Lips painted scarlet. Eyes glimmering.

Spotted an old friend today. I wonder if she remembers me.

I want to scream.

I can't take this anymore. I have to know the truth. I cannot move on. This will gnaw at me my entire life until I know, for better or worse, who or what she is.

I need release. If I can't get help, I at least need answers. I need *something* to happen, or I'll explode.

I open my phone, navigate to Athena's account, and write: okay. You got my attention. what do you want???

The ghost is online. She responds immediately.

exorcist steps.

tomorrow night.

eleven.

Twenty-Three

ATHENA IS ALIVE.

I can think of no other explanation. The *Exorcist* steps are our private joke. The steep, pitch-black stairs a block off the Georgetown campus, the site where Father Karras dies in *The Exorcist*, are famously haunted, and I've always found those steps so slippery with rain and snow that I'm surprised they haven't killed more joggers. Athena and I came here after a poetry reading the first winter after I moved to DC. She dared me to run up the iced-over stairs without stopping. I challenged her instead to a race. I bashed my knee ten steps up, and she dashed past me without a backward glance. She won.

Whatever the fuck is going on here—whatever supernatural or twisted explanation lies behind that Instagram account—it's not some asshole pulling off a prank. It could only be Athena. Only Athena knows what this means to me. The metaphor is too symbolic—my crashing and falling, her dancing all the way to the top.

I know it's a trap. I know that by showing up, I'm playing right into the hands of the ghost, that I'm likely putting myself in grave danger. But I have no choice. This is my only chance to find answers, and I'm desperate now for just a shred of the truth.

I play it as smart as I can. I make sure my cell phone is fully charged. I buy a utility belt and pack it with a flashlight with fresh batteries, a can of pepper spray—thanks, Diana—and a Swiss Army knife. I even buy a string of Chinese firecrackers from a sketchy corner grocery in Chinatown, because I read online that the popping noise can ward off ghosts. It's stupid, I know, but I want to feel prepared. If Athena's ghost tries to murder me on these steps, there's probably no way I can prevent my fate. But I won't go out without a fight.

I think about texting Rory, or even Brett, to leave a record of where I'm going. But if this goes the way I think it might, perhaps it's best I leave no record at all.

I take an Uber up from Rosslyn and get out at Georgetown's front gates. It's a five-minute walk to the stairs, but I don't want to entertain my driver's questions about what I'm doing at the *Exorcist* steps at this hour. School's out for the term. I'm the only one wandering campus tonight. I hurry along the quiet sidewalk of Thirty-Seventh Street, arms folded tight against the wind. It's a moonless dark, and bitingly cold. The Potomac surges against the banks, flush with this morning's rain. It's all very gothic and dramatic. If I were an avenging ghost, I think, this is where I would lure someone out to kill them. All this scene needs is an ominous flash of lightning, and we might get that, too—storm clouds have been gathering all afternoon.

I'm not afraid. At this point nothing could scare me. At this point I would love for Athena to lunge out and attack me, just so I could confirm that she is real, that I'm not insane.

The steps are empty. There's no one in sight for several blocks, and when I hurry down to the bottom of the stairs, I find only the abandoned gas station. It's five past eleven. I double back up the steps, gasping for breath.

I feel like an idiot. Maybe Geoff was right, maybe this was a hoax. Maybe the point was only to scare me.

I'm about to leave when I hear her speak.

"It's *so* good to see you again!"

IT'S ATHENA. THAT'S UNDOUBTEDLY ATHENA'S VOICE, AFFECTING THAT disinterested, so-transparently-artificial-it's-ironic-which-makes-it-real timbre I've heard her employ dozens of times on radio interviews and podcasts. "It's been *aaages*."

"Athena?" She sounds like she's standing at the top. I dash up the rest of the steps and emerge panting back up onto Prospect. The streets are still empty.

"I'm so glad you're a fan of my work."

What the fuck? What is she talking about?

"*Athena?*" I yell. "Where are you?"

"So." Her voice comes from farther away this time. I strain my ears, hunting for the source of the sound. "How've you been?" It seems like it's drifting up from the bottom of the stairs. How could she have gotten down there so quickly?

Unless she's dead; unless she's a spirit, flittering through the air.

"Athena?"

I hear a patter of footsteps on the stairs. Is she running from me? I want to chase her down, but I don't know where to turn;

her footsteps echo from one direction, but her voice sounds from another. I spin around, scanning the darkness for a face, a flash of movement, a clue, *anything.*

"What would you say is your greatest inspiration?" Athena asks suddenly.

Inspiration? What game is this?

But I know the right answers. I know what will lure her out.

"It's you," I shout. "You know that. It's obviously you."

Athena bursts into a peal of laughter. "So I guess my question is, *why*?"

There's something off about her voice. I've only just noticed. It's not the voice you use with your friends. It's pitchy and artificial, like she's putting on a performance. It's the voice you hear from celebrities on game shows, right before they have to describe their first sexual encounter or eat a boiled monkey brain.

Is she okay? Is she being held hostage? Does someone have a gun to her head?

She asks again, in precisely the same intonation, prefacing her question with the same tinkling laughter. "So I guess my question is, *why*?"

"There's no reason why," I yell. "I took your pages, I read them, and I thought they were so brilliant—and I've always envied you, Athena, I just wanted to know what it was like, and I didn't even think about it, it just *happened*—"

"You didn't think you were stealing my work?" Now her voice echoes from somewhere above me. It's strangely garbled this time, like she's speaking underwater. It doesn't sound at all like her. "You didn't think it was a crime?"

"Of course it was. I know that now. It was wrong—"

More tinkling laughter. That same question as before, voiced in an identical manner. "So I guess my question is, *why*?"

"Because it's not fair," I shout, frustrated. She's made her point. She doesn't have to keep toying with me. "You know what kind of stories people want to hear. No one cares about my stories. I wanted what you have—had—but I didn't mean to hurt you. I would never have hurt you, I just thought—"

Her voice rises in pitch again, turns girlie and twee. "I'm a lucky girl, aren't I?"

"I thought you were the luckiest person I'd ever met," I say miserably. "You had everything."

"So you're sorry?" Garbled, distorted, once again. "Are you sorry, June?"

"I'm sorry." My words feel so small, so tinny against the howling wind. My throat aches from holding back sobs. I don't care about maintaining the line anymore. I just want this to be over. "Fuck, Athena—I'm so sorry. I wish every day I could take it back. I'll do anything to make it right—I'll tell your mom, I'll tell my publisher, I'll donate everything, every cent—just tell me you're all right. Athena, please. I can't do this anymore."

A long pause.

When she at last responds, her voice has changed once again. It's lost its pitchy, artificial timbre. It sounds human, and yet completely unlike her. "That's a confession?"

"I confess," I gasp. "I'm sorry, Athena. I'm so sorry, please—come talk to me."

"I see." A pause. I hear footsteps again, and this time they match the direction of her voice. She's standing right behind me. "Thank you, June."

I turn.

A figure steps out of the shadows.

IT'S NOT ATHENA.

This girl looks nothing like Athena. Her face is rounder, plainer. Her eyes are not as massive and doe-like. Her legs aren't impossibly long. She smirks at me as she moves farther into the light, and I have the vague feeling I ought to know her, that I've looked into these eyes before. But I simply cannot place her.

"Nothing?" The girl crosses her arms. "Ruined my life, drove me out of publishing, and you don't even remember me?"

The pieces crash together in my mind then—a tiny face in a Zoom screen, a slew of angry emails, a hiccup in my publishing journey I'd long forgotten.

She's off the project. You won't have to deal with her anymore.

"Candice?"

"Hi, Juniper." She drawls out my name like poison. "Long time no see."

My mouth works, but nothing comes out. What is she doing here? Didn't she move to Bumfuck, Nowhere, Oregon? And since when did Candice know Athena? Is Athena still alive? Is she in on this hoax? Or was it just Candice all along?

"Oh, the look on your face," Candice sneers. "I've been looking forward to this."

"I don't—why—" My brain has short-circuited. I can't articulate my confusion into questions. *"Why?"*

"Simple," Candice sings. "You ruined my life. I ruin yours."

"But I didn't—"

"Do you have any idea how hard it is to get a job in publishing once you're on Daniella Woodhouse's blacklist? They fired me over a Goodreads rating. A fucking *Goodreads* rating. Does that ring a bell?"

"I don't—I didn't—"

"I didn't even get severance." Candice's words spill out of her, a hornet's nest of spite. She talks like she's been keeping this bubbled inside for years, like if she doesn't get it all out she'll explode. "*Unprofessional conduct*, they said. I couldn't pay rent. I slept in a fucking bathtub for weeks. I applied for dozens of openings I was overqualified for. No one would even email me back. They said I was toxic, said I didn't know how to maintain boundaries with authors. Is that what you wanted? Did you gloat?"

"I'm sorry," I manage. "I don't know what you're talking about—"

"'I don't know what you're talking about,'" Candice mimics. "Is that how you get away with everything? By batting your eyelashes and pretending to be a fucking idiot?"

"Really, Candice, I don't—"

"God, stop *lying*!" Candice's voice flies up several octaves then. "You confessed. You finally confessed. I *heard* you."

I wonder then if Candice might not be entirely well. She sounds unhinged. Dangerous.

I take two steps back. My thoughts fly to the pepper spray in my belt, but I'm scared to reach for it—I'm scared any sudden actions might send Candice over the edge.

"God, I've dreamed of this for *ages*." Her voice is flushed and giddy; she sounds high on adrenaline. "I wanted to go public when I got fired—but who was going to believe me? All I had were doubts. You acted so weird about the sensitivity read. And the way you spoke about the novel as if it wasn't your own. As if it was some *thing* you could chop up and polish however you liked." She looks me up and down, and the hungry gape of her mouth makes her look like a ravenous, wild animal—a beast about to pounce. "God. I was right. I can't believe I was *right*."

"I don't know what you think you know." I try to steady my breathing. My mind's scrambling for explanations, possible denials of everything I've just yelled into the darkness. *I was confused. I've been coerced.* "But Athena was my *friend*—"

"Oh yes. Your greatest muse." Candice scoffs. "I've heard that line. Tell me, how long were you planning to steal her work? How accidental was her death, really?"

"It wasn't like that," I insist. "I worked hard on that novel; it's *mine*—"

"Oh, shut up." Candice steps closer. This scene composition is so fucking dramatic. The streetlamp glows behind her, casting her shadow across the steps and across me. It feels like we're in some gothic film. Now the villain's reveal at the climax; now the hero's righteous monologue before I'm cast, screaming, into hell. "I knew you'd never come out and say it. That was the challenge, you know. I figured it out early on. You were never going to admit it, no matter how vicious the allegations got, no matter how much proof there was. You needed to cling to some version of events where you weren't the bad guy. Isn't that right? So I realized the only way to settle this was to make you confess on your own."

She raises her voice, starts projecting, like she's narrating to someone else. Like she's been waiting forever to get her monologue in the spotlight. It's bizarre, but here I am, frozen: a captive, horrified audience. "I thought I'd just mess with you a bit. Rattle you enough to say something circumstantial. Instagram was easy—I know Athena's publicist; she still had her login. At first all I did was fuck around with Photoshop. I wasn't sure if it was working—you kept ignoring my tags—but then I heard you'd attacked Diana Qiu on the street. She said you looked haunted. Turns out white people are more gullible than I thought."

Photoshop? A borrowed login? Is that all it took? "So Athena is . . ."

"Dead and ash." Candice barks out a laugh. "Or are you still hoping to see her ghost?"

"But the stairs . . ." I feel so stupid, questioning her like this. But I can't think of anything else to say. I need it all explained to me, step by step, because Candice is right: part of me still thinks Athena will step out from the shadows any second, cackling, ready to accept my confession. "How did you know about the stairs?"

I *want* Athena to step out. She's the only one I want to confess to. I need true catharsis, not Candice Lee laughing in my face. Not this cruel, childishly simple prank.

"It's Athena's favorite workout," says Candice. "She wouldn't shut up about it on Twitter. Wait, you didn't know?" She registers my expression, then bursts into laughter. "You thought this was *personal*? That's so good. That's *so* good. I hope I got that."

She straightens up. She's holding a camera. She's been recording this whole thing.

She fiddles with the buttons, then plays my own words back at me.

"You know what kind of stories people want to hear. No one cares about my stories. I wanted what you have—had—but I didn't mean to hurt you. I would never have hurt you."

It's utterly damning. It's my voice, without question. She has my face on camera, too, from who knows how many other angles. There is no denying this.

"But the stairs . . ." She zooms forward, and my voice comes out faster, higher-pitched, panicked. I sound so fucking stupid. *"How did you know about the stairs?"*

"Feels bad, doesn't it?" Candice drops the recorder in her backpack. "Watching someone warp your image and tell your story however they choose, knowing you have no power to stop it? No voice? That's how we all felt, watching you. Pretty awful, huh?"

"Candice." My chest deflates. My limbs feel like lead. I know it's pointless even as I say it, but I can't help but go through the motions. I can't walk away knowing I didn't try every possible thing. "Look, please, maybe we can work something out—"

She snorts. "Nah. Sorry, you can't bribe your way out of this one."

"Candice, *please*, I'll lose everything—"

"What would you offer me?" She pulls another camera down from the branches above her head. Jesus Christ, how many cameras are there? "Fifty thousand? A hundred thousand? What's the cost of justice, Juniper Song?" She points the lens right out at me. "How much," she drawls, "do you think Athena deserves?"

I cross my arms over my face. "Candice, *stop*."

"How much do you think Mrs. Liu deserves?"

"Can't you understand what it was like?" I beg. "Even a little bit? Athena had fucking *everything*. It wasn't fair—"

"Is that how you justify it?"

"But it's true, isn't it? Athena had it made. You people—I mean, diverse people—you're all they want—"

"Oh my God." Candice presses a palm against her forehead. "You really are insane. Do all white people talk like this?"

"It's true," I insist. "I'm just the only one who saw it—"

"Do you know how much shit Athena got from this industry?" Candice demands. "They marked her as their token, exotic Asian girl. Every time she tried to branch out to new projects, they kept insisting that Asian was her *brand*, was what her audience expected. They never let her talk about anything other than being an immigrant, other than the fact that half her family died in Cambodia, that her dad killed himself on the twentieth anniversary of Tiananmen. Racial trauma sells, right? They treated her like a museum object. That was her marketing point. Being a Chinese tragedy. She leaned into it, too. She knew the rules. She fucking milked it for all it was worth.

"And if Athena is a success story, what does that mean for the rest of us?" Candice's voice hardens. "Do you know what it's like to pitch a book and be told they already have an Asian writer? That they can't put out two minority stories in the same season? That Athena Liu already exists, so you're redundant? This industry is built on silencing us, stomping us into the ground, and hurling money at white people to produce racist stereotypes of us.

"You're right, though. Every so often someone in this industry develops a conscience and gives a nonwhite creator a chance, and then the whole carnival rallies around their book like it's the only diverse work ever to exist. I've been on the other side. I've seen it happen. I've been in the room when we pick our one spicy book of the season, when we decide who's *educated* and *articulate* and *attractive* but marginalized enough to make good on our marketing budget. It's sick, you know. But I suppose it's nice to be the token. If the rules are broken, you might as well ride the diversity elevator all the way to the top. Wasn't that your logic?"

"Candice . . ."

"Can you *imagine* how they'll fawn over this?" She spreads her hands in the air like she's tracing out a rainbow. "*Yellowface.* By Candice Lee."

"Candice, I beg you. Don't do this."

"If I don't go public, will you?"

I open my mouth, then close it. I can't answer that. She knows I can't answer that. "Candice, please. Athena wouldn't have wanted this—"

"Who cares about Athena?" Candice barks out a laugh. "Fuck Athena. We all hated that bitch. This is for me."

There's nothing I can say to that.

It all boils down to self-interest. Manipulating the story; gaining the upper hand. Doing whatever it takes. If publishing is rigged, you might as well make sure it's rigged in your favor. I get it. I've done it, too; it's just playing the game. It's how you survive in this industry. If I were in Candice's shoes right now, if I had the same kind of narrative gold she's carrying in her backpack, of course I'd do the same.

"Well, I think I have what I came for." She drops the last camera into her backpack, zips it up, and tosses it over her shoulder. "If I were you, I'd get off social media when you get home. Save yourself the agony."

Something sharpens in my chest then. The same feeling I'd always had watching Athena succeed; the vinegar-sour conviction that this wasn't fair. Now Candice is sauntering in front of me, flaunting her spoils, and I can already see how the industry will receive her manuscript. They'll fucking go *wild* for her, because the narrative is simply so perfect: brilliant Asian artist exposes white fraud, wins big for social justice, sticks it to the *man*.

Ever since *The Last Front* came out, I have been victim to people like Candice and Diana and Adele: people who think that, just because they're "oppressed" and "marginalized," they can do or say whatever they want. That the world should put them on a pedestal and shower them with opportunities. That reverse racism is okay. That they can bully, harass, and humiliate people like me, just because I'm white, just because that counts as punching up, because in this day and age, women like me are the last acceptable target. Racism is bad, but you can still send death threats to Karens.

And I know one thing.

I will not let Candice walk away with my fate in her hands.

Years of suppressed rage—rage at being treated like a stereotype, like my voice doesn't matter, like the entirety of my being is constituted in those two words, "white woman"—bubble up inside me and burst.

I throw myself at Candice's waist. Attack the center of gravity—I read that in a Tumblr post once; if someone attacks you on the street, go for their gut and their legs. Unbalance them; knock them to the floor. Then go for something that will hurt. Candice is hardly some hulking, six-foot predator. She's so tiny. Asian women are all so tiny. I sometimes looked at Athena and imagined someone easily scooping her up by the waist. She, and Candice, are like little porcelain dolls—how hard could they be to break?

Candice shrieks as I crash into her. We land on the ground, limbs tangled. Something crunches—the cameras, I hope.

"Get *off* of me!" She flings a fist at my face. But she's punching from below; she's got no momentum, and she's not that strong to begin with. Her knuckles barely tap my chin. Still, she's stronger than I imagined. I can't keep her pinned down—she keeps thrashing beneath me, cursing and screaming, jabbing her palms and elbows at every part of me she can reach. I remember I've brought a Swiss Army knife and pepper spray, but there's no time to unzip my belt; it's all I can do to fend off her blows.

It crosses my mind that we're too close to the steps. We could both tumble, or she could kick me down, or *I* could—

Fuck, no, what am I thinking? There are already people out there who think I murdered Athena. If the police found me at the base of the steps, standing over Candice's shattered body—how would I explain that?

A small voice whispers: *Easily, that's how.*

We were jogging. We're both dressed for it; how hard would that be to believe? The steps were icy, it was raining, and Candice wasn't watching her step. I'd definitely have time to stash the cameras before the EMTs got here. I could dump the whole backpack in the Potomac—or, no, that leaves too much to chance; it's better that I hide it near Georgetown and retrieve it later. If Candice can't talk, who's going to suspect me?

It's fucked up, yes. But I could survive a murder investigation. I can't survive what Candice will do to me if she walks out of here alive.

Candice's thrashes are getting weaker. She's tiring out. I am, too, but I'm bigger, heavier; all I have to do is exhaust her. I pin her wrists to the ground, drive my knees against her chest. I don't want to kill her. If I can just keep her still, if I can get the backpack off, then search her for any hidden recording devices—that'd be ideal; that way we can both walk out in one piece. But if not, if things come down to it—

Candice shrieks and spits at my face. "Get *off*!"

I don't budge. "Just give it," I pant. "Give it, and I'll—"

"You fucking *bitch*!"

She bites my wrist. Pain shoots up my arm. I jerk back, shocked. She's drawn blood—Jesus fucking Christ, it's all over her teeth, all over my arm. Candice thrashes once more. My knees slip off her chest. She breaks loose, coils up, and kicks out at my stomach.

Her foot lands with such force—so much more force than I thought possible from that tiny body. It doesn't hurt so much as it stuns, knocks the air out of my lungs. I reel backward, arms windmilling for balance, but the ground I thought was behind me is not there.

Just empty air.

Twenty-Four

THE DOCTORS LET ME LEAVE THE HOSPITAL AFTER FOUR DAYS, after my clavicle and ankle have been set and I've proven I can hop my way into and out of a car without assistance. It doesn't seem like I'll need surgery, but they want me back in two weeks to check that my concussion has resolved itself. The whole thing costs me thousands of dollars even after insurance, though I suppose I should be grateful I got off this easy.

No police were standing over my bedside when I woke up. No investigators, no journalists. I slipped on the ice while jogging, I'm told. An anonymous Good Samaritan found me and called the EMTs using the emergency feature on my phone, but they'd disappeared by the time the ambulance arrived.

Candice has played this perfectly. Any accusation I make will appear utterly groundless. From the outside, we are near strangers to each other. Our last email interaction was years ago. I don't have her number in my phone. There is no room to suspect foul play, for what motive could there be? It's been storming for days now; the rain will have washed away all fingerprints, all proof of her cameras. Even if I can somehow prove Candice was at the steps that night, this only turns into a battle of verbal testimony that will cost us both thousands in legal fees. What's more, I'm sure I've left bruises on Candice, too—bruises she's no doubt embellished and documented by now. There's no guarantee I'd win.

No. Whatever plays out now will happen in the realm of popular narrative.

I look up Candice's name during the Uber ride back to my apartment, just as I've been doing every few hours since I woke up. It's only a matter of time, I figured. I'd like to see the news the moment it drops. This time, the headline I'm awaiting tops the search results. An interview has just dropped from the *New York Times*: "Former Editor Candice Lee on Athena Liu, Juniper Song Hayward, and the Confession of a Lifetime."

I'm honestly impressed. Putting aside the fact that Candice has managed to retcon her job title from assistant to editor, it's hard to get a *New York Times* piece published in just four days, especially one about a literary feud that passed out of the news cycle months ago. Even Adele Sparks-Sato could never get her think pieces published in the *NYT*; she always had to resort to *Vox* or *Slate* or, God help us, *Reductress*.

But Candice had something no one else had. She had the tapes.

The final paragraph following the interview mentions that Candice is working on a memoir about the whole affair. Of fucking course. She's only begun drafting it, but "multiple publishers" are reportedly "very interested" in acquiring her manuscript. Eden is listed as one of the publishers who have reached out to Candice's agent. Daniella herself is quoted in the final lines: "Of course we'd love to work with Ms. Lee. It would be the ideal way to make amends for the part we played in this tragedy, which we deeply regret."

SO HERE I AM, FINISHED.

I crash through one week, and then another, with painkillers and sleep aids. Consciousness is a burden. I wake up only to eat. I don't taste the food in my mouth. I subsist entirely on peanut butter sandwiches, and after a few days, I stop bothering with the peanut butter. My hair grows ratty and greasy, but the thought of washing it exhausts me. I push myself through the motions of bare survival, but there is no telos, nothing to look forward to, other than marching down the dreadful progression of linear time. This is, I believe, what Agamben would call "bare life."

News of my accident must have circulated around the web. Marnie texts me, Wanted to check in. I heard about the accident, are you alright? I take this to be an attempt to assuage her own conscience in case I die. I don't respond.

Beyond that, not a single other person reaches out. Mom and Rory would drop everything to come to my bedside in an instant, if I told them what happened, but I'd rather shove screwdrivers into my eyeballs than explain it all. My phone chirps one night, but it's only the DoorDash guy with the toilet paper, and I cry into my pillow, feeling profoundly sorry for myself.

When my painkillers run out and I have to face down the agony of cogitation, I while away the hours scrolling numbly through Twitter. My timeline is full of authors begging for attention as usual. Book deal. Cover reveal. Cover reveal. A starred review. A Goodreads giveaway. A plea for preorders. A romance novel cover featuring two white leads looks too similar to another romance novel cover, and the Twitterati aren't sure whether to be mad at the authors, the publishers, the art teams, or White Supremacy in General.

It all reeks of desperation, but I can't look away. It's the only thing linking me to the only world I have any interest in being a part of.

The solitude wouldn't bother me so much—I'm used to being alone; I've always been alone—if I could write. But I can't write—not now, not knowing that I probably don't even have an agent anymore. And what's an author without an audience?

I've wondered, before, how authors who were canceled—and I mean canceled for good reasons, like sexual harassment or using racial slurs—felt after they were iced out of publishing. A few tried to worm their way back in, usually through seedy self-publishing endeavors, or weird cultish workshops. But most just disappeared quietly into the ether, leaving nothing behind but a few tired headlines recapping the drama. I suppose they're living new lives, in new professions. Maybe they're working office jobs. Maybe they're nurses, or teachers, or real estate agents, or full-time parents. I wonder how they feel whenever they walk past a bookstore, whether they get a gnawing desire in their gut for the fairyland that cast them out.

I guess Geoff made his way back in eventually. But Geoff is a wealthy, attractive, cishet white guy. Geoff has endless room for failure. The world will afford me no such lenience.

I do consider suicide. In the later hours of the night, when the ongoing press of time feels like too much, I find myself researching carbon monoxide and razor blades. In theory, it seems like an easy way to escape this suffocating dark. At least it would make my haters feel terrible. *Look at what you did. Look what you drove her to. Aren't you ashamed? Don't you wish you could take it all back?*

But it all seems like so much trouble, and despair as I might, I can't make peace with the idea that I will depart from the world without so much as a final word.

A MONTH LATER, CANDICE SELLS HER TELL-ALL MEMOIR ON PROPOSAL to Penguin Random House for a staggering seven figures.

I scroll down past the deal announcement to the comments. Some are viciously celebratory; others express revulsion at the commodification of a painful, personal tragedy. A few people express disbelief that a first-time writer would earn such a high advance for a book that doesn't even exist yet.

They don't understand. It doesn't matter how well Candice can write. Who knows if she can string together a paragraph at all? Who cares? Athena and I are national news by now. Everyone and their mother will buy and read this exposé. It'll linger at the top of bestseller lists for months. It will surely become one of the most talked-about books in the industry, and when it does, my name will be ruined forever. I will always be the writer who stole Athena Liu's legacy. The psycho, jealous, racist white woman who stole the Asian girl's work.

It's hard to imagine a more total, eviscerating defeat.

But my mind does a funny thing then.

I don't spiral into despair. I don't feel the telltale symptoms of an incoming panic attack. In fact, quite the opposite: I'm utterly calm, Zen-like. I feel *alive*. I find myself composing sentences then, dreaming up turns of phrase, sketching out the contours of a counternarrative. I am the victim of a dreadful hoax. I was cyberbullied, stalked, and manipulated into thinking I was going mad. Candice Lee took my love for my deceased friend and turned it into something ugly and horrible. Candice is the one who exploited me for her art, not the other way around.

Because if Candice is showing off those tapes, then she's revealing that she was at the *Exorcist* steps the night I fell. Then there's no question who that anonymous EMT caller was. And that gives me an opening to make my own accusations.

The truth is fluid. There is always another way to spin the story, another wrench to throw into the narrative. I have learned this now, if nothing else. Candice may have won this round, but I won't let her erase my voice. I will tell our audience what they ought to believe. I will undermine all of her assertions, ascribe new motivations, and alter the sequence of events. I will present a new account that is compelling precisely because it aligns with what our audience, deep down, really wants to believe: that I have done no wrong, and that this is, once again, an instance of nasty, selfish, overdemanding people fabricating a tale of racism where there isn't one. This is cancel culture gone deadly. Look at my cast. Look at my hospital bills.

I will craft, and sell, a story about how the pressures of publishing have made it impossible for white and nonwhite authors alike to succeed. About how Athena's success was entirely manufactured, how she was only ever a token. About how my hoax—because let's frame it as a hoax, not a theft—was really a way to expose the rotten foundations of this entire industry. About how I am the hero, in the end.

I start planning my next steps. First, I'll write a proposal. I can have that done by the end of the day, or perhaps tomorrow morning if I get too tired. But I'll certainly whip it into shape by the end of the week, and then email it off to Brett, assuming Brett hasn't fired me. If he *has* fired me, I'll ask for a phone call, then pitch this to him in person. He'd be insane to say no.

I'll spend the next eight weeks scribbling down all my thoughts and recollections. I can't recycle material from my pseudo-autobiography. No—in that project, I was willing to make myself the villain for the sake of entertainment. In this version, I need redemption. I must make them see my side of the story. Athena was the leech, the vampire, the ghost who wouldn't let me go; Candice her deranged wannabe proxy. I am innocent. My only sin is loving literature too much, and refusing to let Athena's *very* prenatal work go to waste.

The draft will be messy, but that's all right—this whole affair is messy. It's more important to strike while the iron's hot. Brett and I will clean up the typos as best we can, then put the manuscript on submission. Someone will buy that story. Perhaps it'll be Eden—I'd be willing to work again with Daniella, provided she comes groveling, stacks of cash in hand. But I'm expecting a choice. The offers will be many. We'll go to auction. I would not, in fact, be surprised if this project goes for more money than any of my previous works.

A year later, I'll be in bookstores everywhere. The initial press coverage will be skeptical at best, scathing at worst. *White lady publishes tell-all! June Hayward writes the memoir none of us wanted, because this psycho just can't stop.* Diana Qiu will blow a gasket. Adele Sparks-Sato will lose her fucking mind.

But some reviewer, somewhere, will give the book a closer look. They'll publish a contrarian review, because editors who want clickbait always solicit contrarian reviews. *What if we got it all wrong?* And that's all it takes to sow doubt. The netizens who love to argue for the sake of arguing will look for the holes in Candice's story. The character assassinations will begin. We'll all get dragged down in the mud, and when the dust clears, all that will remain is the question: *What if Juniper Song was right?*

And this will become, in time, my story once again.

Acknowledgments

YELLOWFACE IS, IN LARGE PART, A HORROR STORY ABOUT LONELINESS in a fiercely competitive industry. Compared to June and Athena, I am gratefully supported by the most wonderful friends, family, and publishing team a writer could ask for. Many thanks are in order. Thank you to the brilliant folks at William Morrow and Borough Press who turn my scribblings into books: May Chen, Ann Bissell, Natasha Bardon, David Pomerico, Liate Stehlik, Holly Rice, Danielle Bartlett, DJ DeSmyter, Susanna Peden, Robyn Watts, Vicky Leech, Elizabeth Vaziri, Mireya Chiriboga, and Alessandra Roche. You all make HarperCollins feel like home. Thank you to the team at Liza Dawson Associates, who have stood by me every step of the way—Hannah Bowman, Havis Dawson, Liza Dawson, Joanne Fallert, and Lauren Banka. Thank you to Farah Naz Rishi, Ehigbor Shultz, Akanksha Shah, James Jensen, Tochi Onyebuchi, Katicus O'Nell, Julius Bright Ross, Taylor Vandick, Shirlene Obuobi, and all of I Pomodori for laughing with me and encouraging me never to pull my punches. Thank you to Emily Jin, Melodie Liu, and Moira De Graef—my fellow Jingsketeers in arms—for keeping me sane. Thank you to the Bunker for letting me gripe and for making me laugh. Bookstores will always be magical places for me—thank you to all the bookstores and booksellers who have championed my work to readers, but especially to Waterstones Oxford, Barnes & Noble Milford, Mysterious Galaxy, Porter Square Books, and Harvard Book Store, where Emmaline Crooke and Lily Rugo are the absolute best. Thank you to Mom and Dad, who believed fiercely that this writing thing would work out before I did. And thank you always to Bennett, whose love illuminates a world of value.

About the Author

R.F. KUANG IS a Marshall Scholar, a translator, and the Hugo–, Nebula–, Locus–, and World Fantasy Award–nominated author of the Poppy War trilogy and *Babel: An Arcane History*. She has an MPhil in Chinese Studies from Cambridge and an MSc in Contemporary Chinese Studies from Oxford. She lives in New Haven, Connecticut, where she is pursuing a PhD in East Asian Languages and Literatures at Yale University.